Scott Frost is a screenwriter whose credits include *Twin Peaks* and *The X-Files*. He lives in Montana.

By Scott Frost and available from Headline

Run the Risk
Never Fear
Point of No Return

point of
no return

scott frost

headline

Copyright © 2008 Scott Frost

The right of Scott Frost to be identified as the Author of
the Work has been asserted by him in accordance with the
Copyright, Designs and Patents Act 1988.

First published in Great Britain in 2008
by HEADLINE PUBLISHING GROUP

First published in Great Britain in paperback in 2008
by HEADLINE PUBLISHING GROUP

1

Apart from any use permitted under UK copyright law, this publication
may only be reproduced, stored, or transmitted, in any form, or by any
means, with prior permission in writing of the publishers or, in the case
of reprographic production, in accordance with the terms of licences
issued by the Copyright Licensing Agency.

All characters in this publication are fictitious and any resemblance to
real persons, living or dead, is purely coincidental.

Cataloguing in Publication Data is available from the British Library

ISBN 978 0 7553 3395 0

Typeset in Plantin by Avon DataSet Ltd,
Bidford-on-Avon, Warwickshire

Printed and bound in the UK by
CPI Mackays, Chatham ME5 8TD

Headline's policy is to use papers that are natural, renewable and
recyclable products and made from wood grown in sustainable forests.
The logging and manufacturing processes are expected to conform to
the environmental regulations of the country of origin.

HEADLINE PUBLISHING GROUP
An Hachette Livre UK Company
338 Euston Road
London NW1 3BH

www.headline.co.uk
www.hachettelivre.co.uk

As always, for Valerie

No one would do anything if they knew the consequences. A dying detective told me that as he lay in a hospital bed. It seems a natural thing for a cop to understand. The lives of most of the people we deal with have been torn apart by violence in one form or another.

If we could take back just one or two moments in a life and trade it for the assurance of sameness, most people would make that deal in a second. The phone call that began a chain of events would go unmade. The first word of an argument that escalated out of control would be silenced.

And more often than not more people than you would imagine make the same deal to avoid good news. It's what we know that becomes the security we wrap ourselves in to protect us from the dangers around the next turn. It's change that's threatening.

There are moments we control, a choice or a decision that will actually make a difference. The difficult part is identifying the good ones from the bad when you're in the middle of it. Every crime scene is testament to how badly we judge these things.

I know all this is as true as anything I have learned as a cop or a mother. But even knowing it I still didn't walk away when I heard the voice on the other end of the phone. It was nearing midnight when the phone rang. The number meant nothing to me, but the voice, that's what kept me from hanging up. It was a man calling; the connection was bad, the words coming through the white noise of cell towers and spoken in the quiet, measured cadence of exhaustion or fear. I couldn't identify the voice, but at the same time there was a quality to it that seemed to find a place in my memory. Like hearing an ex-lover's voice for the first time in twenty years.

It could have been a wrong number, for all that was said. And I knew just as well it wasn't. It was meant for me.

'It's all true,' he said. 'There's no turning back.'

I should have walked away right then. I should have listened to the voice in my own head that said nothing is 'all true' and hung up. But I couldn't after the next words; just as I couldn't know where it would lead.

'I saw a boy on a bicycle vanish in a flash of light,' he said.

I should have walked away. And if there were second chances, maybe I would. Maybe.

one

It was spring, or what passes for it in southern California. There was new growth on the blackened hillsides around my house from the previous fall's fires; thin green shoots slicing up through a carpet of ash. Only two other houses remained undamaged on the street. The rest had been reduced to their foundations which, in the time since the fire, had taken on the appearance of ruins left by a people who had long ago vanished from these hills. Occasionally the scent of jasmine or a hybrid rose from a distant untouched subdivision drifted in the wind. But when the wind didn't blow, what was left was a strained silence, an uneasy feeling of the calm before the next storm.

My father had swept back in and then out of my life, much like the fires in the hills, except there were no construction companies that specialized in rebuilding the kind of damage he had left in his wake.

Understanding a mystery does not always free you from it as the therapists promise. My work had suffered. Since I had been unable to bring my own father to justice, the belief that I could do that for anyone else had slipped through my fingers. The act of stepping into a crime scene had always been accompanied by a sense of anticipation but now it had been replaced by a certain amount of dread. In every victim I saw my dead half-brother's face. In every suspect in cuffs I saw my father's dark presence.

My health suffered, the winter passing with a seemingly endless string of ailments that no doctor could find the right prescription for. My relationships fared no better. I withdrew from the world. From my daughter Lacy, from my partner Harrison and the love that I continued to leave unsaid.

My daughter, who attended UCLA, had wanted me to sell the house and start over in a place with no past, but I couldn't bring myself to do it. Even bad memories can take on a sort of comfort, or at least familiarity, given time. Most of the neighbors who had lost their homes to the fire had sold their properties to a developer planning a new subdivision. He had made an offer to me but I couldn't accept it. To walk out the door now and hand it over to a builder who would bulldoze it the next day felt like abandoning a piece of earth that had been heavily fought over. It didn't matter that most of the battles I'd waged inside these walls had been losses in one form or another. In a city where nothing lasts, this was Fort Apache, even if what I was preserving by staying were only bad dreams.

Nearly three weeks had passed since the phone call.

It was a Sunday afternoon. I had been in bed all day with the flu, my head feeling as if I had slept on the burner of the stove. My daughter had called to cheer me up, but instead we had a conversation about her future – a topic that the past made us step around carefully. As Lacy was fond of repeating whenever the question of her academic career came up, no one is promised tomorrow, etc., etc. I suggested that didn't necessarily conflict with going into pre-med. She countered, I think only half jokingly, that she was probably better suited, given her life experience, to going into the CIA and becoming an assassin.

I changed the subject and asked about men. She asked if I had slept with my partner Harrison yet. That was when the white sedan pulled up into the driveway and stopped.

'I've got to go, I have a visitor.'

'You never have visitors.'

I hadn't told anyone about the phone call, not because I was keeping it secret. There really was nothing to tell except that two short sentences had slipped into my imagination and I hadn't been able to shake them loose. But that spark of curiosity hadn't happened to me in a long time, and I felt unsure of what it meant.

I promised Lacy I'd call her later to let her know how I was feeling and hung up. My head began to spin as I got out of bed for the first time all day and walked to the window. The woman who stepped out of the car appeared to be in her mid-thirties, thin, with shoulder-length silver-grey hair. Her clothes were casual, but co-ordinated. She walked the way someone who had once been a dancer might. I had never seen her before, I was certain of that.

I slipped out of my robe, threw on some slacks and a shirt and glanced in the mirror as the bell rang. The last few months had added the first grey hairs to my head. My eyes appeared in a perpetual state of exhaustion. By the time I reached the door and opened it she had started back toward her car.

'Can I help you?' I said.

The woman stopped, turned.

'Lieutenant Delillo?'

Her eyes were light blue, nearly green, and from the lines around them I suspected she had slept little recently.

'Yes,' I said. 'Alex if you prefer.'

The only piece of jewelry she wore was a simple silver wedding band. She walked over and extended her hand.

'I was hoping we could talk. My name's Cathy Salem.'

'If you're here about the house, I'm not selling.'

She shook her head. 'Are you all right, Lieutenant?'

Given my quick look in the mirror, I imagined I wasn't exactly what she was expecting, whatever that was.

'Mild flu,' I said.

She glanced back at the rubble of the other homes across the street.

'You were very lucky,' she said.

'That's a matter of some debate.'

I invited her inside and we sat down at the kitchen table.

'How can I help you?' I asked.

'My husband's a policemen ... was, LAPD. He went to Iraq eleven months ago with a private security firm. He was teaching Iraqi policemen to be fair-minded dispensers of justice. I didn't want him to go, but the money was too good to pass up. He said it couldn't be any more dangerous than the gang unit he was with in Rampart. Technically, he was working for the Iraqi government, which is why the Defense Department can only do so much.'

'About what?'

She laid her hands flat on the table, spreading her fingers as if to maintain her balance.

'Three weeks ago he was supposed to come home. He never arrived. The military has listed him as officially missing. They say they're doing everything they can and that I shouldn't lose hope.'

If she was angling for encouragement, her eyes gave no indication of it.

'I'm sorry.'

She looked away. 'It's not what you think.'

I didn't know what I thought, and then she reached into the pocket of her shirt and removed a postcard.

'Something happened to my husband there. The longer he stayed, the fewer calls he made home, and when he did call, it was as if part of him wasn't there.

7

Then just before he was to come home Jack witnessed a bombing. I don't know any of the details, he kept that from me, but from that moment, I knew I had lost him.'

'That doesn't sound out of the ordinary for what he was experiencing,' I said. 'I have some experience with PTSD.'

She nodded. 'That's what I told myself, that he would be all right when he came home, and then he didn't. But the truth was, there was something else to his voice. Then this came. It was mailed from Baghdad the day he was supposed to have left.'

As she handed it to me her hand trembled. The postcard was a photograph of a circus bear standing on a large ball with its front paws in the air. I flipped it over. There was only one line of writing on it and I read it aloud.

'I saw a boy on a bicycle vanish in a flash of light.'

The rush of adrenalin as I read the words made my head spin and for a moment I felt faint. I examined the date on the postmark. It had been mailed the same day I had received the telephone call.

'Why bring this to me? Do I know your husband?' I asked.

Her eyes lingered on me for a moment as if asking a question.

'He was at a seminar on trace evidence you gave several years ago at the Cal State. You must have made an impression on him.'

The voice on the telephone fell into place. I

remembered him, or at least a sense of him. He had seemed out of place amongst the rest of the cops attending. We had drinks afterward. By the second one he told me his wife wanted him to leave the force. He didn't want to quit. He wanted to become a detective. We talked for an hour, maybe more. It was the first and only time a cop had ever asked my advice on love and I ended up lying to him. I told him he could have it all, never mentioning the wreckage that had become my own marriage.

He walked me to my car and asked if I would mind if he called me again sometime for advice. I said no. Three weeks ago he had finally made that call.

She looked at me as if to try and find what it was her husband had seen in me, or perhaps trying to understand if something had happened between us that had remained secret. For the moment I didn't think she needed to know I had received the telephone call from him, or that my advice of the heart had included remaining a cop.

'I don't remember meeting your husband there,' I said.

If my answer was of any consolation to her, she didn't show it.

'Why did you come to me?' I asked.

Cathy Salem took a breath as if it was full of nicotine from a cigarette. 'I received another small package in the mail from Jack four days ago.'

'Is it unusual that mail would be delayed that long from Iraq?'

She shook her head. 'My husband isn't missing in Iraq, Lieutenant.'

'I don't understand,' I said.

'The package was mailed from Trona.'

'I don't know where that is.'

'It's a little town on the way to Death Valley, about three hours north of Los Angeles.'

She reached into the pocket of her linen jacket and removed a battered envelope.

'This was inside of it.'

The envelope was still sealed.

'His note instructed me not to open this, or tell anyone where it came from and to bring it to you.'

Her eyes found mine as if hoping I would provide the answers she didn't have yet.

'Why me?' I asked.

'In his note he said you were a good cop.'

'Nothing more than that?'

She nodded. 'He said I was to follow his instructions, that I must trust him on this, and most importantly that I not talk to any cop but you.'

She slid the envelope across the table to me. I started to reach for it, but stopped and left it where it was.

'Is it possible someone else mailed this for him?'

'No, we drove through Trona every year on the way to Death Valley. Who else would know that? If you've ever been there you would know that no one goes there without a specific reason.'

'And this is the only contact he's made with you?'

Mrs Salem glanced back out the window.

'There have been a few times when I thought some-one was watching me. Maybe it was my imagination.'

I didn't want to ask what I had to next, but there was no way around it.

'There are some questions I have to ask,' I said.

She nodded. 'I've been married to a cop for six years, I know what that can do to a marriage. We had our problems. I didn't want Jack to be a cop; we argued about it. His career was the third person in the room whenever we were together. But whatever problems we had, what's happening now isn't part of them.'

'Are you sure?'

'Yes,' she said without a hint of doubt.

I looked across the table at the way her elegant hair slipped around the line of her jaw. I started to apologize for asking the question when a wave of fever swept through me and I felt as if I had been plunged into cold water. I reached out and picked up the envelope. There was an object inside, a key I thought, though I couldn't be certain.

'Have you considered the possibility that what your husband needs is a doctor and not a cop?'

'My husband is a strong man, Lieutenant.'

'Sometimes that's not enough,' I said.

'My husband didn't ask for a doctor, he asked for you.'

I looked at Mrs Salem and noticed her face was beginning to be surrounded by tiny prisms of light, and I felt light-headed.

11

'What is it you want me to do?' I asked.

'It's not what I want, it's what my husband wants. He picked you, he needs your help.'

The auras began to obscure the details of her face. My body began to tremble with cold and then heat and I felt faint.

'This isn't really what I do,' I said.

'Something happened over there,' said Salem. 'And I think it's followed him here.'

I managed to stand up, thinking I could make it to my bed.

'I'm afraid I don't feel well,' I said.

'Lieutenant?'

The light in the room changed as if a blind had been drawn. Mrs Salem was saying something to me but I couldn't hear the words. I looked down at the envelope in my hand as it slipped from my fingers and disappeared into darkness at my feet. I took a step, started to reach out for the table and lost consciousness.

I could feel a hand gently holding the side of my face but when I opened my eyes I was alone. The kitchen was empty, the walls painted in the soft orange glow of sunset. I was lying on the floor where I had fainted – a pillow had been put under my head, a blanket covered my chest. I had been out for hours.

Outside, a flock of crows were cackling at the sunset. A fly buzzed against a window. I sat up carefully, pulling the blanket around me. Every muscle in my body ached; there was a small bump on my forehead where my head must have hit the table as I passed out. I pulled myself up and sat unsteadily on a chair and the events began to drift back to the surface.

Mrs Salem's white sedan was gone from the driveway. I tried to replay the encounter as best I could. I remembered her elegant hair, and the sadness in her eyes, the postcard, the boy on the bicycle, and the envelope from her husband.

I looked around on the floor where I had dropped the envelope but it was gone. I checked the table and then started toward the kitchen counter when the phone began to ring. I began to reach for it, but hesitated. If I picked it up and it was her . . . I remembered the postcard of the circus bear balancing on the ball. I could let it go and walk away, then I remembered what I had told her husband over drinks when we met. I told him he could have both, that he should stay a cop. I told him the exact thing his wife would not have wanted me to say. On the seventh ring I answered.

'Delillo,' I said.

'Are you all right?' she said.

'Yes, thank you, it was just the fever. It's gone now.'

'I'm sorry, it was a mistake for me to have come to your house.'

Salem's voice had changed from earlier when she was sitting at my table. The strength I had noted before was gone, though what exactly had replaced it I wasn't sure.

'I think it would be better if you forget we ever met,' she said.

'How exactly do I do that?'

There was a pause on the other end.

'The same way I'm going to.'

'Where's the envelope from your husband, Mrs Salem?' I asked.

There was only silence on the other end.

'What happened to the envelope you put on my table?' I repeated.

I heard her take a shallow breath.

'I think you're mistaken, Lieutenant. I didn't put anything on your table.'

I realized it was fear I was hearing in her voice.

'Your husband called me from Iraq the day he mailed the postcard,' I said.

I thought she started to say something, but there was only silence.

'What are you afraid of, Mrs Salem?'

I heard a sound like a wave crashing in the background.

'I'm afraid of the same things everyone else is,' she said, and then the line went dead.

When I slept that night there were long lines of bright flames in my dreams advancing toward my house. And when I didn't sleep, there was Cathy Salem, and the sound of fear in her voice as she lied about placing the envelope on the table. There could be dozens of reasons why her husband had disappeared, and just as many reasons for her to lie about it. Maybe her husband had gone mad over there. Maybe he had strayed over that line that, once crossed, you can never fully return from. And now he was back here, lost in his own fever dream.

I could walk away from that and not look back except for one detail. There were over nine thousand other members of LAPD he could have gone to for help, but instead he had come to me. Why? It certainly couldn't have been because I had once told him that he could have love and still be a cop, as if it were as natural as breathing. On the strength of that kind of advice, he must have thought that Pasadena was awash with unsolved murders from the moment I became head of Homicide.

He had asked for my help, and that could mean only one thing: a crime had been committed. But that still didn't answer the question of what I brought to the table that none of his fellow officers in blue could. Or what that crime was.

I was wrong about those words I heard Jack Salem say over the phone. There is one absolute that is 'all true', from which there is no turning back, and it is the same thing Mrs Salem and everyone else is afraid of.

Death.

two

There were no new cases pending when I walked into the office later that morning. Two gang slayings were the only cases that were open at the moment. Two wasted lives that no amount of police work would ever bring justice to. Pasadena would survive without my presence if I stepped away and looked for Salem. And just maybe I might find something else – a way back to the life I once had. And if not, if all I found at the end was a cop lost in his own personal abyss, then I could turn away having done what I could. That's always the plan at the start – to walk away at the end.

Department of Motor Vehicles records showed that the Salems lived in a condo on the beach, as far away from the streets he patrolled as he could get. A contact with LAPD faxed over the details of Salem's career. Patrol officer four years, IAD a year and a half, once applied for detective and refused. Two and a half years with a gang unit, called CRASH, until the unit's members began to be arrested as quickly as the street

17

thugs they were assigned to investigate. While with the gang unit he had once been investigated for excessive use of force and was exonerated.

In every aspect, every report, he appeared to be an entirely average policeman. So much so, his profile was nearly interchangeable with any other cop. He had neither too much nor too little ambition. He could have drifted along until early retirement and lived a nice, comfortable, suburban life. Then twelve months ago he took a leave of absence to work for ISC – International Security Consultants – providing training in Iraq to the new police force.

Why did he do that? What was there inside of him that wasn't present in his jacket file? Was he a patriot, a true believer? Did he want adventure, or was it just the money? And if it was the money, why did he need more of it? Was there a secret addiction, or just dreams of a better house, a sailboat or a college fund for a child they hadn't had yet?

I stared at his photograph. I had remembered almost everything about the one meeting we had, except for his face. He had short, light brown hair, brown eyes, was of average height, average build. He could walk by you a dozen times in one day and you wouldn't remember ever seeing him. He might have been a high school social studies teacher. But instead he went to Iraq and had been swallowed up and spat out.

I dialed the Salems' number and got the machine. His voice was on the recording.

'You've reached Jack and Cathy, please leave a message.'

His voice didn't match the picture or résumé. It was why I remembered our meeting: deeper than you would have expected, as distinctive as the rest of him wasn't. But the person who had spoken on the telephone from Iraq sounded like a shadow of the man who had recorded this message.

I left a message for Mrs Salem to call me, then dialed Harrison and asked him to step in my office. A moment later he walked in and sat on the edge of my desk. At age 39 he was ten years younger than me. His blond hair was turning sandy. His green eyes still went through me with the most casual of glances. The crescent-shaped scar on the corner of his left eye was a constant reminder of the price he had paid for becoming my partner.

'You don't look so good,' he said.

'I had the flu over the weekend.'

His eyes drifted over my desk and Salem's files.

'Could you close the door?' I asked.

He looked at me for a moment, then walked over to the door and shut it.

'I'm going to take a couple of days off,' I said.

Harrison studied me for a moment. It wasn't the first time I had said those words in the past months and I could see the worry in his eyes.

'Professional or personal?' he asked.

'I'm not sure yet.' I looked at him for a moment. 'Don't worry, I'm not going home and locking myself in the house.'

19

Harrison nodded, though it would take more than words to convince him that I was taking even a tentative step back into the world.

'Have dinner with me tonight,' he said as if testing me.

I shook my head. 'There's something I need to do.'

He glanced down to my desk and the open files. Harrison tried to mask the surprise in his eyes, but didn't quite manage it. Since I discovered the abuse I had suffered by my father's hands, and that he was a suspect in several unsolved murders, my work as a cop had felt pointless.

'Does this file have something to do with it?'

'It's part of it.'

'Is it important?'

I nodded, though in truth I wasn't sure if I was talking about Salem or myself.

'There is something you could do for me,' I said.

'Anything,' Harrison answered.

'I need you to make a few inquiries.'

I had to know about ISC, and questions coming from an explosives expert would raise fewer eyebrows than ones coming from the head of a homicide division.

'Would you look into a security firm named ISC?' I said.

'Is there something I should know about?' Harrison asked.

'I'm just doing someone a favor,' I said.

'An LAPD cop named Salem?'

20

I nodded.

'Since when did you begin doing favors for LAPD?'

'This isn't for LAPD.'

'Interesting favor.'

'Why do you say that?'

'There's an LAPD personnel file on your desk. You tell me to close the door, and then ask about a private security firm that until a few years ago when they became respectable were called mercenaries.'

'You're suggesting something?'

'They're still just mercenaries. Beyond that I don't know enough to suggest anything.'

I shook my head. 'It's just a favor.'

'Then I am suggesting something – discretion,' Harrison said.

'I'll be back in the office in forty-eight hours.'

I gathered up Salem's records, stood up from the desk and started to take a step when Harrison's hand gently landed on my forehead.

'I think you still have a little fever.'

I closed my eyes and leaned into his hand for a moment. There was little about me Harrison didn't know, including that I was in love with him. He had nearly lost his life while saving my daughter, bathed me when my skin was stained with blood, helped me uncover secrets to my own past more painful than one could imagine. But each time we had begun to step across that chasm called love I had retreated back to the safety of my isolation.

'What's going on, Alex?'

21

I looked at him for a moment. A dozen times or more over the past months Harrison had tried to save me from myself, and I had rejected all his offers, both professional and personal, not because I didn't need saving, but because something inside me seemed to know I was the only one capable of climbing out of the darkness my father had plunged me into.

'Someone handed me a secret, that's all. I'm going to ask a few questions, and then I'll be home.'

Harrison looked me for a moment as if questioning whether I still remembered the meaning of the word.

'You certain you know what you're doing?' he asked.

His hand slipped from my head and I glanced into his eyes.

'Don't worry, it's only my own secrets that have proved dangerous.'

'Let me help,' he said.

I briefly took his fingers in mine.

'You can't,' I said.

Harrison began to ask another question and then let it go.

'I'll have it for you by the end of the day,' he said, and then I turned and moved toward the door.

'I'll see you back here in two days,' Harrison said. 'You need anything else—'

'You'll be my first call.'

We looked at each other for a moment, then I walked out of the office.

★

Cathy Salem was the first place to begin. I dialed her number again and left another message, waited an hour, called yet again, with no result, then began the drive across town to her home in Manhattan Beach.

Spring seemed to have already passed into summer as I headed down into the basin and out toward the ocean. A layer of smog hung over downtown and the Valley to the north. Waves of heat shimmered off the pavement and hoods of cars. The view toward the coast was like trying to see through a brown paper bag.

It took two hours to get across town and then south through traffic. A big-rig had jackknifed on the 405, spilling its load of running shoes across the road, setting off a feeding frenzy as drivers opened their doors and began tossing boxes of Nikes and Reeboks on to the back seat before enough California Highway Patrol officers arrived on scene to restore order. A family of Salvadorians with three kids actually stopped their car and were trying on shoes as if this was just another uniquely LA form of shopping.

The condo was a block from the beach – a white two-story stucco building just like the half-dozen next to it, each with a small courtyard in front large enough for a chair, table and five square feet of grass. I parked and walked up to the front door. The curtains were drawn. A Hispanic gardener was in the next yard blowing the half-dozen loose leaves on the tiny plot of grass out on to the street.

As I reached for the bell I stopped; the front door

was open several inches. I called out Mrs Salem's name but if she heard me over the sound of the leaf blower no response came back. I glanced over to the gardener, who was still intently blowing every last blade of grass. He was the fittest-looking gardener I'd ever seen, and he held the leaf blower as if it were a weapon. His pickup with the tools of his trade must have been parked out back because it wasn't anywhere in sight out front. I noticed he had an earpiece and was nodding his head to music.

I pushed the door open all the way, flipped a light switch and stepped in. On the floor of the living room a cordless phone lay on the carpet in several pieces as if it had been stepped on, but nothing else in the room was out of place.

'Mrs Salem?' I said, and again there was no response.

A phone machine on an end table next to the couch was untouched. My messages were there and then two calls with no message, made from a number with a 619 area code, each of them made at nine at night. I wrote down the number and then stepped over to the dining table.

A map of California had been spread out, a pad of paper and pencil next to it as if notes had been made, but none was present. Next to the notepad a photo album lay open – pictures of a smiling Jack and Cathy on a vacation in Death Valley. The smile on his face transformed him. There seemed to be nothing average in the happiness exhibited, and nothing ordinary in the spark present in his eyes. In that moment of time with his wife, he could have been an extraordinary man. Maybe he was, and maybe this was the man who went to Iraq. And the man I read about in his personnel file was just a ghost.

The spare bedroom and den off the living room appeared untouched. As I started toward the stairs to the second floor, something in the kitchen caught my eye and I stepped in. A long grocery list was held to the refrigerator door with a magnet. The faint outline of something behind it was visible through the thin paper. I lifted up the grocery list; underneath was another photograph. Jack Salem standing on a dusty Iraqi street wearing a dark commando sweater, jeans and combat boots. His arm is round the shoulder of an Iraqi boy who looked to be eight or nine years old. They're both smiling broadly. The boy's hands are tightly clutching a shiny new bicycle.

I pulled the picture out from under the magnet and stared at the image. I didn't want to think what I was thinking. I wanted to walk out the door and leave it all behind and not look back, but the sound of his voice over a bad phone connection wouldn't let me. 'I saw a boy on a bicycle vanish in a flash of light.'

I looked at both their faces in the picture. Was this how nightmares began – hidden in a moment of joy? I slipped the photograph into my shirt pocket and started up the stairway.

On the last step before the landing on the second floor, a thin strip of torn duct tape lay stuck to the carpet. On the wall of the landing a picture hung off-center. In one corner of the frame a thin crack in the glass sliced toward the center. From behind the door at the end of the hallway I heard what sounded like fingernails on a chalkboard.

I pulled my Glock from the holster and moved toward the door. The door to the master bath was open, the bathroom empty. Through the open window the steady drone of the leaf blower continued. I stepped to the master-bedroom door and waited for the sound again, but there was only silence.

Carefully I turned the handle until the latch cleared, then pushed the door open and raised the Glock. The curtains were drawn, the room nearly pitch-black. Something seemed to move though I couldn't see what it was.

'Police.'

I held the gun into the darkness where I thought the movement had come from.

A barely audible 'police' came out of the darkness, sounding as if it were from an old radio recording.

I took a step, the gun pointed toward the sound of the voice.

'Don't move,' I said then reached out for the light switch and flipped it on. On the floor in the corner, a large birdcage lay tipped over on its side. The grey parrot inside began shrieking and flapping its wings.

The rest of the room was empty. I walked to the foot of the bed. Whatever struggle had knocked the birdcage to the floor had started here. The mattress had been pulled a foot off the foundation, the bed-spread, blanket and top sheet were thrown to the floor; the fitted sheet on the mattress had been pulled nearly off and torn down the center.

Two dresser drawers were pulled open as if some clothes had been quickly grabbed. All the clothes in the drawers were women's; her husband's drawers were unopened.

The fear I had heard in her voice on the phone had come alive in this house. I holstered the Glock as I imagined Cathy Salem being surprised in her sleep by the intruder walking into her room. In panic she must have tried to run toward the window, knocking over the birdcage, and then returned to the bed in a hopeless effort to seek protection from a thin sheet of cotton until it began to tear in her hands. They bound her with duct tape, and carried her out, knocking the picture in the hallway and cracking the glass.

I walked over to the door and took one last look around to make sure I hadn't missed a detail. My heart began to pound. What violence does to a physical place, the story it leaves in everyday objects, and the new meaning they're given is sometimes more frightening than the evidence it leaves behind on a body.

Outside the back window in the alley I heard the gunning of an engine and the squeal of tires. I rushed down the stairs and out the back door. At the end of the alley a dark sedan paused at the corner then drove away out of sight. On the road in front of the Salems' garage the leaf blower lay discarded, its motor still running. The muscled gardener with the earpiece was nowhere to be seen.

As much as I wanted another explanation for what had taken place here, I knew there wasn't one. A line had been drawn halfway round the world from that little boy clutching the bicycle to this house, and that line was still moving, wrapping itself around me as it headed toward whatever abyss the Salems had already fallen into.

three

I dialed the contact at LAPD who had given me the information on Salem, an IAD detective named Jackson. He didn't mind doing favors as long as they didn't involve too much work. The call I had made to him that morning had been easy for him, pull a personnel file, read a report. It took nearly two minutes and three transfers before he picked up.

'I thought one call a day was enough,' Jackson said.

I told him what I thought had happened at the Salems' home.

'You're there now?' he asked.

'Yes.'

'No forced entry, no witnesses and no one reported her missing?' Jackson said.

'I'm reporting her missing,' I said.

'How well do you know her?'

'I don't.'

'What exactly is your interest in this?' Jackson asked.

'I met her husband once, she asked me to look into something.'

There was a pause on the other end of the phone, not unusual for an IAD cop whose business is to distrust every word coming out of most cops' mouths, but this was different, something had changed for him since we had talked in the morning.

'What something?' he asked.

I remembered the words in Salem's letter to his wife that no one other than me should know about the possibility that her husband wasn't in Iraq.

'It was of a personal nature.'

'I thought you said you didn't know her, yet you're doing something of a personal nature. What exactly was your relationship with Salem?' Jackson asked.

'There is no relationship.'

'You're in his condo.'

'I can have my own crime-scene people here in half an hour if you're not interested,' I said.

'What interests me is a detective from another jurisdiction asking personal questions about one of our cops, looking at his file, and then making claims about his wife who is going through an emotional crisis.'

Even for an IAD cop Jackson's reaction had gone off the rails of what I would have expected. He was treating me as if I was a suspect in something. The question was why, and that I had no answer to. Was he just protecting his own turf, or something else?

'What is it you think is going on here?' I asked.

'I think a cop is sticking her nose in where it doesn't

belong. If there's a problem with one of our people, it's our business.'

'You gave me his file.'

Jackson whispered something under his breath, probably to someone looking over his shoulder.

'I'm doing you a favor here.'

I realized the reason Jackson wasn't interested in what I had to say was because he already knew everything I had told him, right down to the torn sheet and the talking bird. It was what I knew and hadn't told him that interested him and, not getting it, he had just given me a friendly warning to stay away.

'I haven't told you one thing you didn't already know, have I?'

'We're on the same side, Delillo,' he said.

'Was the gardener one of your people?'

If silence can register surprise, I may have just heard it.

'We'll take care of this, go back to Pasadena,' Jackson said.

'Where's Mrs Salem?' I asked.

Jackson took a long, deep breath.

'Is she all right?' I repeated.

'I don't know . . . don't ask anything else.'

'Sounds like good advice,' I said.

'I'm glad you think so,' Jackson said and then hung up.

I slipped the phone into my pocket and walked over to the car. A heavy marine layer was moving in from the ocean, its dense gray fog beginning to creep around the corners of the condo. Was the gardener an LAPD officer? Or was someone else interested in the Salems, watching me right now? And if so, why? I glanced casually around but if anyone was here I couldn't spot them.

'We'll take care of this,' Jackson had said. Take care of what?

To the east there was still sunlight over the San Gabriels as I drove away from the shroud of clouds moving in over the coast. I dialed Harrison and asked him to trace the number I had retrieved from the machine in the condo. Two minutes later he called me back.

'The number's from a pay phone from a town in the high desert,' Harrison said.

'Trona?' I asked.

'How did you know that?'

'It's on the way to Death Valley,' I said. 'You have an address on it?'

'The eighty-four hundred block of Trona Road. You want to tell me what's going on?'

'A little boy on a bicycle vanished in a flash of light.'

Harrison let that pass. 'Where are you?'

'I'm supposed to be going back to Pasadena where I belong,' I said. 'You know anything about Trona?'

'Driving through it gives you a preview of how the end of the world might look. It's a mining town, potash or borax if I remember. It's also surrounded by a military installation, China Lake Weapons Center.'

'And you mention that because?'

32

'ISC has a training facility there.'

I checked the time. It was already after four o'clock, it would be dark by the time I drove the three hours north.

'What else did you find out about ISC?'

'They incorporated just about the time the Third Army was pulling down Saddam's statue in Baghdad. Their corporate offices are here in LA, sixty-some employees, mostly ex-Special Forces or Rangers, a few former SAS from the UK and some South Africans. They have one of the higher casualty rates of any of the firms operating in Iraq – four dead, twice as many wounded. One of their employees is listed as missing in action.'

'Salem.'

'That's right.'

'Anything else that stands out?'

'Two of their employees have committed suicide since returning to the States.'

'When?'

'Last year.'

'Do you know where?'

Harrison checked his notes. 'Both were in southern California, I don't have the specifics.'

'What about their work in Iraq?'

'They have a contract to train the national police force, the rest is providing security for private firms or individuals.'

I pulled to a stop in a long line of cars waiting at the entrance to the 405 and the 10.

'How did you know Salem was missing?' Harrison asked.

'He asked for my help.'

'Before or after he went missing?'

'Both.'

'How is that possible?'

'I don't think Salem's missing. He's hiding.'

'From what?'

'I don't know. But I think his wife is in trouble now too.'

'You're not coming back to Pasadena, are you?'

The light over the distant San Gabriels faded as the marine layer crept overhead. I looked around at the faces of the drivers in the other cars. They all stared straight ahead, a few talking on phones, all with the same tired, determined look.

'See what you can find out about those two suicides,' I said. 'I'll be back in the morning.'

'You're going to Trona.'

'Yes.'

Harrison didn't say anything for a moment as the long line of cars around me finally began to move.

'Why are you doing this?' he asked.

I pulled on to the freeway and headed north on the 405 instead of east on the 10 toward home.

'I suppose I'm doing this for myself,' I said.

'I don't imagine it would do any good for me to say you shouldn't do this alone.'

I drove for a moment in silence.

'No . . . but I like that you would say that.'

Harrison began to say something else but stopped himself.

'I'll be here when you get back,' he finally said.

I slipped the photograph of Salem and the little boy with the bicycle out of my pocket and set it on the dash. What was his name? Was he alive, dead? Was there a little boy behind that smile, or a deadly flash of light?

'Thank you,' I said to Harrison.

I put the photograph back in my pocket and then hung up. Ahead, the long line of tail lights rising up into the Santa Monica Mountains began to vanish into the fog.

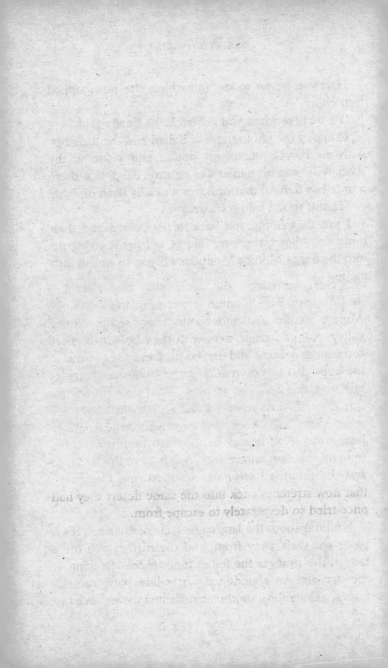

four

Desert surrounds the mountains that ring Los Angeles. The Sonoran stretches to the south, the Mojave to the east and north. Early settlers found valleys full of strange trees with their branches raised toward the heavens and named the trees after Joshua in the hope that salvation and escape from the desert lay just over the next rise of hills. What they found was Pueblo de Los Angeles, a small settlement on a small river that had been in existence since before Jamestown. And just as the Spanish took it from the Indians, the new immigrants took it from the Spanish, and the promised salvation vanished into the sprawl that now stretches back into the same desert they had once tried so desperately to escape from.

Nothing about the landscape feels permanent. It's a place you walk away from, and the further you drive into it, the stranger the follies that are left decaying in the dry air. An abandoned waterslide park, motels, mines, gas stations, mothballed airliners, even an early

37

paleo-man site set among extinct cinder cones seems testament to the fact that the desert is a precarious place to dream.

The sun had been down an hour when the glow of Trona's lights faintly lit the sky to the north. There was no moon to light the landscape spreading out beyond the beams of my headlights. No other cars had passed me coming or going for nearly an hour. I could be anywhere. A single coyote standing on the edge of the pavement with a large snake dangling from its jaws had been the only living thing I had seen since sunset, and a reminder not to stray too far from the light.

I tried to imagine what it was that Salem believed he could find here that didn't exist somewhere else, but couldn't. Was it sanctuary or flight? Was there something in this desert that reflected what he had found in the blowing dust and chaos of Iraq? Maybe an answer to a riddle about a boy and a bicycle? Or had he come here like so many before who had run out of options and were left with nowhere else to turn.

The first lights from houses began to dot the surrounding desert like stars in the darkness. The air that a moment before held the crisp chill and sage scent of the desert seemed to warm a few degrees and had a faint powdery taste. As I passed the bullet-ridden sign welcoming me to Trona, the glow of a large chemical plant appeared around the bend, looking like a version of Vegas gone terribly wrong.

Banks of lights lit up large silver and white industrial buildings that appeared on the edge of decay. A chain-link fence topped with razor wire surrounded the plant which stretched into the darkness. Two large smoke stacks towered over everything else. A low mechanical buzz emerged from the buildings as if a swarm of insects were descending on the town out of the darkness.

I passed a boarded-up gas station, a restaurant and a small playground, its slide and jungle gym looking as if they had been twisted by a windstorm. What plant life existed was covered in a fine dust. Somewhere in the darkness I thought I heard a radio playing, but the sound vanished.

I checked my watch. If the pattern of the previous two nights continued, the caller who had dialed the Salems' condo would be stepping to the same phone booth in little over half an hour. I pulled over next to a row of small identical houses that must have been built by the company for workers. They were boarded up and covered in the same powdery dust as everything else. Two large palm trees clinging to life decorated one yard. In another sat an old wooden fishing boat large enough to have worked the ocean. The faded street number on the house put me three blocks from where the calls had been made.

Several blocks away a car pulled on to the highway then stopped, its headlights shining in my direction. I instinctively switched off my lights and the vehicle began to move again, driving a block before turning off and vanishing into the darkness.

I switched my lights back on and drove toward the

center of town. On the left a school's football field appeared to be little more than the dusty soil of everywhere else except it had been painted blue. A single motel with a green neon vacancy sign glowed above two cars in the parking lot. Most of the store-fronts were shuttered. Down a side street a sheriff substation next to a sign that read Bus Station looked to be the only other going concern.

A block ahead a small deli and liquor store in a bunker-like stucco building appeared to be still open. A dozen feet from the entrance the phone booth where the calls had originated sat on the edge of the light spilling out the door. I turned round and drove back to the motel to get a room.

The coffee shop next to the motel was still open, though the only occupant appeared to be the waitress standing at the door smoking a cigarette. I parked and stepped into the motel's office. The room was paneled in knotty pine, the walls decorated with framed pieces of barbed wire, and old rusting mining tools. Postcards of Death Valley decorated the counter under a sheet of yellowed glass.

A door behind the counter was halfway open. From behind it I could hear the voices of a man and a woman talking over the sound of a television. I let the door to the office close and the voices abruptly stopped, A moment later the door swung open and a young woman who appeared to be in her late twenties stepped into the office. Her hair had been dyed a bright shade of red. Her eyes had the tired look of a meth abuser. I pulled my jacket over the Glock on my hip, trying not to advertise that I was a cop. She looked at me for a moment then turned and closed the door behind her.

'On your way to Death Valley?' she asked.

'How did you know?' I asked.

She laughed and placed a registration card in front of me.

'Why else would anyone come here, unless you want to see the Pinnacles?'

'Pinnacles?' I asked.

She pointed out into the darkness beyond the plant. 'Past the dry lake. The astronauts practiced walking on the moon there. Some people believe they filmed the whole thing here and never went to the moon at all. I wasn't born yet though. I don't have an opinion on that. Do you think they walked on the moon?'

I nodded. 'I think they did.'

I finished filling out the card and slid it across the counter. She picked it up and looked it over.

'Well, maybe they did land on the moon, but I don't see how it's changed anything,' she said.

'A friend was supposed to meet me here, I'm wondering if you've seen him?'

I slipped the picture of Salem and the little boy out of my pocket and showed it to her. She looked at it a moment, then shook her head.

'He hasn't been here. He your boyfriend?'

'Something like that.'

41

She took a key off a hook, and then glanced over her shoulder at the closed door behind her.

'Some days I have one, some days I don't.'

'Which is he today?' I asked.

She leaned on the counter and handed me the key. 'He was in the army over there, he had a parade and everything when he came back, now he just watches TV. Everything dies here. If I see your friend, I'll tell him what room you're in.'

As I got back in the car, the young woman remained at the counter for a moment, staring out into the darkness. The cop in me wanted to go back in and bust the guy behind that door, who no doubt was waiting for her to return so he could get her high. The mother in me wanted to take her by the hand and lead her away from this place. And I knew just as well that neither would help her find what she wanted. As I began to drive away, the girl switched the vacancy sign off and disappeared through the door behind the counter.

I drove back down to the deli and liquor store and parked across the street in the shadow of an abandoned storefront. I checked my watch. If no one walked to the phone and made a call within the next ten minutes, the three-hour drive would have been for no reason. Finding anything in this town seemed at best a remote possibility. I could check with the sheriff substation, or walk into the ISC training facility but that would be exactly the thing Salem would not want me to do.

The headlights of a beat-up Mustang appeared

around the corner then pulled in and stopped outside the store. Three young men in T-shirts and jeans jumped out and rushed inside. A minute later they emerged with twelve-packs of beer and drove off. Two minutes passed, then another. A BMW drove by on the highway headed north but didn't slow.

I glanced at my watch as a pickup truck pulled on to the highway a block away and slowly drove past the liquor store. I couldn't see the face of the driver, or tell if he or she had glanced in my direction. If the call were going to be made like the others, it would have to happen in the next minute.

The truck drove another block then made a U-turn and drove back to the store, pulling in and stopping next to the phone booth. Thirty seconds before the call needed to be made the door of the truck opened and a man stepped out. Long hair and a baseball cap obscured his face. He looked over six feet, with powerful shoulders. He glanced around the parking lot then he walked to the phone booth, stuck his finger into the change slot, and walked into the store.

That was it. No phone call – unless he needed change from inside the store, and if so he would be back within moments to call the Salems' condo. A minute stretched to two, then three and he hadn't returned to make the call. I started to pull out my cell phone to call Harrison and tell him I had wasted three hours when I saw movement in the rear-view mirror.

I dropped the phone in my lap and started to reach

for my Glock when a gun was thrust through my open window and placed against the side of my face.

'Take your hand away from your waist and place it on the steering wheel.'

I did what he said.

'Who the fuck are you?' he demanded.

I was able to turn my head enough to see that it was the man with the long hair who had stepped out of the truck across the street.

'I don't answer questions with guns pointed at me,' I said.

He pulled the hammer back on the automatic.

'Start,' he said.

'I'm a friend of Jack and Cathy,' I said.

'What are you doing here?'

'Jack asked me for help. I'm looking for the man who called their house for the last two nights at nine o'clock. I'm guessing that's you. If you want to know anything else, put the hammer down and take the gun out of my face.'

He didn't move for a moment, and then he reached over with his other hand and lowered the hammer, but didn't move the gun.

'Tell me something I don't know,' he said.

'When you dial that number again tonight you still won't get an answer.'

'How do you know that?'

'She's missing,' I said.

He held the gun for another moment then swiftly lowered it and tucked it into his belt. I turned and looked at him. He appeared to be in his early forties, though the lines around his dark eyes made him look much older. His shoulder-length hair was streaked with grey. A large scar wrapped around the hand that had held the gun. I had never seen him before.

'You a cop?'

I nodded. 'Pasadena.'

'Show me.'

I slipped my badge off my belt and handed it to him. He stared at it for a moment and then gave it back.

'Who else knows about the calls?'

'Anyone who's been inside their house, which probably includes whoever has Cathy.'

He quickly looked around at the surrounding darkness and empty homes with the practiced eye of someone who has spent time in dangerous places. And from the way his eyes were darting back and forth, I guessed maybe too much time.

'You have a name?' I asked.

He quietly whispered, 'Son of a bitch,' as he peered into the open second-floor window of a boarded-up house.

'Miller . . . Would you know if you were followed?'

'I think so, and I don't think I was.'

He turned and looked at me. 'You didn't see me come up behind you. In my world you're already dead.'

I imagined his world wasn't a place I would want to linger, and one he may never find his way out of. His face had the drawn look of a man who slept little, and stayed awake pumping his system full of adrenalin, amphetamines, or cup after cup of coffee so he could keep an eye on the darkness. If I was right about who he was, he had served with Salem in Iraq. And what he brought home wasn't the kind of war stories told on couches to grandsons and daughters.

'Do you know where Jack is?' I asked.

Miller looked at me and shook his head. 'You could be anybody.'

'So could you,' I said. 'Unless you want to begin talking, this conversation ends now.'

He leaned in close and looked into my eyes. I could smell the faint odor of whisky on his breath.

'He called me before his tour ended, said he was in trouble and asked me to meet him here. I've come back every night just like he said, but he never showed up.'

'You served with Salem in ISC?' I said.

Miller looked at me for a moment. His dark eyes seemed to swallow all light as if it was an enemy to be fought. What they had witnessed I couldn't imagine. The faint traces of a smile appeared on his lips.

'Served,' he said softly, losing the smile. 'Do I look like a waiter?'

'Tell me about ISC.'

'Tell you? What do you think you're going to do here, wave your badge, arrest the bad guys?'

He looked at the stars and shook his head.

'To know who the bad guys are you have to know who the good ones are, but you can't. They all look the same. You getting this, Lieutenant?'

A breeze rustled the dried fronds of a palm tree and

46

he turned as if he had just stepped on a tripwire. Across the street a cashier stepped out the door to the store and lit a cigarette. In the distance a car engine revved then faded away. Miller scanned the street for a moment, and then turned back to me.

'Go home.'

'I know about the boy on the bicycle.'

I saw the surprise register in his eyes, and then discomfort. In his world, surprise was what got you killed.

'Do you?'

'If you know where he is or are trying to protect him, I can help.'

He shook his head. 'Haven't you heard? He's missing, poof, just like that. Here today, gone . . .'

'What happened over there?'

'I left before things got bad—' he stopped himself. 'No, they were bad then too . . . I left before they got worse.'

'What got worse?'

'You're a civilian, you wouldn't understand.'

I slipped the picture of Salem and the boy out of my pocket and held it up for Miller to see. He stared at it for a moment then began to reach for it as the sound of tires spinning on gravel drew his attention to the darkness down the empty road.

'We're on the same side, Miller.'

He looked at the picture for a moment then I slipped it back in my pocket.

'What if there's more than two sides, Lieutenant?'

47

'Salem tried to send me something, I think it had to do with what happened before he left Baghdad.'

Miller stood absolutely still as if he were trying to hear the meaning within what I had just told him.

'You said he tried. What happened?'

'It never got to me.'

'So you don't really know what it is you're looking for?' he said, and then glanced toward one of the empty buildings.

'You want to tell me?'

'I don't know what happened after I left, but I can guess given the direction things were taking.'

'What happened?'

He looked out toward the darkness. 'I think you should just go home, Lieutenant.'

'No,' I said.

He thought for a moment. 'I was just trying to help a buddy, I don't want to be involved in this.'

'I think it's a little late for that.'

He stared into the darkness, shook his head and whispered something to himself.

'Three miles north,' he said, glancing toward the highway. 'There's a dirt road to the left. Four miles in is an old stock tank. I'll meet you there.'

'What is it you can tell me there that you can't here?' I asked.

'It's what I can show you. You need to see for yourself. Then I'm done with it.'

Before I could react he reached into the car and took my cell phone off my lap.

'I may need that,' I said.

'Not while you're with me.'

Miller stepped back from the car and held up the phone.

'Unless you've changed your mind and want to go back to your little world.'

'I make you nervous?' I said.

His eyes caught mine for just an instant. Any doubt that this man would kill without a moment's hesitation vanished.

'The only thing that makes me nervous is making mistakes,' he said. 'If the people who are after Salem are who I think they are, they don't make mistakes. Wait here twenty minutes, don't use the pay phone, don't talk to anyone. Another twenty minutes you'll be at the tank. If you're late, you'll never see me again.'

'And if you're not there?' I said.

He nearly smiled. The man leaning against the door to the liquor store looked in our direction and then tossed his cigarette into the darkness and stepped back inside.

'Then we'll know you were followed,' said Miller, 'and I'm dead and your life expectancy just got shot to hell.'

Miller slipped his gun out from under his shirt and held it casually at his side as he walked back to his truck, got in and drove away in the opposite direction he had told me to go.

five

I didn't like the idea of driving into the desert, but turning around and heading back to what my life had been seemed an even worse choice. Twenty minutes after Miller left I drove north out of Trona into the desert that rose and dipped as it left the lights of the plant and the few inhabited houses behind. The dirt road was just where he said it would be three miles north. Nothing marked its presence and from the look of the track few cars ever used it.

I took note of the mileage and turned on to the powdery sand and drove toward a series of small hills that were little more than dull shapes in the darkness. If the girl at the motel was right and the astronauts had trained here to walk on the moon, I couldn't imagine a better place. Boulders as big as cars seemed to have been spread about like a child's game of jacks. Dying Joshua trees lay bent over in the sand as if they had run out of air and collapsed.

A mile from the junction another road connected

from the south and I stopped. In the beam of the headlights a set of fresh tire tracks disappeared into the distance ahead. I reached down and rested my hand on my Glock and stared at the point where my headlights gave into the darkness.

If Miller was correct and there were more than two sides, then how would you know who was good and who wasn't? Does such a thing as truth even exist if everyone is telling lies? What would the boy with the bicycle say to that? Could I trust Miller, or Salem or even his wife? Or was truth something that had lost all meaning somewhere between Baghdad and a slowly dying town in the high desert?

I turned off the engine, leaned out my window and listened for the sound of another vehicle ahead in the darkness. Nothing. Maybe the track was days old. Or maybe someone was waiting just beyond the reach of my headlights and the desert swallowed the sound the same way it was taking Trona one house at a time.

Twenty feet ahead, a snake came zigzagging out of the darkness, crossing the road. I reached down and turned the ignition back on, eased my foot on to the accelerator and began following the other tire tracks in the sand. After two miles the lights of Trona were becoming little more than a faint glow over the hills. As I passed three miles, the glow vanished completely as the hills around me appeared to grow in height.

I dropped into a small ravine that crossed what appeared to be a dry stream bed then rose back up around several large boulders and stopped. The posts of a gate lay broken on either side of the road. Beyond that a rusting steel tank and a small windmill with most of the blades missing stood at the limit of the headlights. I grabbed a Mag-lite from out of the glove compartment, shut the engine off and stepped out, leaving the headlights on.

The tracks of the other car continued on past the tank further into the hills. I listened for any engine noise, but the only sound was the screech of an owl and the twisting of the blades of the windmill in the slight breeze.

I was two minutes early according to Miller's time-table. The tank was set amongst a series of hills that formed a bowl around it. From what I remembered of the contact I had had over the years with the San Bernardino sheriff's office, its chief occupation in its desert jurisdiction was body recovery. The sound of gunshot here would travel no further than the sur-rounding hills and no one knew I was here except for a man who had held a gun to my head forty minutes ago. I reached into the car and turned the headlights off, walked over and knelt down out of sight next to the tank.

Miller's two minutes passed and there was no sound of an engine, no footsteps emerging from the darkness. The air was colder here than in Trona. I tucked my knees in tight and wrapped my arms around my chest to fight off the chill. I watched the hands of my watch pass another three minutes and then another with no appearance by Miller.

A meteor burned across the sky toward the north and seemed to plunge into the hills. I pressed my back against the steel tank, which still held some of the sun's heat. As my eyes adjusted to the starlight I began to see the movement of bats above the sand, and then saw the footprints. They could have been a day old or a week or an hour, I couldn't tell. I reached down and slipped the Glock out and rose to my feet.

The prints moved past where I had been kneeling and around behind the windmill. I pressed myself against the tank for another moment then stepped out of its protection and listened for the sound of a hammer being cocked or the faint click of a round being chambered.

The high-pitch squeaks of bats were the only sound. I followed the tracks around the windmill and up a narrow trail through the rocks leading to the hill behind the tank. A few feet from the top of the hill I stopped. A new chain-link fence eight feet high had been erected across the trail. In the darkness I could just make out the neatly severed links where a hole had been cut large enough for a person to climb through. I flipped on my flashlight for a moment and scanned the trail. The footprints continued through the fence and disappeared over the top of the rise.

I climbed through the opening and followed the trail to the top, knelt and eased myself up over the edge to see what lay ahead. The hillside dropped steeply away, opening to a small valley enclosed on three sides by another set of hills. What looked like the main street of a small town stretched down the center of the valley. The street appeared to be paved. I counted a half-dozen parked cars and as many as twenty buildings stretched the length of a city block.

Not a sound rose from it. Not a single light shone in any building, and nothing moved except for a coyote that crossed the road at the far end of the buildings. I thought it might be a mining town that had been abandoned, or a failed subdivision of Trona, but neither felt right. The trail I had followed to the top of the hill continued no further, and the footprints seemed to vanish.

I walked carefully down the hillside around cactus and sage. Passing a crevice in a rock I thought I heard the rattle of a snake and kept moving as quickly as I dared in the darkness without losing my footing.

At the bottom of the hill I walked to the edge of the road, which seemed to have been stopped in mid-construction. Most of the buildings were two stories. I walked over to the nearest and stood next to the corner. It wasn't a mining camp or a failed venture of expansion. The building I stood next to appeared to be new and made of poured concrete and brick.

I slipped round the corner and walked to the entrance to the building and stepped inside. As I cleared the doorway I saw a figure standing in the corner to my right and raised the Glock.

'Police,' I said.

The person didn't move, didn't make a sound. I

took a step; the figure was covered from head to toe in the long flowing robes of a Muslim woman. Her face was covered except for a thin opening over her eyes, though in the darkness I couldn't see them.

'It's all right,' I said.

She remained absolutely still. I started to give her another command, then stopped and walked across the room until I was just a foot away. I lowered the Glock then reached out and took hold of the cloth covering her head and gently lifted it.

The blank eye of a mannequin stared into the room. The other eye and portions of the face had been blown away by gunshots.

'ISC,' I whispered to myself.

The training facility Harrison had told me about. I looked at the partially blown-away face of the mannequin. The damage the high-velocity rounds had done was not so different from what a human body would endure. I slipped the hood back over the head then walked back outside. Was this what Miller had wanted me to see? And if so, why?

In the doorway to the next building something was lying across the threshold. I walked over. It was the sandal-covered foot of a male mannequin dressed as an Iraqi peasant. The simple shirt it was wearing was torn to pieces by bullet rounds. A large hole in the plastic was where its chest should have been. I started to move on, but stopped. Further into the room a half-dozen other mannequins, some of them of children, lay scattered about the floor where they had been raked by bullets; pieces of fabric and plastic were scattered across the room.

In a doorway at the back of the room was another figure that I couldn't quite make out. I crossed the room, pieces of the shattered limbs snapping under my feet. As I got closer I recognized the boots on the mannequin in the doorway as army issue desert boots. The figure of a soldier was leaning against the wall, wearing full combat fatigues and holding a toy M-16. A single bullet round had pierced its face, leaving a hole about the size of a fifty-cent piece in the middle of the forehead. The back of the head was entirely blown away.

What kind of training had been going on here? A dead soldier, dead women and children. Is this how you train for stepping into a nightmare? Or was this something else? Was this where Salem's nightmare began? In a pretend town where pieces of plastic could do nothing more than stare silently back as rage was practiced day after day.

I looked at the scattered remains in the room and they began to take on an all too real presence. A voice in my head began to repeat over and over to get the hell out of here. And no matter how many times I told myself that it wasn't real, it took little imagination to hear the screams and cries of real people half a world away. I pushed past the soldier out the side door into an alley between two buildings and froze after two steps. In the middle of the alley was another mannequin, a boy riding a bicycle.

A small backpack hung from the figure's shoulders. Was he carrying his schoolbooks, bread for his mother, or a flash of light? I walked over to the bike and examined the mannequin. No bullets had torn it apart. Its face had the dull smile of a model displaying beachwear in Pennys. The walls of the two buildings on either side of the alley were pockmarked with impact holes. Scattered in the dirt around me I noticed pieces of debris. I knelt down and picked one up. It was a twisted bicycle spoke. I tossed it back into the dirt and then stared at the pack on the mannequin's shoulders and started to reach for the zipper to open it. The sound of a car engine became audible and headlights swept down the center of the street.

The vehicle was at the other end of town, moving in my direction. I ran back to the doorway I had come out of and ducked inside next to the mannequin of the soldier. A moment later the vehicle reached the alley and stopped. It was a large black SUV, its diesel engine sounding almost alive in the darkness. The dark glass of the driver's side window began to lower and I stepped back against the figure of the soldier as the beam of a flashlight shot down the length of the alley. The light swung back along buildings on the other side of the alley then swept back and stopped as it reached the doorway. The light moved slowly up the length of the door frame and stopped. Only then did I notice where chunks of concrete had been blown away by gunfire in the wall where I was standing.

The light moved further into the doorway and I

stepped away from it. The plastic arm of the soldier slipped from the rifle and landed on my hand just inches from the light. I eased its arm off my hand, moving it away from the light, then chambered a round in the Glock and waited for the quick burst of automatic fire. A few seconds passed silently, then another few without firing. I took a breath. This wasn't a casual inspection. They were looking for something or someone.

Had they seen my car up beyond the fence? Was that why they were here? Was Miller behind the wheel holding the light, or neatly tied up in the back? The light lingered on the door frame for another moment as if waiting for me to make a mistake, then was turned off and the SUV continued moving.

It drove down to the end of the road and stopped where I had descended the hill, then turned round and sped back the length of the street and left. I crossed the room to the door and waited until the sound of the SUV had vanished into the distance, then rushed back to the hill and climbed up to the fence.

From the top of the rise I could hear the SUV in the darkness but couldn't see any hint of its lights. I stepped back through the fence and took one last look at the street and buildings below. A pretend town with pretend violence and pretend victims. If a law had been broken here, it wasn't one that was written in any book or statute. But what war were they rehearsing for here? Or was it not a war they were training for at all, but something else? Was that what Salem was hiding from?

The sound of the SUV faded and I followed the trail down to my car. I drove back across the dry wash and through the dips and rises of the small hills. As I approached the road coming in from the south I saw a vague shape moving in the darkness beyond the range of my headlights. It appeared to be little more than a shadow, but shadows don't move at fifty miles per hour. I stepped on the gas and gripped the steering wheel. My tires spun on the loose gravel and the car began to fishtail as I approached the crossroads.

The dark shape appeared to be gathering speed. I reached to pull my seatbelt on but the car began to swerve on to the shoulder toward a pile of rocks. I let the belt go and brought the car back on to the gravel.

In the darkness I began to see the outline of the SUV as it approached the intersection. I pressed harder on the gas and flew through the crossroads as the SUV spun on to the road in a cloud of dust then appeared again in my rear-view mirror, coming out of the darkness and gaining speed.

Before I could react I felt the impact of the truck on my rear bumper. I began to swerve, corrected back on to the road and then the truck hit me again harder and my head hit the headrest as if someone had pulled me by the hair. The rear of the car began to spin and the front wheels slipped on to the shoulder. I tried to correct but the wheels had lost all traction. The car began to turn sideways and I saw the shape of a Joshua tree appear in the windshield and just as quickly vanish.

'No no no,' I began to say without realizing it.

I pulled hard on the steering wheel, turning it back on to the road. The front wheels began to grip and the car started to shudder as the wheels bounced over the washboard. I heard the roar of the truck's engine. The right side of the car began to spin and I shot back across the road and was lifted off the seat as the car went into the air.

'Don't,' I said.

I saw stars in the sky. An empty coffee cup flew past my face and hit the roof. Loose change floated in the air and all sound fell silent. Everything seemed to freeze for an instant. I took my foot off the gas as the stars vanished. I tried to reach for my gun, but I couldn't move against the force of the car's inertia.

It all happened in a blink of an eye. A Joshua tree swept past my window and I felt the jolt of the front tires hitting the sand. Loose coins pelted the windshield and hit me in the face. I flew backwards, hitting the seat. The post of a fence appeared in the lights. I heard the snap of wood. I tried to find the brake and was jolted forward toward the windshield when the flash of the air bag filled my vision.

All the air rushed out of my lungs. I tasted the bitter residue of the bag's explosive cap and everything stopped. There wasn't a sound. Not from the car, or the desert. Even the stars appeared to vanish. I remembered for a brief instant that I had been a mother, and then even that slipped away.

six

Had a minute passed, a few seconds? I tried to take a breath but it was as if a hand was held over my mouth. I tried again and again and finally the air came rushing back into my chest and I sat back in the seat and opened my eyes. There was the smell of sage in the dust floating in the car. The beams of the headlights bored two holes into the darkness.

My hand slipped down to my side until I found the Glock and took hold of it as I opened the door and rolled out into the sand, swinging the weapon across the surrounding darkness.

I heard movement behind me and I began to swing the weapon when I felt a hand grab my neck and then another one took my wrist. I tried to squeeze a shot but the Glock was already out of my hand and I felt myself being lifted and then the ground came rushing at me and my face hit it and my mouth filled with sand.

'Bitch,' a voice said.

I tried to move and my face was pressed harder into the sand.

'Take her hands,' the same voice said.

I could see some dark boots, but nothing more as the hand pressed down on my neck. Someone took both my hands and pulled them out in front of me.

'This isn't your business.'

I tried to say I was a police officer.

'You're nothing,' he said. 'This is what happens to nothing.'

My head was jerked back by my hair and a piece of tape stretched across my eyes. Then I felt hands on the waistband of my slacks and the button snapped and fabric begin to tear.

'No,' I said and tried to shake free only to be pressed harder into the sand. Then my slacks were pulled down my legs.

'You're not a policewoman any more.'

His hand took hold of my underwear and tore it from me.

'Do you understand?' he shouted in my ear.

Tears began to fill my eyes.

'You're nothing, do you understand?'

I began to gasp for breath and his hand pressed in between my legs.

'Nod your head that you understand.'

I could feel my body begin to shake. His hand pressed harder into me and pain shot up the length of my body like a knife.

'Nod your head,' he shouted.

The hand holding my neck took hold of my hair and started to move my head up and down.

'Say it,' he shouted.

I tried to shake my head and his hand pressed harder.

'I'm nothing,' I said barely above a whisper.

'You see, you're nothing, now we understand each other.'

The hand between my legs pulled away.

'Shoot her,' he said.

I heard the chambering of a round and then the gun was put against my ear.

'Now?' said another voice.

'Shoot her.'

The barrel pressed harder against my ear and I heard the motion of the trigger. I began to scream and the trigger clicked and the hammer fell on an empty chamber.

'Shoot her, goddamn it,' he shouted again, and again I heard the chamber on the automatic move and it was pressed against my ear.

'Shoot her in the head.'

I began to scream; it came from a place I couldn't control – a wild, horrible place.

'Shoot her!'

The trigger clicked and again I felt the heavy thud of the hammer falling on the empty chamber. The man on top of me leaned in next to my ear, his body pressing me into the sand.

'This is our world, not yours.'

The gun was pressed against my head again.

'You will be killed. Do you understand? Walk away.'

My entire body was shaking uncontrollably. I couldn't speak, couldn't react to his voice at all.

'I don't think she understands,' he said.

I heard the blast of the shot. Every muscle, every nerve in my body reacted and I began to shake. I didn't feel his weight leave me, or the other man release my hands. My body continued to shake like a child's, gasping for breath as the tears flowed from my eyes. I don't know how long it was before I moved. I tried to say something, I tried to talk myself back but the only words I continued to hear were in my head as I said, 'I'm nothing.'

I reached down and pulled my pants back up to cover myself, then pulled the tape off of my eyes, barely noticing the pain as it pulled against my skin and eyebrows. Even the smallest movement took forever to manage as muscles struggled to respond.

I pushed myself up and then crawled over and pressed against the security of the car. In the sand ten feet from the car I could see the Glock. I took a deep breath, took hold of the door handle and pulled myself up. My head began to spin and I closed my eyes until it passed.

In the distance I heard the sound of a semi shifting gears on a distant highway. I took a step and then another toward my weapon, waiting for the sound of the shot to come out of the darkness and hit me in the back, but it didn't come.

I knelt down to the gun, picked it up, brushed the sand off of it and turned round. The SUV was gone. I walked back to the car and sat down, took the Glock in both hands and pointed it out toward the desert. Tears began to mix with blood coming from my nose and gather on the corner of my mouth. I was still trembling. As hard as I tried I couldn't hold the gun still.

'You bastards,' I whispered, spitting out grains of sand that were still in my mouth.

I could still feel his hands on my waist pulling on my pants.

'Work it,' I said, trying to be the cop I had been just moments before.

I closed my eyes to try and find a detail that I could hold on to but all that did was bring back the feel of his hands, and the fall of the hammer against my head. I wiped the blood and tears from the corner of my mouth and took hold of the Glock again with my shaking hands.

'Stop,' I said, trying to still the tremors. 'Stop it, stop it, stop . . .'

I squeezed the trigger, firing a shot into the desert. Then I fired again and again and again and began to scream until I had emptied the clip and drained the last of the terror from my shaking hands.

'He wore a ring,' I whispered.

I saw it as the tape was put over my eyes – a military ring. The kind given to officers when they graduate from one of the academies.

Why wasn't I lying in the sand with a bullet in my head? I tried to make sense of it. They could have put me in a hole in the desert but they didn't. I couldn't hold on to the logic. With every step I took toward reason, I took one back to the sound of the hammer falling, and the feel of his hand.

'This is our world,' he had said.

I thought of the pictures of hostages in bare empty rooms with blindfolds around their eyes half a world away. What they had done to me, the precision wasn't by chance. It came from practice. It came from having done it over and over until pressing a gun against another human being's head and reducing a woman to little more than a thing becomes second nature.

In an instant I was little more than an animal. They didn't kill me because in their world, as they called it, whatever threat I had posed had been eliminated. When their victims walked out of those dirty little rooms in Baghdad, they would move like frightened animals, trying to stay in the shadows, not drawing attention to themselves. And every time they heard a shot, or a knock on the door, or a stranger brushed past them on the street, they would be back in that room, held down, waiting for the sound of the hammer falling on the chamber that contained a bullet.

A few feet away in the sand my underwear lay in several pieces. I walked over and picked them up. My hand trembled slightly as I slipped them into the pocket of my slacks.

'You've made a mistake,' I said silently.

I turned and looked at my car. The front end rested against a cactus, but it didn't look too terribly damaged. I walked over, got in and then removed the empty clip from my gun and replaced it with the spare I carried but never needed. The engine started right up and I placed the Glock on the seat tucked under my leg.

I backed up over the fence post. The tires spun slightly in the soft sand but I made it back on to the road. I wound the three miles back to the junction and stopped. For a brief second I thought of turning left and heading away from the glow of Trona to the south. I flipped down the visor and opened the mirror to look at myself. The blood in my nose from the air bag's impact had begun to dry. Mascara streaked my cheeks; there was sand and pieces of dried grasses in my hair.

I wanted to kill the man who had held me down. I wanted to hold my gun against the side of his head and pull the trigger. And then do it again and again until there was nothing left of him.

'What's happening to me?' I whispered to myself, then closed the mirror.

I reached down and pulled the Glock out from under my leg and chambered a round, then turned right and headed back to Trona.

seven

Three miles isn't very far to travel to return to what you thought had been your life. Five minutes of driving, seven or eight if you stretch it out. I stretched it out. Twice headlights of vehicles came out of the darkness behind me, and each time I reached down and slipped the Glock out from under my leg and held on to it until they passed.

I drove in through the first abandoned houses and realized something had changed. The light was different. The heavy scent of a burning building hung in the air, along with the dust from the plant. I rounded the turn into the center of town and saw the flashing lights of several fire trucks and sheriff's vehicles in front of a low stucco building with bright orange flames shooting out of the few windows. A small Greyhound bus sign hung above the door where two firemen were directing the stream of water.

I remembered the envelope Mrs Salem had placed on my table. It could have held the kind of key from a bus-station locker. It could have been anything, and this fire could just be old wiring, and the gun placed against my head was all a misunderstanding. It could wait until morning.

I drove on to the motel and parked outside my room. The young woman who had been in the office was sitting on a rail fence next to the parking lot. I picked up the Glock and covered it with a sweater I had in the back seat and got out.

'A man asked about you,' she said as I got out.

She reached down and unsteadily picked up a bottle of beer at her feet, swaying a little from her high as she did. I stepped over. She looked at me for a moment and briefly lost the haze of whatever high she was on.

'I guess he found you,' she said.

'I had an accident,' I said.

The dullness in her eyes returned and she laughed joylessly. 'I've had accidents like that.'

'Was it the man I showed you the picture of?'

'Maybe . . . I forget faces.'

'Was his hair long?'

She shook her head.

'What did he look like?' I asked.

'Kinda like Ken.'

'Ken?'

'You know, the doll. Ken, the dreamboat.' Her eyes lingered for a moment on the dried blood in my nose, then she looked out into the darkness. 'Dreamboats aren't what they used to be.'

'Did he get a room?'

She shook her head and gestured down the road. 'He just drove off.'

She took another drink from her beer and looked at the blood on my face.

'You want me to call the police for you?' she asked.

I shook my head. 'I am the police.'

I turned and started for my room.

'Do you think there'll still be buses without a station?' she said.

I stopped and looked at her. 'You don't have to stay here, you can leave.'

She gazed at the beer in her hand as if it were a ticket out of here.

'I leave every day,' she said, and then drifted back into her high.

The room, like the office, seemed to have been modeled after a sixties television version of what the west had been like. The paneling on the walls had brands inked on them. I locked the door and jammed a chair up against the handle and then ran a bath. I placed the Glock on the edge of the tub and then sank into the warm water.

There was still sand in my hair. I washed the blood away from my nose, and my elbows and knees which had been scraped where they were forced into the sand. Shampoo and soap did little to remove the sensation of his hands on me, or stop me from reaching for the gun every time a board creaked or a car drove by outside. Closing my eyes only brought back the sound of the hammer falling on the empty chamber. Twice I got out of the tub, wrapped a towel around myself and took the gun to the door to make sure it was still locked, and then checked and rechecked the windows to see if they were latched.

At 2 a.m. I finally lay down in bed, but each time sleep began to approach I heard another sound and rose from the bed with the Glock in hand and stood by the door, listening until I was certain there was no one outside.

I made plans. In the morning I would try and find Miller if he was alive, and then talk to the sheriff about the fire at the bus station and what he knew of ISC. Then I would get the hell out of Trona. I turned the TV on, turned it off, picked up the phone to call Harrison and Lacy but put it down each time before dialing a single number.

I tried to sleep in the chair, then back on the bed and then repeated the process again and again. Twice in the night on the shallow edge of sleep my heart began to beat uncontrollably and I picked up the gun, pointed it at the door and began to squeeze the trigger until my heart slowed and the panic passed.

What sleep did come produced only more anxiety that I had missed the creak of a window opening and that I was no longer alone in the room. At 5 a.m. I saw the glow of headlights through the curtains pull up and stop outside the motel. I took the Glock in hand and walked over to the door. I heard footsteps in the gravel outside.

The steps stopped outside and a fist pounded on my door three times.

'Sheriff's deputy, please open the door.'

I raised the Glock and stepped over to the window to peek out, but I could see nothing other than the white light of the headlights. I raised my Glock toward the door.

'Hold your ID up to the window,' I said.

'I just want to ask you some questions,' the deputy responded and then banged on the door again.

'I'm a police officer,' I said.

There was a hesitation on the other side.

'Then you have nothing to worry about, do you? Do you have a weapon?'

'Yes.'

'Put it on the floor and let me see your empty hands when you open the door.'

I held the gun toward the door.

'Your ID,' I said.

'Open the door now,' he repeated.

I started to squeeze the trigger when I heard the crackle of a police radio.

'Open the door.'

I held the gun for another moment, then lowered it and placed it on the carpet. I stared at it for a moment as if I'd just had a piece of me removed.

'The gun's on the floor, I'm unlocking the door.'

Nothing came back from the other side. I pulled the chair away from the doorknob, and then reached up to the deadbolt. My hand began to shake and I had to turn the latch with both hands. As soon as the latch cleared the jamb, the door flew open, hitting me on the shoulder and knocking me backwards.

'On the floor, face down, arms spread.'

In the dim light the deputy appeared to be in his mid-thirties, heavily built. His 9mm was pointed right at my chest. I looked down at the floor and shook my head.

'I can't do that. My ID's next to the bed.'

'Lie on the floor, face down, now.'

I shook my head again. 'Cuff me if you want, but I can't lie down like that. If you want to shoot me, you'll ruin both our careers.'

He took a step toward me, stopped, and then seemed to reconsider.

'Place your hands on the back of your head and turn around.'

I did as directed. He stepped up behind me and took my left wrist, snapped the cuff on it, then placed both my hands behind my back and secured the second cuff. His hands quickly patted me down then he sat me on the edge of the bed.

'Would you like to tell me why you're in my room?'

He picked up my gun and then my ID on the nightstand.

'Lieutenant Delillo, Pasadena PD?'

'That's right.'

He held out my phone. 'This belongs to you.'

I nodded. 'A man named Miller had it.'

'Did he drive an old pickup?'

'Yes.'

The deputy glanced over to the chair next to the door and then at my bruised nose and scraped elbows.

'Did Miller do this?'

I shook my head. 'I drove into a pile of sand.'

'Do you know where Miller is?'

The name tag above the deputy's badge read Gilley.

'I was supposed to meet him but he never showed up.'

'I don't suppose it would do any good to ask you why you were meeting him,' said the deputy.

'Not at the moment,' I said.

He walked over and removed the cuffs then handed me my badge and gun.

'I think you'd better come with me.'

We drove back into Trona without any conversation. The first light of dawn was turning the horizon shades of purple and orange. The eeriness of the empty streets and desiccated landscape and buildings began to take on a feeling of violence that had happened just moments before. At the burned-down bus station Deputy Gilley turned down a dark side street. Miller's truck was parked halfway down the block, the only vehicle on the street. We pulled up to it and got out.

'Is this his?'

I nodded. 'It's what he was driving. What is this about?'

'Several witnesses said they saw this truck circle the bus station before it caught on fire. I guess you know nothing about that?'

I shook my head.

'The truck's registration says he's from Los Angeles,' said the deputy.

'I've only met him once and it was here,' I said. 'I'd like that address.'

He nodded. 'I don't suppose you know anything about this either.'

He walked over to the truck and pulled back a tarp covering the bed. Inside were a number of aluminum and wooden cases and chests, and several nylon duffel bags. Deputy Gilley reached in and opened one of the aluminum cases. Inside were several assault rifles and scopes, along with what appeared to be grenades.

'Your phone was on the floor under the driver's seat, along with two nine millimeter automatics. Neither of the weapons have serial numbers, and from what I've seen in these boxes, neither does any of this.' The deputy looked at me. 'One of the other cases has some pretty sophisticated com and surveillance equipment, all of it high-end military stuff. All the makings for the start of a nice little war if that was his intention. Was that his intention, Lieutenant Delillo?'

'I honestly don't know.'

'Well, I honestly don't know whether to believe you or not.'

The deputy shook his head, then reached into another case and removed a grenade.

'Incendiary, incredibly hot. Nice way to burn a bus station down. Do you have any idea why he would want to burn down our little bus station?'

'No.'

'You don't have many answers to anything, do you? Are you here as part of an investigation?'

I reached into my pocket and handed the deputy the picture of Salem.

'I'm looking for him.'

Gilley studied it for a moment, shook his head. 'Is he a suspect in an investigation?'

'He's a cop,' I said.

The deputy glanced at it again then gave it back to me. 'I've never seen him.'

'He had been working for ISC,' I said.

That caught Deputy Gilley's attention. 'The mercenary outfit.'

'What can you tell me about them?' I asked.

He shook his head. 'Not a damn thing. They have a training facility in the desert. The few people I've met haven't been terribly interested in talking with a cop. My guess is they're tight with China Lake.'

'The naval weapons center?' I said.

The deputy nodded.

'Why do you say that?'

'I've seen vehicles come and go. Some official, some not. From the look of the people inside them, I figure none of them are regular soldiers. China Lake is supposedly an air combat and weapons center, but the people I've seen aren't flyers.'

'What would you call them?' I asked.

'Special operations,' he said. 'Or goddamn spooks.'

In the distance, the strange white surface of the dry

lake bed next to the town began to gather the coming light and seemed to glow.

'What's so important about a small-town bus station, Lieutenant?'

'Were there lockers in the station?'

The deputy nodded. 'A row or two, maybe a dozen at most. You think something was inside of one?'

'I'd like to take a look, if it's all right.'

I heard something move on the gravel behind me, grabbed my Glock and spun round. A middle-aged man in running shorts and sweatshirt stopped short, his eyes staring at the gun, his face turning pale in fear.

'Lieutenant,' Gilley said, but I didn't hear him.

The sound of the hammer falling on the chamber went through me again.

'Lieutenant,' he repeated.

I stared at the jogger for a moment then slipped the Glock back in the speed holster. My hand was shaking like a leaf in the wind.

'I'm sorry,' I said to the man.

He looked at me for a moment then turned and started running back the way he had come. Deputy Gilley was staring at my shaking hand, and then motioned with his hand to his nose.

'You're bleeding.'

I reached up and touched a thin line of blood streaming out of my nose. The deputy walked over to the squad car and returned with a small box of Kleenex. I took a few and held them against the flow of blood.

'Are you all right, Lieutenant?'

'The air bag in the car,' I said.

'That's not what I mean,' he said, glancing at the jogger running away.

'I'm fine. I didn't get much sleep.'

He didn't believe a word.

'I was with a Marine recon unit during the ride north from Kuwait,' he said. 'It's just my opinion, but it takes more than missing a nap to do what you just did.'

Gilley looked at me for a moment.

'What happened to your wrists?'

I didn't know what he meant until I looked at them. A faint bruising had risen, where I had been held down in the sand. I stared for a moment, the grip on my wrists coming back all too vividly. I wanted to tell him, or at least I wanted to tell someone, but the moment I even entertained the idea, I could feel the gun pressing against the side of my head.

'I'm all right,' I said, less than convincingly.

Before Gilley could respond, another deputy drove up and stopped to secure Miller's truck.

'I'd like to go look at the bus station now,' I said.

The jogger at the end of the street hesitated as he turned the corner and looked back in my direction before disappearing out of sight.

'Then I'd like to go home,' I said.

Heat still rose from under the ashes of what had been the small seating area inside the station. The roof had collapsed and burned, all that remained of the structure was the walls and the partially melted Greyhound sign that hung loosely over what had been the entrance.

'Like I was saying,' said Deputy Gilley. 'Incendiaries burn hot.'

'Where were the lockers?' I asked.

He motioned to the far wall.

'The only reason the floor is still here is that it was concrete,' he said.

I walked over to the far wall, stepping around the larger pieces of the fallen roof that were still giving off heat. The lockers had melted into a neat pool of aluminum on the floor. All that was left of their structure were the steel bolts that had secured them to the walls, and even those had sagged in the heat.

'If there was something in one of these, it's gone now,' said Gilley.

The acrid odor of the burned structure made it difficult to breathe and I nodded in agreement. We stepped back out of the wreckage as the first rays of the sun were rising over the mountains to the east.

Deputy Gilley drove me back to the motel and we both sat silently for a moment when he pulled to a stop next to the Volvo.

'I'm just a second-year deputy, Lieutenant,' said Gilley. 'What I do here is handle domestic abuse, drunks, the odd body left in the desert, and car accidents, but I'm pretty good at it.'

He looked at me for a moment.

'I'm wondering about your accident last night.'

'I missed a turn, skidded off the road,' I said.

He nodded. 'That can happen on the sand and dirt around here.'

'I should have been more careful,' I said.

'Of course it doesn't matter how careful you drive if someone pushes you off the road, and from the small dents in your back bumper, I would say you were pushed.'

We looked at each other in silence.

'I've also seen bruising like you have on your wrists of women drink driving suspects who had to be restrained. I also saw it in Iraq in prisoners who had been interrogated.'

I opened the door of the squad car and got out.

'You're right, you are a good cop,' I said.

'Whatever happened to you last night, this isn't the end of it, is it?' he asked.

'No, I think it's just beginning,' I said.

'If I find out any more about Miller, I'll let you know.'

'Thank you.'

'And maybe I'll have a talk with the occupants of one of those vehicles coming from China Lake. I'm guessing they might be driving a big SUV.'

He put his squad car in gear and drove away.

I checked my room to make sure I had left nothing behind then walked back out to the Volvo to leave. The young woman from the office was waiting outside. Her eyes were red from drink and whatever else she had indulged in, but the fog that had clouded them the night before was gone.

'I thought of something about the guy who asked about you last night,' she said. 'I don't really remember his face, but I did remember somethin'.'

'What did you remember?' I asked.

'He had on a big gold ring, might have been like anchors or something on it.'

'Which hand was it on?'

'Right, I think.'

'Thank you,' I said and got in the car.

'You're a cop, aren't you?' she asked.

I nodded and she took a breath and looked down at her feet.

'Is there something you need?' I said.

She looked out toward Trona. The sun had risen far enough in the sky for all the warmth of the light to have been replaced by a bright washed-out hardness.

'A walk on the moon,' she said then turned and went back toward the tiny office with the cattle brands stamped on the walls.

As I headed south toward LA, past the massive plant and the empty houses, a north wind began to sweep across the dry lake bed next to the town. When I passed the painted football field I checked the mirrors to be certain that I wasn't being followed, and then checked again and again every few hundred feet, but there was nothing there. As I drove further from Trona, all I could see behind me was a gathering cloud of dust.

eight

I knew why Salem had disappeared. I had seen and felt what he was running from. And now I wanted to do the same. I couldn't walk back into headquarters the way I was. It wasn't the clothes, no one would notice the small tear in my slacks or understand how it was made if they did. It wasn't even the light bruises on my wrists. I could cover those with a long shirt or touch them up with a little makeup. It was what I saw in my own eyes in the mirror I didn't want anyone else to see. Or what I didn't see. I didn't see me.

The fall of the hammer, the pull of the trigger, the steel of the barrel against my skin, that was what I saw. I saw weakness and shame. I saw the person I had been vanish in the time it took to be stretched out in the sand and manipulated like a plaything.

I knew what terror was, but this was different. This was calculated and with a purpose. It grew out of a twisted sense of righteousness that believed war was a form of violence immune from the weakness that is in

85

the human heart. This was what Salem was running from, I knew it as clearly as if he had told me on the phone that night he had called from Iraq. Maybe he had.

I could walk away, do as I had been told and not look back. I knew part of me wanted to. And I knew the part of me that mattered the most, the part that had raised a daughter, and become a cop, would be lost if I did. Those men holding me down in the sand would have won their war without ever firing a shot.

But how to do it? How did I find that person again? It would be so much easier just to disappear.

LA was covered in a thick blanket of clouds that dappled the windshield with mist as I drove down into the city. I could see five or ten cars ahead but no more. The sprawl and strip malls and lawns and pools and the nine million people spread out in neighborhoods of Mexican, Russian, Chinese and every other color and language from everywhere on earth had vanished like everything else. My world had been reduced to a small circle that extended little further than my own reach.

I drove home to my blackened neighborhood. The sound of hammers nailing the frames of new houses together sent a jolt through me with each blow. I recognized several people as I drove up my street but didn't look at them, didn't make eye contact, sank down in the seat and pretended I wasn't there.

I thought I would feel something when I walked into my house. I thought being home would make a difference, but I was a stranger. What allowed me to feel anything had been taken, or had been pushed so deep inside I couldn't find it.

There were messages waiting. Harrison had called with information on one of the suicides I had asked him to look into. Lacy had called because I had not called her for a day. And Deputy Gilley had left a message that he was going out to China Lake to talk to an officer he knew. I just let them go.

I threw the clothes I had been wearing in the trash, and then stood in the shower holding my Glock until the hot water began to cool, and the faintest reflection of the person I had been before driving into Trona flickered in the mirror, if only for an instant.

I dressed and drove into downtown, parked a block from headquarters and just watched the squad cars come and go. I didn't want to walk through the squad room. I didn't want a room full of cops watching me. I didn't want them to see the hesitation in my eyes that accompanied even the smallest of thoughts. I didn't want them to see the weakness in me.

I dialed Harrison's number three times before I stopped hanging up before the first ring. When I finally let it go through, he picked up immediately.

'Where are you?' Harrison said.

'The car,' I answered.

'Lacy called me looking for you, I left some messages last night—'

'I need to meet you,' I said.

'Where?'

I knew every inch of Pasadena; I had been a girl

there, a young wife, mother, and cop. I couldn't think of a single place.

'Are you all right?' Harrison asked.

An unmarked squad car pulled out of the station and passed by. It wasn't one of ours, the driver was Jackson the IAD officer from LAPD I had talked to about Salem. I started to ask Harrison about it, but stopped myself. They would know I was right outside if I asked that. I watched him drive away then looked around. The number of people walking past on the sidewalk began to feel threatening and I locked the door.

'Alex?' Harrison said.

'The arroyo . . .'

There would be fewer people, no cops.

'Parking lot of the aquatic center,' I said.

'I can be there in ten minutes.'

I hung up without saying anything else and waited for Harrison to pull out of the parking lot. He drove past me without looking in my direction. I waited another minute watching the lot, making sure no one was trailing along behind him, then pulled out into traffic and drove down Colorado until I dropped down under the bridge and into the arroyo.

The parking lot was nearly empty. Harrison was parked in the center, leaning against the door of the unmarked squad. I hesitated at the entrance to the lot, checking my mirrors, then drove in and stopped twenty feet from where he had parked and unlocked the passenger door as he walked over and slipped inside.

I dropped my hands into my lap but I could see that he had seen the bruises before I hid them. He looked into my eyes briefly then at the deflated air bag on the steering column, then turned and closed the door behind him.

'I hit a cactus last night.'

'Are you all right?'

I placed my hands back on to the steering wheel.

'I jammed my wrists.'

Whether he believed me or not, he didn't press the issue.

'Did you find what you were looking for in Trona?'

I started to answer but was unable to form a single word for a moment. Looking into the face of a person who was part of my life seemed to push me back into the sand with the gun at my head instead of away from it. I quickly checked the mirror.

'Are you sure no one knows where you went?' I said.

He nodded. 'What's happened, Alex?'

I stepped out of the car and walked over to a bench and sat. Harrison waited a moment then walked over and sat next to me.

'It's important that no one knows what's happening.'

'What is happening?'

I watched a jogger pass on the street then looked up to the rim of the arroyo and the houses that clung to its edge.

'All those windows, I should have picked a different . . .'

I closed my eyes and tried to stop the flood of paranoia running loose inside. Overhead, a flock of parrots came flying down the valley, their manic screeching going right through me as if I had touched a live wire.

'We are alone, aren't we?' I said.

Harrison nodded. 'No one knows where we are.'

'Why was Jackson at headquarters?'

Harrison looked at me for a moment, took a breath. 'He was talking to Chavez.'

'About?'

I could see Harrison didn't want to answer.

'Tell me,' I said.

'LAPD suggested you were romantically linked with Salem, and were harassing his wife and that she had gone into hiding to get away from you.'

I looked into Harrison's eyes. 'Did he believe him?'

'Chavez told him to stick it.' He looked at me silently for a moment. 'You don't have to ask what I think.'

A boy on a bicycle began approaching from the other end of the parking lot. I stared at his face, trying to read his emotions, then my eyes drifted to his feet on the pedals, pushing the bike closer to us. I took hold of the bench with both hands and squeezed tight to keep myself from getting up and moving away. The cyclist turned and rode out into the street and down the arroyo.

'Alex?'

I looked away from the bicycle.

'You mentioned one of the suicides,' I said.

Harrison's eyes followed the cyclist for a moment then nodded.

'One of them graduated from the same high school, the same year Salem did. Just a few months after his death, Salem joined ISC.'

It took me a moment to place the detail he was talking about.

'They were friends, or at least they knew each other.'

'It would seem. There was no connection that I could find with the other, nothing about that death raised any flags.' Harrison looked at me for a moment. 'I don't know what happened, but I know you,' he said softly. 'If I'm to help you, I need to know as much as you can tell me.'

I shook my head. 'You can't help. No laws have been broken in Pasadena.'

'What's happened, Alex?'

I reached into my pocket and handed Harrison the photograph of Salem and the boy. Harrison looked at the picture for a moment.

'This is Salem?' Harrison said.

I nodded. The images from the previous night began to come back.

'I was driving . . . it was late, and I was forced off the road . . . I hit the air bag and was stunned. By the time I crawled out of the car . . .' The words left me as easily as a breath. I looked down at the bruises on my wrists.

'The war's come home,' I said.

Harrison handed me back the photograph and I

stared at the smiling face of the little boy.

'I think ISC used, or is using, children as weapons. I think they gave them gifts like bicycles and turned them into killing machines. They may have refined it in Trona.'

Harrison looked at me in silence for a moment.

'Do you have evidence of this?' he asked.

'If I did, I would be dead now,' I said.

Harrison looked at my wrists.

'I believe Salem had or has evidence,' I said. 'It could have been in the bus station in Trona, but that burned to the ground last night. There could be others who served with him who also knew. I may have met one.'

I reached into my pocket and removed my card that had the address of Miller's vehicle registration on it and gave it to Harrison.

'Colin Miller?' said Harrison. 'He served with Salem?'

'He said he did. I don't even know if he's alive now. I don't know if he was telling the truth. I can't even tell you what side he's really on because I don't know who to believe or trust. I need to find the others that served with Salem.'

'As a private company, without a court order there's no way to get a list of ISC's employees,' Harrison said. 'An assault on a police officer would be cause for a warrant.'

I shook my head. 'It's more complicated than that.'

'How?' Harrison said.

'A deputy sheriff in Trona thinks ISC may have a connection to China Lake and a special operations unit.'

Harrison sat back on the bench and took a breath. 'If there's a connection between ISC and the military, or a particular unit . . .' Harrison didn't need to finish the sentence; he just turned and looked at me.

'Then I just fell down the same rabbit hole that Salem disappeared into,' I said and looked at Harrison. 'What can I do?'

'See if you can find out anything about Miller.'

'What else?'

The sound of mariachi music playing somewhere drifted across the parking lot.

'Then walk away, just like they told me,' I said.

'I'm not going to do that.'

'Yes you are, you're going to do just that.'

Harrison reached over and gently touched one of my wrists. I pulled away from him.

'Don't,' I said.

'What else happened last night?' Harrison said.

The sound of the music was lost as a helicopter flying up the arroyo drowned it out. I watched the chopper pass until it was beyond the Rose Bowl then looked back at Harrison and shook my head, unable to tell him.

'Professionals,' I said. 'They were very practiced.'

'Can you make an ID?'

I almost laughed. 'I can identify a ring with anchors on it . . . maybe. A dark SUV, could have been a Ford or a Chevy, unless it was something else. It most certainly was black, unless it just looked black on a moonless night. And I can testify under oath that there were at least two people, maybe three, probably no more than five who held me down, and a . . .' I let the rest go. 'I was a hell of a cop last night,' I said softly.

Harrison's eyes held on mine. Of all the men I had known he had the unique ability never to seem to pass judgement with just a look.

'The ring could belong to a naval academy graduate,' Harrison said.

'That doesn't narrow it down much.'

The sound of the mariachi drifted off again as a late model Chevy the color of cotton candy drove out of the lot and turned south. A kid on a skateboard slapped it against the cement and I spun round, my heart pounding against my chest.

'You can't do this,' Harrison said.

'If I walk away, they've won their war.'

A bright yellow school bus pulled into the parking lot and over to the aquatic center. A group of high school kids, all of them seeming to have long blond hair and looking impossibly perfect, jumped out and ran through the gates toward the pools.

'Is there a surviving next of kin for the suicide victim who knew Salem?' I asked.

Harrison hesitated to answer.

'I can find out, whether you tell me or not,' I said.

'The wife. Maya Torres. She moved to Ontario after her husband's death.'

I handed Harrison a card. 'I need the address.'

He hesitated then reluctantly wrote it down and handed it back.

'How did he die?'

'Gunshot wound to the head. Coroner's office found no evidence of foul play.'

'Where exactly did the bullet enter?'

Harrison shook his head. 'The coroner found no cause to think—'

'Where was he shot?' I demanded.

'The right temple, next to the ear.'

A shudder went through me and I got up from the bench and steadied my breathing.

'Was it a contact wound?' I asked.

Harrison looked at me for a moment and then nodded. 'The barrel was pressed against the head with enough force for the ring of the muzzle to leave a burn mark on the skin.'

If I closed my eyes I could hear it all over again. There were four distinct sounds, like a four count in a measure of music.

'Can you get me the case file?'

'I'll try.'

'I have to go,' I said and started back toward the car.

'I could follow you,' said Harrison. He stood up.

I stopped. 'You won't, though.'

'How do you know?'

'Because I'm asking you not to . . . because if anything happened to someone I cared about . . . I've

95

already told you more than I should have. Trust me on this. Please, just get me the file.'

His eyes held mine for a moment and then he looked away.

'Promise me,' I said.

He shook his head.

'If I get in trouble, I'll call you. That's the best I can do.'

'You're already in trouble.'

I nodded. 'For far too long. This is my chance to end it.'

I placed my hand on his chest. His hand reached up and took hold of mine.

'Promise me,' I said.

Harrison closed his eyes and then nodded. I slipped my hand from his.

'Is there anything else about the suicide I should know?' I asked.

Harrison took a breath, thought it over for a second and reluctantly answered.

'He had planned to take his kids to Disneyland the following day.'

I took a step away.

'How did you know about the wound?' asked Harrison.

For a moment there wasn't a sound, not a single bird, no voices, not even the constant hum of distant traffic, just the rhythm of my own breathing.

'A music teacher in school once said I was tone deaf,' I said. 'She was wrong. I always heard every note perfectly.'

Harrison clenched his left hand into a fist.

'When should I tell Chavez you'll be back?'

His eyes locked on mine and refused to look away until I answered. I took another step, started to shake my head but stopped.

'When I know the way,' I said, then turned and didn't look back.

nine

Miller's address on the car registration was an empty lot between an Armenian grocery and a thirty-dollar-a-night transient hotel in Hollywood. How much of the rest of Miller was also a forgery I could only guess. Forty minutes after driving away from the aquatic center Harrison had called me with as much information as he could find on Miller – nothing. Not a birth certificate, social security card, driver's license, military record. No credit cards, bank accounts. Whoever the man I had met was, he had lived in the shadows so long the light was a stranger to him.

Were there others who knew what had happened, as he suggested? Or had he led me to that empty spot in the desert so that a gun could be put against my head? Did the words of a ghost mean anything except to those already dead?

There was little doubt in my mind that former Green Beret Albert Torres had been killed. The act of pressing a weapon against one's own head and pulling the trigger makes it difficult to create the kind of searing of the skin his wound had received. And if that truth held up then there was also little doubt that he had reached out to his old friend from high school before the bullet silenced him. Salem had gone to Iraq to solve the murder of a friend. What he found instead in the dust and the chaos was a nightmare that had followed him back home.

The light was already beginning to fail as I drove east toward Ontario. The heavy fog and mist that shrouded the basin had begun to move east toward the desert, spreading its grey light across the dark green mountains in thin white streaks.

Maya Torres' address was on a dirt road tucked up against the base of the San Gabriels. A large sign with a bright shiny picture of a tile-roofed condo promised a new future for anyone coming to this spot in Rancho del Sol.

There were only a handful of other homes waiting out the arrival of the future and a wrecking ball spread out on acre lots. Tall eucalyptus trees stripped bare by the wind lined the road, their pale bark covered in dust the color of bone. Torres' house was a small box-like structure that appeared as if it had slid down the mountain and come to rest where it now sat. The wall seemed out of square, the small porch looked as if it were still in the process of falling. A row of dead roses lined the driveway where a white minivan was parked. Brown tufts of dried grass dotted the front yard where a lawn had once grown.

I parked the car across the street and stepped out. The blinds on the front window parted just enough for me to know I was being watched as I walked toward the front door. This wasn't a place where one brought a family to heal. This was a hiding place.

As I stepped on to the small porch, the front door opened and a woman in her early thirties stepped out. She was blonde, her tired features masking what had once been cheerleader-like beauty.

'What do you want?' she asked.

I started to answer, but lost the words. I had been asked that question thousands of times in thousands of interviews. I looked into her blue eyes that looked as if they had been holding back tears from the moment her husband's life had been taken. I want the same thing as you, I thought. I want it to end.

'If you're looking for a home site you have to go to the developer's office.'

I held out my ID.

'You're a police officer?'

I nodded. 'Are you Maya Torres?'

She hesitated before answering.

'Yes.'

'Your husband,' I said. 'There're some question—'

'My husband's dead.'

'I'm a friend of Jack Salem. My name's Delillo. I need your help.'

She studied my ID intently, then looked up and down the road until she appeared satisfied that I had come alone. She looked back inside the house, then back at me.

'Why?'

'Because Jack isn't missing in Iraq.'

Torres appeared to juggle several thoughts for a moment, then she stepped back inside the house and I followed. The living room looked as if it had been furnished with cheap rental furniture. A couple of chairs, a couch that appeared as if it had been used as a bed and a small TV with a bent antenna sitting on top; there was nothing personal, no photographs, no family heirlooms.

Torres closed the door behind me and pressed her body against it. I looked around the room and into the adjacent small kitchen and dining room. Something else was missing. There was nothing anywhere that hinted at the presence of children.

'Where are your children?'

The lock on the deadbolt slid shut with a click.

'They're safe,' Torres said.

I turned and looked at her. Next to the door leaned a pump-action shotgun.

'That won't protect you from the people who killed your husband,' I said.

Her eyes found mine and held on as if I had thrown her a lifeline.

'How do you know about my husband?'

'I'm a homicide detective, I read the medical examiner's report.'

'Then you know the case was closed.'

I nodded.

'So why are you here?'

'I think Jack went to Iraq to try and find out who killed your husband.'

We looked at each other in silence for a moment.

'He found out about more than your husband's murder,' I said.

'And now you're trying to find him.'

'Yes.'

Torres shook her head. 'Then you're dead too.'

'Will you help me?' I asked.

'My husband was a Green Beret, Lieutenant, he wasn't afraid of anything or any man. And they killed him. That little badge won't protect you any more than it did him.'

'Cathy Salem is missing. Before she disappeared she came to me for help,' I said.

'I'm sorry, I don't know you. I can't help you.' She started to turn to the door.

'Please,' I said.

She stopped and took a breath. 'The law doesn't exist for the people who killed my husband.'

'When your husband came back, did he tell you anything about what happened over there?'

She nervously glanced back into the house. 'No, nothing.'

She was clearly lying, but what about?

'I don't think that's the answer you really want to give me, is it?' I said.

'It's the only answer I have. I was a wife, he loved

me, he loved his children, but soldiers don't share things with wives.'

'I was in Trona last night. I saw ISC's training base.'

She looked at me for a moment. 'You live in a simple world, Lieutenant. I think you should go back to it before more people get hurt.'

'It's too late for that,' I said.

'You're alive, it's not too late. And I have two little girls who don't need to lose their mother and their father. Unless you can bring my husband back, then I can't help you.'

'What about Jack Salem? He went there because of your husband.'

She started to turn toward the door but stopped. 'What do you want from me? I gave, my family gave, only I didn't even get a folded-up flag. My husband was a good man, a good soldier, and it didn't matter because . . .' She stared at me for a moment. 'He didn't choose this war, he just went, and it broke his heart, and now he's dead.'

'They used children as weapons,' I said.

She stared at me with a look that suggested nothing I could have said would have surprised her.

'Who? ISC, the army, CIA, our government, theirs? How do you know who's good or who's bad in a place like that? You tell me, and then tell me which one of them put a gun to my husband's head and shot him?'

'Do you know a man named Miller? He said he worked with your husband.'

Torres stopped, looked at me for a moment, then picked up the shotgun and raised it at me.

'Who are you?'

I held out my hands, away from my weapon. 'I'm a cop, just like I said.'

Torres' index finger reached up and clicked off the safety.

'I'll ask you one more time,' she said.

'I need the names of the men who served with your husband at ISC.'

Behind me I heard the sound of a door slowly opening.

'It's all right, Maya,' said a voice.

Torres shook her head. Her arms began to quiver from the weight of the gun. 'I don't believe her.'

'I do. You can put the gun down.'

Torres hesitated, and then lowered the weapon. I turned round. A woman was standing in the doorway. I stared at her face for a moment before I recognized Cathy Salem. Her elegant grey hair had been dyed black and cut short. She walked across the room to the window, parted the blinds and looked out at the road.

'Are you alone?' Salem asked.

'Yes,' I said.

She turned round. The events of the last forty-eight hours appeared to have aged her many years.

'What happened at your condo?' I asked.

She took a breath. 'Fiction.'

'I need more of an explanation than that,' I said.

'The day I came home after visiting you I found it

ransacked. I decided it would be better if I disappeared.'

'Has your husband tried to contact you?'

She shook her head.

'Was your husband on the job when he joined ISC?'

'Yes,' she said, walking over and taking the gun out of Torres' hands. She leaned it next to the door. 'At the beginning he was, anyway. Every night he would e-mail me when he first got to Iraq. That began to change after several months. His e-mails became less frequent, then finally stopped altogether. He stopped talking to LAPD too.'

'Do you know who he was working with at LAPD?'

'A captain in Robbery Homicide, Smith. I never met him. I don't think many people within the department knew about it. I think they were afraid of where it might lead.'

Her eyes drifted for a moment, stared blankly across the room. I wondered if she was looking at a past that had been forever lost.

'It was his chance to be the cop he had always wanted to be, to help a friend.'

'Do you know why Jack didn't want you to talk to the police?' I asked.

She nodded. 'I think he thought he had been betrayed. I don't know by whom, he never said. I think he thought he was protecting me.'

'Have they told you anything?'

She shook her head. 'Just that they're doing what they can.'

I reached into my pocket and removed the photograph of her husband and the boy with the bike. She looked at it with a mixture of love and dread.

'Did Jack tell you about this?'

She closed her eyes for a moment and shook her head. 'Not in so many words, but my guess is he's the boy who died in the explosion just before he was to come home.'

'What did he tell you exactly?'

'He said he had seen an American officer and a little boy killed. One moment they were there, the next they were gone.'

'Nothing else?'

'He said he was living in a house of mirrors.'

'Do you remember the date it occurred?'

She nodded. 'No matter how much I'd like not to. First week of March, it was Tuesday the second.'

'Is there anything else you can remember about the conversation?'

She nodded. 'He was frightened.'

'The envelope you placed on my table. Where is it?'

She looked at me for a moment. 'It was taken from our house, it's gone.'

'Why didn't you leave it with me?'

Her eyes found mine for a moment, and then looked away, trying to hide what I recognized as embarrassment.

'Our marriage had problems. I wondered if the reason he had contacted you was because . . .' she shook her head. 'I was stupid.'

'The answer's no,' I said.

Cathy Salem's eyes held on mine for a moment. 'I should have told you everything.'

'I probably would have done the same thing,' I said.

I looked over at Maya Torres. 'Why did you pick up the gun when I said the name Miller?'

'There was no one named Miller in ISC with my husband.'

'You're sure?'

She nodded. I turned to Mrs Salem.

'Does the name sound familiar to you?'

'What did he look like?' she asked.

'Early forties, long hair streaked with grey, dark eyes. He had a scar that wrapped around his right hand.'

She shook her head.

'You're sure about the scar on the hand?' Torres said.

'It held a gun to my face, I couldn't miss it.'

Torres walked over and looked out the window.

'That meant something to you?' I asked.

Her eyes focused on some piece of the past.

'My husband did two tours in Iraq before he left Special Forces for ISC,' she said. 'There was a man in Delta who had a scar that wrapped around his hand like a snake. I met him once at a barbecue before they were deployed the second time. His name wasn't Miller; it was Taylor, I think. He stayed mostly apart from everyone, talked very little.'

'Is there a reason you remember him?' I asked.

'I asked my husband about him on the drive home. He said at a party full of dangerous men, he was the one you wouldn't want to meet alone at night.' She looked at me in silence for a moment. 'If he killed my husband, that means the government did it. Was it him?'

'I don't know.' I turned to Salem. 'Do you know the names of any of the other men who were with your husband in Iraq?'

'Just one, his name's Crawford. I saw him at the airport when I went to pick up Jack and he wasn't on the flight.'

'Did he say anything to you?'

She nodded. 'I think he knew something was wrong. He gave me a cell phone number if I ever needed anything. I think they were friends.'

'Do you still have it?'

Salem nodded and walked over to a bag and retrieved an address book. She wrote the number down on a card and brought it back.

'It's an LA number,' she said and handed it to me. 'He called me once asking if I had heard anything about Jack. I tried calling him a few days later but all I got was a message.'

'Has he called again?'

'No.'

'If someone took that envelope, then I don't think you're in danger any longer.'

I walked over and handed her a card with my number.

'But I think it would be better if you let me know where you are if you move.'

She looked at me, her eyes full of sadness. 'I'm afraid that . . .' she hesitated.

'Go ahead,' I said.

'I'm afraid the man my husband was is gone.'

'Is there something he said you haven't told me?'

Salem glanced at Torres and then nodded. 'Jack called me that night I came to your home. Most of what he said didn't make sense. He was angry, scared. He told me to get out, to find a place to hide because the end was coming. He had already seen what it looked like.'

'A flash of light,' I said.

Salem nodded. 'I'm afraid he's going to do something.'

'What?'

She shook her head. 'He kept repeating that the law is dead. What do you think that means, Lieutenant?'

I walked over to the door and opened it. Darkness was beginning to fall. The thick clouds had dropped down to ground level. The landscape vanished into the mist little more than a hundred yards from the house. I turned and looked at Salem. The sense of hands gripping my wrists returned for an instant.

'It means he's living a nightmare,' I said.

ten

What I knew now was that Salem had gone to Iraq as a cop to try to solve a crime. He had gone out of friendship and loyalty, and maybe even ambition, and he had returned with none of it intact. But what had he returned as?

I drove with his words running through my head, hoping to god they wouldn't stick. 'The end is coming . . . the law is dead.'

Whose words were those? They didn't belong to a cop, or a husband. They came from a set of circumstances that didn't exist in nature. Only we could create that kind of hell. I didn't want to understand, and I knew just as well that there was no avoiding it. The moment I had been held down in the sand and heard the fall of the hammer on an empty chamber I had stepped into the same nightmare.

Traffic had slowed to a crawl through the fog and mist. The usual sense of space that is present even in the dark in LA had been reduced to just a few feet.

Passing cars felt closer, as if crowding together for safety or because of fear of what was just out of sight. The endless lights that usually stretched to the mountains or toward the blackness of the Pacific had been reduced to the faint glow of strip malls and car dealerships that lined the freeway, with no more light than a closet door left ajar.

I dialed the number of the LAPD IA officer Jackson and left a message for him to call me unless he wanted the entire world to know they had sent a cop into a war zone. Before I reached the edge of Pasadena he called me back. From the sound in the background on his phone I guessed he was at a party or a restaurant.

'Tell me what you know about Salem and the investigation into the murder of Albert Torres,' I said.

'I don't know what you've imagined, but it's not something I know about, or would consider talking about if I didn't know the facts,' said Jackson.

'I think you can do better than that,' I said.

'What I know is that you're personally creating a lot of pain for the wife of an LAPD officer who you probably had an affair with.'

'I just left Cathy Salem. I can get you in touch with her if you like, then you two can talk about it.'

There was nothing but silence on the other end.

'Did you know that the law might be dead?' I said.

I thought I heard the sound of ice in a glass.

'Where is she?' Jackson asked.

'I imagine if she wanted you to know that she'd have told you. I think there's a certain lack of trust on her part given that your department sent her husband into the middle of a nightmare to solve a crime that took place on the streets of LA.'

'I don't have any idea what you're talking about, Lieutenant,' Jackson said, which may in fact have been the first truthful thing he had said to me. If Cathy Salem was correct, the circle of people with knowledge of the investigation into ISC probably didn't include an IA officer.

'What is it you want?' Jackson said.

'I want to know the law isn't dead, and I want the taste of sand out of my mouth.'

'I'm too busy for this—'

'I want to meet the cop who was looking over your shoulder when I called you from the Salems'.'

'There wasn't anyone—'

'Smith,' I said. 'Captain, Robbery Homicide.'

Jackson hesitated.

'I want to meet him tonight,' I added.

Jackson took a breath. 'I'm not sure that can be arranged.'

'Try telling him my next call is to the *LA Times*.'

'That would be a very bad idea,' Jackson said.

'I haven't come across many good ones in the last forty-eight hours. You have thirty minutes. I'll wait for your call,' I said and hung up.

Jackson called back in less than five minutes.

'You have a hell of a sense of timing, Delillo. I guess you hit a nerve. You'll find him on the four hundred block of Figueroa in Wilmington.'

Wilmington was next to the harbor. In the fog the drive would take more than an hour.

'It will take me a while to get there,' I said.

'He'll be there. Just show your badge to a black and white, they'll direct you,' Jackson said.

'He's at a crime scene?'

I heard the clink of ice cubes again and then the line was dead.

If the modern Los Angeles is a city built on dreams, Wilmington was the Philip K. Dick nightmare that kept it moving. A neighborhood on the edge of the harbor, built around one purpose, to turn eight hundred thousand barrels of crude oil into gasoline and every other fuel that keeps the dream moving twenty-four hours a day, seven days a week. Every lawnmower, leaf blower, every truck loaded with oranges, or wine, Gucci bags, ninety-nine-cent flip-flops, every meal in every restaurant, movie studio, jail cell or beach-front mansion, every SUV carrying soccer moms, every limo, Hyundai, Porsche, every gardener's Ford pickup, every news helicopter, cop car, or tractor digging graves at Forest Lawn was plugged right into a few square miles of steel tanks, gleaming pipes and flame-topped stacks burning off the by-product of turning crude into fuel.

When I turned off the 110 on to Figueroa, not even the fog could mask what took place beyond the razor wire and chain-link fences. The lights of the refineries reflected off the mist with a glow that was full of tiny prisms sparkling like rainbows that extended for blocks. There was no scent of the ocean even though it was little more than a mile away. The air held an odor that was closer to shoe polish than brine. A thin film spread across the windshield with each swipe of the wiper like a drop of oil spreading on a pool of water.

A few blocks south, three LAPD black and whites blocked a side street. Crime-scene tape stretched across the road beyond the squad cars. There were none of the curious onlookers who usually gather round a gang slaying. Whoever had died here probably meant little to the local streets; Robbery Homicide didn't waste their time on anything but the most high-profile murders.

I pulled to a stop behind one of the squads. In the darkness beyond the yellow tape I could see the large black SUV favored by Robbery Homicide brass. My heart rate began to soar and I had to fight the spreading sense of fear to keep from putting the car in reverse and speeding away.

Rapping on the glass of my window brought me back to the moment. A patrol officer who appeared to be sixteen years old was motioning me to roll down my window. He had a buzz cut like a Marine. I glanced at his fingers resting on the side of my window for a ring with an anchor, not because I suspected there would be one, I just couldn't stop myself.

'You can't stay here, lady.'

I rolled down the window and held up my badge.

'I'm looking for Captain Smith,' I said.

He examined my ID for a moment then handed it back.

'He's expecting you?' he asked.

'Yes.'

An older cop, clearly the senior of the two, stepped over.

'She's a cop. Pasadena. Says Smith is expecting her.'

The older cop looked at me for a moment.

'Then I guess you better let her in,' he said.

The younger officer looked past the crime-scene tape as if he was staring into the Promised Land.

'You can't drive in there.'

I opened the door and stepped out. The faint hint of roasted corn from a tortilla factory a block away mingled with the refinery's heavy scent.

'And don't touch anything,' he added, his eyes holding an edge of disdain that I should be able to walk past the tape into the darkness while he had to stand watch so far from the action.

I stepped past the officers and under the tape and started toward the crime scene. The block was lined with small mom and pop businesses and a number of empty storefronts. There was only one street light, which in the heavy fog did little more than illuminate a small circle directly below. The hum of the machinery turning crude into gas sounded oddly like a ventilator in a hospital room.

Some work lights had been set up where the SUVs and ME's van were parked. More crime-scene tape had been stretched around a large pickup parked next to the curb. A detective approached me as I walked up toward the edge of the lights. He carried himself with the swagger I had come to expect from Robbery Homicide. His clothes were more expensive and stylish than regular detectives'. The black trench coat was probably Italian.

'You Delillo?'

I nodded.

He motioned for me to follow him around the perimeter tape to one of the SUVs.

'Captain Smith,' he said, nodding toward a cop talking on a cell phone sitting in the open passenger side of the big Suburban.

I walked over and Smith glanced in my direction then turned away and continued his call. When he finished he slipped the phone in his pocket and came over. Smith appeared to be in his early fifties, reminded me a little of Steve McQueen, right down to the turtleneck he wore instead of a tie. In the darkness his eyes seemed to be the same color as the nickel-plated 9mm in the speed holster slung under his shoulder.

'I need to know when the last conversation you had with Salem was,' he said, forgoing any introductions.

'Why?' I said.

Smith stared at me for a moment as if he had misheard my answer. When I made no attempt at another one he reached in his jacket pocket, slipped a stick of gum out and slowly began to unwrap it.

'Because he needs my help.'

117

'If Salem wanted your help, why did he come to me instead of you?'

He finished unwrapping the gum and began to carefully roll it up into a tight ball.

'I really wish I knew the answer to that myself,' Smith said.

He put the gum in his mouth and chewed it a few times then reached up, took it out of his mouth and tossed it into the darkness.

'Come with me,' said Smith, walking past me and stepping under the crime-scene tape.

I followed him over to the large black Ford pickup parked next to the curb. The driver's door was halfway open; the truck's lights were still on. A crime-scene investigator and another detective were going over the door of the truck for prints.

'I need the scene for a moment,' Smith said and the investigator and the detective immediately stepped away, leaving us alone.

'This is why Salem needs my help,' Smith said. 'Take a look.'

I stepped over to the door and looked inside. The odor of violence, of spent powder and blood and flesh hung heavily in the moist air. The driver was a white male, slumped forward, his face pressing against the air vents in the dash, his left arm awkwardly caught in the steering wheel. What appeared to be multiple gunshot wounds had torn apart the left side of his head. His ear had all but vanished. Flesh around the wound was darkly stained from the heat of the powder. Pieces of tissue, bone and blood were spread across much of his shirt. On the seat next to him sat a 45 caliber revolver that he had apparently been unable to use to defend himself.

My heart rate began to soar, and I had to fight the urge to turn and run. How many times had the hammer landed on an empty chamber before it found one containing the round that killed him?

I drew a breath but no air seemed to reach my lungs.

'Those are contact wounds,' I said, turning to Smith.

He nodded. 'The gun was probably pressed right against his ear.'

I tried to hide the spreading panic that must have been in my eyes by turning away from Smith and staring into the cab of the truck, away from the body.

'Do you have an ID?' I asked.

'Yes.'

I looked at the victim's face pressed against the dash; there was nothing familiar about it, but I knew him. Or I knew all I really needed to know. I knew what the gun had felt like pressed against his ear. I knew his last moment on this earth had been filled with such fear that it blanked out every other moment that had made up his life. If he had kids, or loves, regrets or dreams, they had vanished with the sound of the gun's hammer. I knew that he would have done nearly anything to survive, and that the last emotion he would have experienced would have been a fleeting awful shame.

'Who was he?' I said, barely above a whisper.

'Meet the CEO of International Security Consultants – ISC,' said Smith.

eleven

I took a step back from the truck and looked up toward the glow of the refinery through the fog.

'Oil,' I said softly.

One of the tall stacks rising above the glow of the lights erupted in a bright orange flame.

'What did you say?' asked Smith.

The orange flame burned brighter for a moment then gradually disappeared into the blackness.

'I was wondering if this stops, or if this just keeps going and going until it's gone, or we are.'

'I don't think the short money's on us,' Smith said.

I looked back at the body slumped against the dash.

'What was his name?'

'Burns.'

'I'd like to look at his hands, if that's all right,' I said.

Smith looked at me for a moment, trying to calculate if he was behind a curve he hadn't seen coming.

'You expecting to find something?' he asked.

I shook my head. 'I don't know.'

'Knock yourself out,' Smith said.

I forced as deep a breath as I could manage and then leaned in next to the body to examine his hand, which had fallen through the steering wheel. There was a silver wedding band on his ring finger, the rest were bare. His right hand, which lay on the seat next to the revolver, had no rings on at all.

'Do you know him?' asked Smith.

I stepped back and glanced at the dead man's face, or at least what I could see of it. His left eye was open in death, dull as faded glass.

'No, I don't,' I said, stepping away from the truck.

'But you were looking for something?'

I turned to Smith. 'It is what we do, look at death the way other people read a newspaper. That's the same wound as Albert Torres suffered, only it's going to be difficult to mask it as a suicide with the gun on the other side of his body.'

Smith looked over toward the other detective and the CSI, then walked several more steps away from them and I followed.

'If I'm going to help Salem, I need to know everything I possibly can,' he said.

'Help him?'

Smith nodded, his eyes holding much more than what had been spoken aloud. I glanced over toward the other detective who looked our way, then over toward the cab of the truck.

'You think Salem did this?' I said softly so no one could overhear us.

Smith nodded. 'It's a possibility.'

'Does anyone else know this?'

'Not yet, but this isn't the kind of secret that keeps,' Smith said, glancing toward the refinery.

'Are you certain about this?' I asked.

He shook his head. 'I'm not sure about anything, but in the end someone has to be blamed. And the weakest always lose. Now I need to know what you know.'

'Salem didn't come to you for help, he came to me. If you want my assistance, I need to know why.'

Smith took a tired breath. 'Because I didn't believe him.'

'About what?'

'He was telling stories that just couldn't be true.'

'A boy on a bicycle,' I said.

Smith's grey-blue eyes locked on mine for a moment. 'There was more than just that.'

'I would have thought that would be enough.'

'It's not the "what" that's dangerous, it's the who.'

'You think this goes beyond ISC?'

'Salem thought so, but he couldn't prove it. And even if it was true, it was so far over his head, there was nothing he was going to be able to do about it.'

I looked over to the truck. 'What makes you think he did this?'

He stared at the truck for a moment. 'Come with me.'

Smith began walking back to his SUV and I followed. When he reached it he got in.

'Get in and close the door,' he said.

I hesitated, or rather my body seemed to react all on its own as if my memories now had a mind of their own. Smith looked at me, sensing my apprehension.

'There's something you need to hear,' he said then reached into his jacket pocket, removed a cassette tape.

I took hold of the handle above the door and climbed in.

'Close it,' said Smith.

I looked outside, quickly trying to plot an escape route into the darkness, then I reached out and pulled the door shut.

'No one has heard this other than the technician and he didn't know who he was listening to.'

He hit play. The recording was full of pops and crackles.

'Is this a wire tap?' I asked.

Smith nodded.

'It was recorded three days ago. It's only a partial of the conversation, the beginning was missed.'

The recording began: *'You know what I see when I close my eyes?'*

'That's Salem?' I said.

Smith nodded. 'The next voice is Burns.'

The tape continued.

'No, I don't know.'

'I see how it all ends.'

'And how is that?'

'We've killed them all, that's the way to do it, one at a time, then two at a time, hundreds and then thousands.'

'You're tired, Jack.'

Salem laughed.

'Come in and we'll straighten it all out.'

'You're just a bellhop, you carry their bags, that's all,' said Salem.

'What are you, Jack?'

'You know what I am. I'm a policeman, I arrest people, I even have a badge, but you can have it, they don't work any more. The law's dead, here, there, everywhere. And the only way to fix it is to break the law that isn't there, isn't that funny? It's like one of those things that is but isn't . . . a double negative or an anagram. That's it, same letters, different order, different meaning, isn't that funny?'

'That's not what it is, Jack.'

'What is it then? You tell me.'

'It's the way it is,' said Burns.

The recording dissolved into static for a moment and then cleared.

'You're a bastard,' said Salem.

'Come in, Jack.'

'It's too late, I have a plan, you want to hear it—'

'No I don't—'

'I'll tell you anyway. You should know it. Everyone dies. The children. Me. You. Every bastard son of a bitch and all the grey men in suits whose work you do.'

'That's not a plan, Jack.'

'Sure it is. I'm already dead, and so are you, you just don't know it.'

'You're out of your fucking mind.'

Smith stared silently at the cassette player for a moment then reached over and turned it off.

'The call abruptly ended there.'

He ejected the tape, slipped it back in his pocket and then turned to me.

'That sounds like a threat in any language,' he said. 'When I run out of any other options, I'll have to act on it.'

A tiny drop of oil product fell on to the windshield and began to spread across the glass in bands of color then gradually dissipated until it was gone. I looked over toward the truck and the body of Burns.

'Have you found anything in the truck that ties the killing to Salem?' I asked.

'An anonymous caller reported the shooting, they said a man matching Salem's general description was walking away from the truck just after the shot.'

'A witness on this street, in this fog and darkness?'

'Convenient, isn't it?' Smith sat in silence for a moment. 'That's not the Jack Salem I knew. The man on that recording sounds capable of putting a gun to a man's head and pulling the trigger.'

'He blamed Burns for Torres' death?'

Smith nodded. 'Burns or someone working for him. As to what took place in Iraq, who did what – things begin to lose clarity.' Smith looked at me and tried to force a smile. 'There don't appear to be any happy endings here.'

'I need to know some things,' I said.

'If I can tell you, I will.'

'Salem thought you, or someone with LAPD, had betrayed him. Why?'

Smith's eyes turned inward, examining some piece of the recent past. I didn't need much explanation to know that it wasn't a happy trip.

'He thought that because he had been,' Smith said.

My hand settled on the door handle.

'I did it, but not the way it sounds.'

His eyes landed on my hand wrapped around the handle.

'I wasn't aware betrayal had a second definition,' I said.

'It became clear to me that our communications had been compromised. What he was saying and seeing was too dangerous, and was way beyond our ability to do anything about it. Even if it was true, which has yet to be proven.'

'Children being used as weapons.'

He nodded. 'Walking into a war to solve a murder . . .' he shook his head. 'Salem was yelling fire in a theater full of people holding Molotov cocktails. I tried to pull the plug, bring him home; when that didn't work I thought if he believed no one was listening to him he would give it up. His communications got more erratic, he began to see enemies in every shadow, behind every door. He eventually cut off all contact.'

'The last thing Salem said to his wife was that the law is dead,' I said.

Smith stared out into the darkness and took a breath. 'He wasn't seeing things clearly.'

'Torres was his friend.'

He nodded.

'And so was a little boy with a bike,' I said.

Smith settled back into the seat and stared into the fog. 'I've tried to imagine where this all stops. None of the outcomes is good. Either one of my own is a killer and I have to go after him, or he's being made a patsy. And if that's true . . .'

Smith continued but I didn't hear the words. I wanted to be away from all of this. I wanted to turn the clock back as far as it would take to be unaware and safe in its comforting ignorance, but I knew it didn't work that way. Even if I stepped out of this truck, handed in my badge and kept walking, there would be nowhere I could go, no hiding place remote enough from what I now carried inside.

'It's possible Salem found that proof he was looking for,' I said.

Smith turned to me.

'I think he hid it in a locker in a bus station or airport.'

'You're sure?'

'He wrote his wife from Trona. Last night the bus station there burned down. If it was there, it's gone, but if he moved it before that, then it still exists.'

'Trona? ISC has a facility there.'

I nodded. 'A deputy there believes ISC may have ties to a unit at China Lake.'

'How do you know this?'

'I was there last night.'

'You were in Trona?'

I nodded.

Smith started to reach for my left arm and I instinctively pulled it away.

'What happened?' he asked.

I hesitated for a moment, then reached over and rolled up my left sleeve, revealing the bruises on my wrist.

'It was explained to me that I should go back to Pasadena.'

Smith stared at my wrist. From the look in his eyes, there seemed to be little need to furnish the rest of the details.

'That was why you wanted to look at Burns's hands?'

I nodded. 'Maybe I'm alive because they thought a woman would do as she was told and walk away, or maybe they just didn't want to kill a cop.'

'It might not be that,' Smith said.

He reached out and took hold of the steering wheel and gripped it tightly.

'You know something I don't?'

'You said you met with a deputy up there?'

I nodded.

'A San Bernardino County deputy was killed this afternoon. They found his squad car at the bottom of a steep ravine in the high desert. It rolled at least three hundred feet before coming to a stop.'

My heart began to beat against my chest and I struggled to stop the panic trying to spread in my gut. This was what it was like for Salem, I realized. This is what you feel when there is no law, and everyone passing you on the street or driving in the car becomes an object to fear.

'Do you have a name?' I asked.

Smith shook his head. 'Initial reports said it was an uninvolved accident.' Smith studied me for a moment. 'You think it could be him?'

'He said he was going to take a drive out to China Lake and talk to an officer he knew.'

I took out my cell phone and called the number Gilley had given me. A woman answered.

'San Bernardino County sheriff's department.'

'I'd like to talk to Deputy Gilley.'

There was a pause on the other end.

'Who's calling?'

'Pasadena PD, I talked with him this morning.'

'Just a moment.'

She transferred the call and a male voice picked up.

'How can I help you?'

'I would like to talk to Deputy Gilley.'

'You're with Pasadena?'

'Yes.'

'Tom Gilley died in an accident this morning . . . Is there something I can help you with?'

Smith looked at me. 'I think you should hang up.'

'He found a pickup this morning in Trona loaded with military equipment,' I said.

There was long pause.

'I have no record of any pickup.'

'That's impossible, I was with him when he found it.'

'Hang up,' said Smith.

'No pickup was found in Trona. What did you say your name was?'

My hand tightened around the phone, my heart began to beat heavily against my chest.

'Is there something you want to tell me?'

'No.'

'Hang up,' said Smith.

'Can you be reached at this number?' said the voice.

I closed the phone and ended the call. Outside the window of the SUV the fog appeared be moving across the ground like swirling currents of water.

'He never got to China Lake,' Smith said, looking at me.

'Or never made it home,' I said.

We sat in silence for several moments.

'Does the name Taylor mean anything to you?' I asked.

Smith shook his head.

I wrote down the cell number Crawford had given Cathy Salem and held it out. 'I need a location.'

'That would take a court order.'

'I don't think Salem has that kind of time,' I said.

'Who is it?'

'If we're going to break the law, I think it would be better if you didn't know.'

131

Smith reached out and took the card. 'I'll see what I can do.'

I opened the door of the truck and stepped out.

'How many partners are there in ISC?' I said.

'Three, including the late Mr Burns. A South African named Henkel, and an American named Russell.'

'Do you know where they are?'

Smith shook his head.

'What about their offices?'

'Empty, not even a scrap of paper left on the floor. Their operations in Iraq shut down within days after Salem disappeared.'

He picked up a file on the seat next to him and pulled out two copies of California drivers' licenses and handed them to me.

'Henkel and Russell. Since there's no law against disappearing, there's not much I can do to find them. Maybe you'll have some luck.'

I stared at their pictures for a moment; neither looked like the stereotype one assumed came with the word mercenary. If I had to guess, I would have said they were high-school teachers.

'Who's Taylor?' Smith asked.

I glanced over toward the pickup and Burns's body.

'The man you don't want to meet alone on a dark street.'

twelve

'Everyone dies. The children. Me. You. Every bastard son of a bitch and all the grey men in suits.'

How dark must the heart grow for these words to become one's own? How hard did Salem resist them? How easily are we seduced? Is that the secret the grey men know when they send others into violence? That it is our nature to give in, to be weak by embracing the illusion of strength that violence gives. That succumbing to our worst instincts is far easier than holding on to what is good and decent.

The other voice in my head didn't buy it. It was no illusion that held me into the sand, turned me into a frightened child, and tried to take away every piece of myself I cared about. And when I finally face that man with the ring who pressed the gun against my head and pulled the trigger, that same voice will be telling me to draw my weapon and fire and keep firing until the last breath of air had left his lungs. Maybe then I would fully understand Salem's words. And then I would be just as lost as him, and the grey men would have another victory.

It was nearing midnight when I pulled on to the 110 and followed the fleet of tanker trucks leaving the refineries with their loads of fuel to keep LA moving. As I headed toward downtown I tried to put the pieces together as I would for any other investigation. Were Burns's hands covered with Albert Torres' blood and that of a boy on a bicycle? Was that why he was dead? Had he pulled the trigger, pressed the detonator, given an order, or followed one? If Salem's words were true, then Burns was no more than an errand boy. And if that were true, where would the violence stop? There wasn't enough crime-scene tape in all the departments in all of Los Angeles to isolate what was yet to come.

A white Mustang was parked on the other side of the cul-de-sac as I approached my house. It wasn't one of my neighbors, since the lot it was parked in front of was still little more than a charred foundation. It could be teenagers hooking up or getting high or both. And it could be my imagination that fueled the rise in my blood pressure. My headlights swept across the rear window as I turned into the driveway. There was no silhouette in the car.

I pulled up in front of the garage and stopped, then reached down and slipped my Glock out of its holster. The fog appeared to press against the windows of my car. I could see little more than a dozen feet, which wouldn't even give me a clear shot at making it to my front door.

'You're being foolish,' I said silently to myself.

I turned the ignition off and listened for the sound of movement, then opened the door, stepped out and started walking. As I reached the edge of the driveway I heard the faint click of a car door open.

Run.

I tightened my grip on the Glock and forced myself to stop and swung the weapon up. I could see nothing in the fog. The voice in my head wouldn't let up.

Run.

I took a backward step, keeping the gun raised to where I believed the Mustang to be.

Run.

I took another step and another, then gave in and turned and ran the remaining steps to the front door. As I reached for my keys, I heard footsteps on the pavement of the driveway. I fumbled the keys, grabbed the wrong one, then the right one, slipped it into the lock and then turned round and raised the weapon.

'If you take another step I will shoot you,' I said.

The dull shape of the figure stopped moving at the edge of the front walk.

'Raise your hands where I can see them.'

'Are you Lieutenant Delillo?' said the figure.

'Raise your hands,' I repeated.

The individual's hands rose from his side.

'I've been waiting a couple of hours, I need to talk.'

I turned the key in the door, pushed it open, reached

inside and flipped on the entry light.

'Walk toward me until I can see you,' I said.

'Please put the gun down—'

'Do it now! One step at a time, arms raised!'

He took a step and then another and I told him to stop. He had short-cropped brown hair, late twenties, dressed in jeans and a loose shirt that hung over his belt.

'Take another step into the light. Then reach down and raise your shirt above your waist, one side at a time.'

'I don't have a gun,' he said.

'Do it.'

He stepped forward then followed the instructions. As he reached for his right side, the silver ring caught the light and I saw the anchors. I rushed forward and pressed my Glock against the side of his face before he could react.

'Please,' he said, his voice cracking.

'Who are you?' I yelled.

He tried to answer but his voice faltered. I pulled the hammer back on the Glock and pushed it against his face until his knees buckled and he dropped to the ground.

'Who?' I repeated.

'Please.'

'Who the hell are you!'

He took a short gasping breath then managed a word.

'Navy.'

'Tell me about the ring, do you wear it all the time? Do you?'

He nodded his head. 'I'm a naval officer.'

I pressed the gun harder against his face. 'Why are you here?'

His voice faltered again, then managed a few barely audible words. 'Friend of Tom Gilley's . . .'

I stared at the barrel of the gun pressed into the flesh of his cheek just in front of his ear.

'Don't,' he begged.

My hand began to shake as I stared at the man cowering on his knees. I pulled the gun away and eased the hammer down.

'Tom Gilley the deputy?'

He nodded. I stood absolutely still for a moment, then my stomach began to turn and I thought I would be sick.

'Get up,' I whispered, but he didn't hear me. 'Please, get up.'

He raised his head and when I looked at the fear in his eyes I felt ashamed and turned and walked over to the front step and sat down, trying to stop myself from trembling.

'I'm sorry,' I said.

I looked over at him, sitting up on his knees, trying to catch his breath as if he had just run a sprint. He tentatively looked toward me, his eyes asking why I had just done this to him. I tried to speak but couldn't and instead set the Glock on the step next to me and buried my face in my hands.

I don't know how much time passed, two minutes, or four, as I replayed what I had just done, and how the gun had felt in my hand as I stood over another human being, pressing it against his head.

When I looked up, the man was sitting on the step a few feet away from me, staring out into the fog. His eyes glistened with a thin film of tears.

'You're the officer Gilley was going to see at China Lake this morning?' I said.

He nodded.

'You saw him then?'

'Yes.'

'You have a name?' I asked.

'Lowenstein . . . James. First Lieutenant.'

'How did you find me?'

He took a moment to catch his breath. 'Tom told me to call you if I found anything out. I tried calling Pasadena PD, then I found this address on the web and took a chance it was you. I've been waiting two hours.'

He looked at me as if trying to apologize, as if he had been the cause of what I had done to him.

'I didn't mean to sneak up on you, I just wasn't sure it was you.'

I shook my head.

'It's my fault,' I said, which seemed pitiful compensation for what I had done.

He took a slow, deep breath, holding on to it as if he had just tasted air for the first time.

'What is it you do at China Lake, First Lieutenant?'

'I'm in materials and distribution, a supply officer.'

'And you don't think Tom Gilley had an accident?'

He looked at me and shook his head. 'It doesn't make sense.'

'Why?' I asked.

'Tom wanted to know if I had heard if there were any special units stationed at the Lake that didn't seem to belong or were different or out of place.'

'Did he mention ISC?'

The lieutenant nodded. 'And a pickup truck filled with high-tech surveillance equipment. He also said something had happened to a cop in Trona, and that it may have a link to the base.' He looked over at me. 'That cop was you, wasn't it?'

I nodded. 'Was he right about a unit that didn't seem to fit?'

'You hear stories, rumors about things, but those are always going on, I never really took them very seriously, and if they were there, it's not my job to know.'

'What kind of stories did you hear?'

He stared into the fog for a moment. 'The usual stuff, secret weapons, units. Special ops guys are like rock stars, they dress different, act different . . . they're what everyone would like to be, so who cares what they do, it's a war . . . But I was curious.'

Lowenstein took a breath and closed his eyes for a moment.

'I started going back through some paperwork. The military's very good at keeping records, mountains of it, right down to every nut, bolt and bullet. Everything that comes in to the base comes through our office.'

He paused as if not wanting to go on.

'What do you know about China Lake?' he asked.

'Not very much.'

'It's a weapons center, we test things, develop the better missile, warhead, guidance system, bullet, you name it. I found a small program with the designation "Havoc". I asked around. Nothing.'

'Is that unusual?'

He nodded. 'The only things that go on at the Lake that everyone has heard about, or has an idea what it does, are the things that are supposed to be secret, but no one had ever heard of this, not even a rumor. Then I went through the requisitions I could find. The materials they were receiving didn't match a program with a name like that. They didn't seem to match anything that goes on there.'

'What kind of things?'

'Everyday things. Toasters, flat screen TVs, iPods, phones, cameras, things you find in any house or car.'

'Bicycles?' I asked.

Lowenstein nodded. 'So either some admiral is buying presents for his family, or something else is going on, so I kept tracking the stuff as far as I could. It all went to Iraq.'

'Were any personnel listed in connection with Havoc?'

'The only reference to any personnel was the transfer of remains from Baghdad to Germany to Arlington National Cemetery for interment.'

'When did that happen?'

'Beginning of March. The seventh, if I remember.'

The lieutenant stared into the darkness for a moment, and then lowered his head.

'Can you tell me why any of this is important enough for a man to die on a road in the desert?'

'What makes you so certain that Gilley didn't die in an accident?' I asked.

He turned to me. 'Until you put a gun to my head I wasn't certain of anything . . . One look at you and I knew all this was real.'

He shook his head, then closed his eyes for a moment as if trying to suppress the thought.

'When Tom Gilley left the base he said he was driving back to Trona for a meeting. The road Tom died on wasn't the road back to Trona, wasn't anywhere near it. What was he doing out in the high desert?'

thirteen

When Lowenstein left, I locked myself in the house and walked from window to window, staring out into the fog and darkness until I was certain he hadn't been followed. When I was satisfied I was alone I lay down and tried to get some sleep, but when I closed my eyes I was standing over the lieutenant again, pressing the gun to his face.

'One look at you and I knew all this was real,' he had said, and he was right.

What I knew now about the men who had held me down in the sand was that it had been harder for them not to kill me than to have just terrorized me. What I knew about myself I didn't want to know, but how do you unlearn or un-feel something once that box inside has been opened?

Was I closer to Jack Salem or further from him?

I ran a shower and stood under it until the water began to lose its heat and turn cold, but I didn't get out, or turn the water off. I wanted to feel something other than what I had felt standing over the lieutenant holding the gun, even if it was just the trembling of the cold. I had wanted to pull that trigger more than I could fathom. It was as pure and as uncomplicated an emotion as I had ever known. And I wanted to be rid of it, to pretend it wasn't my own, but the cold water couldn't wash it away. If anything, it seemed to push it deeper inside where it took hold like a tightening fist around my heart.

When I began to tremble so much I could barely grip the shower handle I turned it off and sat down on the cold porcelain, pulling my knees to my chest. It would be so easy to step off into the same hole Salem had vanished into, where the law was dead. I had walked up to its edge. But I couldn't.

I whispered my old mantra that had helped me through countless crime scenes.

'Work it,' I whispered. Step back from the edge. Be a cop again. There was something there that Lowenstein had told me about that I hadn't connected. I resisted it. It would be easier just to let go.

'Arlington National Cemetery,' I said. 'A dead American.'

I stood up, wrapped a towel around myself and walked into my daughter's room to the desk where her computer still sat and stared at the blank screen. Cathy Salem had been the first person to mention the death of an American in Baghdad the first week of March. Lowenstein was the second one to mention it. Find it, put them together. I began to go through newspaper archives online for the first week of March.

The week had been a particularly cruel one in Baghdad, even by the standards of a city gone mad. I knew all the images; they had been repeated every day until sitting at home it had begun to take on the feel of normality. The vehicles in flames torn apart by explosives, masked gunmen, exhausted GIs, angry crowds, horrified men and women searching for a child or lover in the chaos. And the endless train of dead and wounded being borne on the shoulders of those left to pick up the pieces.

In a week where so many died, only one number stood out from the rest. A single American was reported killed on the second of the month. Newspaper after newspaper passed on the screen. The few details offered didn't change or add any more insight. A single casualty among so many had lost the importance of specific detail. A bomb had gone off outside a small café frequented by foreigners, or the few that remained anyway. The American had been a captain, no unit designation or name was given. The number of Iraqi dead was listed as six, including a child.

Only one photograph appeared on the net documenting the scene. None of the major daily papers had run it. A French news agency had it on their wire service. It was unremarkable when compared to others taken in moments of horror. It could have come from a 'day in the life' kind of series except that in Baghdad that meant a scene of a shattered storefront, twisted tables, chairs and glass spread across the bloodstained sidewalk. A single boot of a victim was just visible underneath an upturned table.

I nearly scrolled past the photograph, giving it little more than a glance except that among the chaos was a figure in jeans and a black sweater, an M-16 held at his side. He was looking to his right into a large crowd of people as if something had just caught his eye. There's no expression in his face, no sense of emotion at all, as if he were wearing a mask. His left hand is stained with blood.

I knew what was behind his eyes. Nothing. The things that connected him to his past life were gone. That was now the province of memory, and memory was slipping through his fingers. He was standing on the edge, or had just taken the first step into the abyss. He had seen a boy disappear in a flash of light.

'Jack Salem,' I said.

It wouldn't have been long after this that he had vanished. I enlarged the picture to the limits of the screen, hoping to find a detail that would point in the direction he had gone. His expression was empty of emotion, but his eyes were focused.

'What are you looking at?'

I followed his line of sight across the street to where the crowd of Iraqis stood. A woman in a black burka was shaking a hand in the air. A man casually smoked a cigarette, others stood with arms crossed, a few appeared to be chatting, all their faces held an exhausted emptiness. But none of them was what Salem was looking at.

I focused on the crowd of onlookers and enlarged it until it was the only portion of the photograph on the screen. The camera had caught another individual I hadn't noticed before – the face was white, slightly blurred as if the camera had frozen his movements in mid-stride. There was nothing distinct about the face or his expression. He could be anyone.

'A schoolteacher,' I whispered to myself.

I walked into the dining room and retrieved the copies Smith had given me of the driving licenses of the two remaining partners at ISC, came back to the computer and compared the pictures.

'Russell,' I said.

He was holding something in his right hand – a weapon maybe, but it didn't look right. I scrolled down and enlarged the picture again. It was a cell phone, and it was opened as if he had just made a call.

'You bastard,' I said softly.

If I was right, he was holding a weapon. He had killed a little boy, an American officer and six others with a telephone call. I widened the view of the picture until Salem was visible again. I tried to imagine what his eyes had just witnessed. If he had been sitting at another café he would have had to watch it all play out in front him with no more ability to change the outcome than he would have had sitting in a theater watching a movie.

I widened the photograph to its original frame, taking in the entire street. I looked at the upturned chairs and the pieces of clothing littering the pavement. The boot visible under the table was the sand-colored combat boot of a GI.

If what I was looking at was a murder scene, who had been the intended victim? The dead American captain whose burial at Arlington National Cemetery was orchestrated by a program out of China Lake? If that was true then Salem's presence at the same time in a city the size of Baghdad didn't fit, the coincidence was too great.

That put Salem sitting at the table with the American. They would have been at the café, maybe having coffee, and Salem was telling him what ISC had been doing, or confronting him because Havoc was part of it, or – least likely – the captain had just been horribly unlucky and in the wrong place.

In the middle of their conversation Salem looked up to see the boy he had given the bike to riding toward him. His first reaction may have been to smile, and he started to wave, but then stopped when he heard the ring of the cell phone. And with each ring the little boy would have got closer and closer, and just before the flash of light Salem might have realized what was about to happen and started to move or shout, and maybe the boy understood and he started to turn the bike away enough to save Salem's life before his own vanished in a flash.

I stared at the photograph for a moment, half wishing I was wrong with my thinking, then noticed some distinctive curved metal amongst the debris scattered across the pavement and I knew I wasn't.

'Handlebars,' I whispered softly.

ISC had tried to kill Salem using a little boy he had befriended as a weapon and a cell phone as a detonator. But they had missed him, leaving the soldier and six Iraqis dead. And Salem began to run because he was being hunted, he ran all the way back to Trona, and then it began to unravel. A deputy was killed because he had been perceived as a threat. And then one of the men who had packed the bike full of explosives was murdered, either to silence him or because a cop believing the law was dead had reached out from the darkness and pulled him in.

I printed a copy of the entire picture and one close-up of Russell then shut the computer down and walked over to Lacy's bed and lay down. I wanted to cry, and I wanted my old life back, but wanting wasn't enough.

Sleep provided little rest. The images came just as fast out of dreams as they had flashed by on the computer screen, and the more I tried to turn them off, the faster they came, one after another seeming to blend into a single image that held a piece of every face of every victim. The ringing of the phone finally put an end to it.

'Delillo?'

'Smith,' I said.

I sat up on the edge of the bed, feeling more exhausted than when I lay down.

'I think I know why Salem ran,' I said.

'So do I,' said Smith.

I waited to let him go on but he didn't.

'Why do I think we haven't come up with the same answer?' I said.

Smith took a deep breath. 'We found a print on the door of Burns's truck. We've just issued a warrant for Salem's arrest.'

'How many prints did you get?' I asked.

'One good one.'

'A single clear print? What was the word you used – patsy? It could have been placed there.'

'That doesn't happen in my world.'

'This isn't our world, Smith,' I said.

'It's out of my hands.'

'They tried to kill him, and in the process murdered an American captain and six Iraqis. Salem ran because he would be dead otherwise.'

'You can prove this?'

I looked over at the photograph sitting next to the bed.

'No,' I said.

'Then you really have nothing.'

'You sent him there, you can't abandon him.'

'I sent him there to solve a murder, not to get involved in a war.'

'But you didn't tell him how, did you? There were no classes on the subject at the academy. You put him into an asylum and expected him to remain sane.'

'Salem made his choices,' he finally said.

'Did he? Like the little boy on the bike made his?'

'If I could—'

'You can't,' I said cutting him off. 'We don't get to play that game.'

Smith fell silent for a moment. 'I have an address to go with that number you gave me. If I thought Salem was there, you wouldn't be getting this.'

'I wouldn't have given it to you if I believed it was Salem.'

'Then I guess we understand each other.'

'Where is it?' I asked.

'Catalina Island. The house looks right over the harbor and the pier.'

I wrote down the address.

'If you think this might help Salem, do it quickly,' Smith said.

'Thank you.'

'Don't thank me. Whoever is sitting in that house can watch every person stepping off a boat on to the island. Someone like that may not want visitors.'

'I'll keep that in mind.'

'Be careful, Lieutenant.'

fourteen

It was shortly before dawn when I reached Long Beach to catch the first express boat of the day to Avalon. Where the water began and the fog ended was nearly impossible to tell in the darkness. The aromas of cooking from the restaurants along the waterfront, and wisteria and car exhaust mixed with the scent of kelp and brine, gulls and diesel until they all seemed to be coming from the same large pot boiling somewhere in the fog.

The waiting room in the terminal was filled mostly with day laborers on their way out to tend residential gardens or serve or cook in the island's restaurants. I scanned the few non-Hispanic faces for the possibility of threat. There was a young couple with scuba equipment. A middle-aged man who appeared to be returning home from a mainland business trip, and a woman with two sleepy young children.

I waited until the last possible moment to board, watching for any late arrivals, then stepped off solid land and took a place alone on the front deck in the open air as we slipped moorings and headed into the fog toward the channel.

I had never understood the solace people find in the ocean. Cold dark water that can swallow ships holding more people than some small towns never filled me with the peace some found in it. The scents and sounds of life shared with nine million other people had always been the tides that brought rhythm to my days. The sound of a school bus stopping to pick up kids, a jet taking off, a passing car radio, the conversation from the next table where every other word is lost and you begin to fill in the blanks on your own.

But passing the last jetty and turning into the open ocean, the sense of dread that usually accompanied the dark water wasn't there. The engines came to life and the boat rose up and began to plane across the surface. I closed my eyes and let the fine salty spray fall on me and for the first time in twenty-four hours I couldn't remember the feel of sand pressed against my face, and the faint odor of sage, the touch of a stranger's hand, and the paralyzing fear that came with the sharp click of a gun's hammer.

It would take a little over an hour to reach the island. The further we headed into the channel, the thicker the fog grew until I could no longer see the stern of the boat from where I stood on the bow. Occasionally the churning engines of a much larger ship passing somewhere near could be heard for a moment before fading away. A pair of dolphins appeared out of nowhere and briefly surfed along the boat's wake, then just as quickly disappeared. The silvery wisp of a flying fish broke the surface, gliding briefly over the swell, then it folded its wings and vanished back into the dark water.

I had a daughter who meant more to me than anything in the world, a job I cared about, a partner I was probably in love with, and the harder I tried to picture any of it, the further it seemed to slip away, like the beautiful dream you try to hold on to in the middle of the night but can't. One fleeting moment had changed all of it. And I was powerless to alter the direction I was going. The only way back that I saw was to follow it to the end – to fold up my wings and slip into the dark water without so much as leaving a wake.

The engines of the boat throttled back and we settled into a glide across the rolling surface. I stared into the fog, looking for any hint of land, and then as if a curtain was raised we drifted through a wall of fog and into sunlight which lit the dark water, turning it a deep emerald blue, and a wall of lush green vegetation rose up in front of the boat.

We rounded a point of land and the town of Avalon came into view, built around a small harbor with the old casino on the north end and the pier on the south. From the water the town looked as much a movie set as a place where actual lives were lived. Conceived by a man whose empire was built on nothing more than chewing gum, it was the perfect blending of fantasy and reality, an island in the ocean with its own herd of buffalo where tourists float in glass-bottomed boats, watching young women dressed as mermaids.

Sailboats and motor launches filled the small sheltered bay. Restaurants and palm trees and tourist shops lined the waterfront. We pulled up to the pier and the rumble of the engines fell silent, replaced by the sound of gulls and salsa music drifting out of an open window on shore. As the lines were secured and the gentle rocking of the boat stopped, I looked up toward the houses in the surrounding hills that formed a natural bowl around the town.

Before leaving the mainland I had located the address on a map. If Smith was correct, a soldier was behind one of those windows looking down on me. Crawford had picked this spot the way a soldier would, a place with high ground and concealment. He would be at that window for every boat, watching, waiting for the one individual to step on to the island that didn't belong, and from that moment he would have the advantage.

I stepped off the boat on to the pier, trying to appear like a tourist, and keeping my jacket over the Glock on my waist. The day laborers quickly dispersed toward their jobs. The locals returning from the mainland chatted with each other as they walked toward the waterfront.

If Cathy Salem had been correct about Crawford, he had been a friend of her husband, and he had come here trying to elude the same men her husband had fled, or at least some of the same memories. But how could she know? A chance meeting in the airport and a single phone call. If she was wrong, the meeting hadn't been by chance, and he may have helped pack a bicycle full of explosives and told a young boy where he could find his friend Salem, patted him on the back and given him a push as he pedaled off down the street.

The locals all headed in their own directions and I was left alone. I tried not to look up toward the windows looking down from the hills, but couldn't stop myself. He was there; I could feel his presence the way one does in an interrogation room with one-way glass.

If I was lucky, the person Crawford expected to step on to the island looking for him wasn't a mother in her forties. But thinking like that probably didn't exist for a man who could only find security on an island. I was the only one left from the boat to watch, so his eyes wouldn't leave me. And they could follow me right to his door.

As I walked along the pier a cold wet breeze fell on the back of my neck. I turned to see the fog moving in over the end of the pier. The sailboats in the harbor, the casino on the north end all disappeared back into the grey light. A mechanical beacon began pulsing with the advance of the fog. The green hills above town and the window where Crawford stood vanished into the clouds.

I quickly rushed across the street past a restaurant and stopped on the corner. From inside the kitchen I could hear the sound of a man singing softly in Spanish about two dead lovers. Somewhere in the fog the sound of footsteps on pavement rose and then faded.

I left the souvenir shops and restaurants and started up the hill. Bougainvilleas tumbled over fences and retaining walls lining properties. The first blossoms of jacaranda trees were beginning to open with their bright violet flowers. He had come as far as he could from the dull light of Baghdad, and it probably still wasn't far enough to escape what he carried inside, whether it was murder, or just the ache of witnessing and not acting.

The house sat away from the others around it, down narrow steps lined with a hedge of rosemary beyond a bright blue picket fence. The adjacent homes had rental signs in the small yards and not a sound came from either. I opened the gate and gently closed it behind me and started down the steps. The house was a small, neat bungalow, painted the same blue as the fence, and looked prominently down on the waterfront. The front door was solid wood; the drapes were drawn across the windows on either side.

I slipped my Glock from the speed holster and held it at my side. A dog began barking manically somewhere in the fog. I started to reach for the doorbell, then stopped; a single drop of what appeared to be blood stained the threshold of the door. I pressed myself against the wall between the door and window and slipped my phone out and dialed Crawford's number.

A cell phone began to ring inside the house then

abruptly stopped after three rings with no message or answering service; it was more like it had been turned off. I leaned in toward the window and listened for a sound from inside but there was nothing. I hit redial on the phone and this time there was only silence.

I stepped under the window and walked over to the side of the house and looked around the corner. Two windows looked out on to a small grass yard and a steep ivy-covered hillside. I eased along the wall to the first window. A mattress placed against the glass blocked the view inside. The second window was covered with what appeared to be towels. I stepped to the far corner and glanced round it into the back yard.

A small stone patio, littered with empty beer and liquor bottles, had been laid out to the edge of the hillside that fell away into the mist. A table and four chairs were placed near the edge. Binoculars and two half-empty beers sat on the table. Open French doors led into the house.

I stepped round the corner, listening for any movement from inside, then eased along the wall until I reached the edge of the doors. The smell of stale beer and cigarettes drifted out from inside. I pressed myself back against the wall for a moment, took hold of the Glock with both hands and then swung round into the open doorway, raising the weapon.

My eyes took a moment to adjust to the darkness inside. It was a living room with a small open kitchen to the right. A wooden chair lay smashed in one corner of the room. The red tiled floor was covered with more beer and liquor bottles, a few of which had been shattered as if thrown in rage. Take-out food containers littered the kitchen counter. An AR-15 rifle mounted with a scope and a pump-action twelve gauge with a folding stock lay on the small leather couch.

I stepped inside and crossed the room, holding the weapon on the open door that led to the bedroom and bathroom. An empty bed frame sat in the middle of the room, the mattress having been propped against the wall to block the window. Clothes littered the floor; the wall opposite the bed was marked with small-caliber bullet holes.

I stepped to the bathroom door. The sink was bloodstained, as were two small towels that lay in the bathtub. Bottles of unidentified pills were scattered across a small shelf next to the sink. From their color and shape I guessed they were amphetamines. The house was clear.

I walked back into the living room, my eyes now fully adjusted to the dim light, and saw what I had missed before. Against one wall of the room was a small folding card table with a computer and printer on it. I stepped over to it. The floor around it was covered with pictures, and then I realized so were the walls, dozens of pictures were pinned and taped to nearly every usable space.

I reached down and picked up one of the photographs on the floor. It was of an Iraqi woman, her clothes partially torn from her body. Her eyes were closed, her face unmarked and beautiful; the only giveaway that she was dead was that one of her legs was gone, and the crimson pool of blood she seemed to be floating on.

Outside, the sun broke through the fog and the light in the room began to warm. I set the picture on the table and my heart began to pound against my chest as I looked around the room. They were all photographs of the dead. Women, children, men, some wearing the traditional loose flowing clothes of Shiite or Sunnis, others in western-style shirt and pants. There wasn't a single picture of a living, breathing soul. Some of the faces held a kind of peace that seemed impossible, given the circumstances of their deaths. Other victims' tormented expressions reflected the violence that had claimed them in ways that were difficult to look at. The most frightening of the images showed two corpses whose heads were covered by dark bags – their nightmare somehow more vivid and measurable knowing the darkness it took place in.

I resisted the urge to turn away and get out of the house as quickly as I could. The psychic weight the room held was palpable. It seemed almost surprising that the walls of the house could sustain such a burden. What it had done to the man who had taken the pictures and then covered these walls I couldn't imagine.

'What kind of penance is being paid here?' I said silently.

The sun broke through the fog completely and light began to fill the room. I started to turn and then froze when I saw the shadow of a figure behind me spread across the floor, and heard the sound of a revolver's hammer being cocked.

fifteen

'**A**re you here to kill me?' he said.

I held my hands clearly out to my side and didn't make another move.

'No,' I said.

'I didn't think they would send a woman. I saw you step off the boat. You didn't look like a tourist, and you weren't carrying a briefcase or shoulder bag, so you weren't here on business. I was going to take you while you were standing on the pier, but I let you go. I decided you were here for an affair, I thought you had that desperate lost look. I guess that's why they chose you. It was smart of them. Over there I would have killed you without thinking.'

I shook my head. 'I may be desperate, but I'm not here to kill you.'

'I should have seen the gun under the jacket.'

'No one sent me, I'm a police officer.'

He was silent for a moment then I heard his footsteps move closer to me, stopping just a foot or two

163

away. I could hear his breathing, and smell the booze on his breath.

'Turn around,' he said. 'If you move the hand holding the weapon, you're dead.'

'I believe you, I won't move it.'

I slowly turned around. Crawford's clothes hung loosely on him. His eyes had a deep-set, drug-strung-out weariness to them. He appeared to be powerfully built, but the weeks spent inside these walls had taken their toll. A bloodstained bandage was wrapped haphazardly around his left forearm and wrist. His weapon was pointed right at my face.

'ID,' he said.

I carefully reached into my jacket, removed my ID and badge and held it out.

He took it with his left hand and examined it in quick darting glances, barely removing his eyes from me.

'Delillo.'

I nodded.

'Why has a lieutenant come all the way from Pasadena to visit my humble island getaway?'

'I'm trying to keep Jack Salem alive.'

His eyes focused for a brief instant and he took a deep exhausted breath.

'A man of principle . . . and a fool's errand,' he said softly, and then lowered his gun to his side and tucked it into his belt under his shirt.

'If I've misjudged you, then this is your opportunity, Lieutenant,' Crawford said.

He looked into my eyes and I knew that at least part of him was hoping he had made a mistake and that I was here to put an end to it all. I glanced at the gun in my hand for a moment then slipped it back in the speed holster.

'Who were you expecting to get off that boat?' I asked.

'It's not who, it's what. I'm expecting justice to step off that boat.'

'Are you guilty of something?'

He suppressed a smile, as one would do with a bad joke. 'Look around, Lieutenant, what do you think?'

'I think I see a lot a pain here,' I said.

'Ladies and gentlemen of the jury, the defendant has been charged with the crime of nation-building.'

I had seen rooms where serial killers kept records of their kills, like a hunter's trophy room in a suburban basement, but this was different.

'What are you doing here?' I asked.

'Not following orders.' Crawford saw that I didn't understand. 'An experienced officer once told me to never look at their faces, so I didn't.'

'You're saying you're responsible for all this?'

'Me, us, them, the unit, the coalition, those magnificent men in their flying machines . . . I have taken part in many successful operations.'

He walked over to the wall and pulled a picture off and handed it to me.

'That boy committed the treasonous crime of being eleven years old.' He stepped back and stared at the wall. 'That one was eight, he was thirty-one, she was twenty-two, he was seventy-three . . .'

His voice trailed off and he stared in silence.

'The prosecution rests, your honor, the defendant disobeyed orders and looked at their faces.'

He turned toward the open French doors.

'You've been injured,' I said.

Crawford looked down at the bandage and shook his head. 'Just indecisive.'

He walked over to the kitchen counter and began going through the assembled bottles until he found one that still had beer in it.

'Would you like a beer, Lieutenant? If you don't mind my saying so, you look like you could use one.'

I shook my head. He gave the bottle a quick shake and then emptied it in one gulp.

'Burns is dead,' I said.

He turned and looked at me.

'Someone put a bullet in his head.'

Crawford smiled, though there was no joy in it. 'That deserves a fresh one.'

He walked over to the refrigerator and removed another beer.

'A warrant's been issued for Salem's arrest,' I said.

He stopped at the counter, looked up at the ceiling, thoughts dancing in his eyes.

'And you think he's an innocent man?'

'It's possible.'

His eyes fixed on mine and then he opened the beer and drained it in one long gulp.

'Do you actually believe that innocence still exists? What is it that brings you to this astonishing conclusion?' Crawford said.

'Salem was working undercover trying to solve the murder of Albert Torres. He believed ISC was responsible because of what Torres had witnessed in Iraq.'

'A real goddamn boy scout, isn't he?'

'ISC was using children as weapons.'

Crawford turned and looked at me. 'That kind of talk can get a person killed.'

I slipped the picture of Salem and the boy out of my pocket and placed it on the counter in front of Crawford. He stared at it for a moment, showing no reaction, no emotion whatsoever, then his eyes drifted away.

'But you already know all of this,' I said.

He smiled or at least what now passed for a smile. 'I think we called the boy Ace.'

He glanced at me, then walked over to the open doors and looked out through the breaks in the clouds at the water.

'It's why you're here,' I said. 'Why you're waiting for someone to step off that boat, it's why you decided to look at all these faces.'

'Why I'm here is my business.'

I reached into my jacket and removed the picture I had printed of the explosion at the café and walked over to Crawford.

'ISC used that little boy to try and kill Salem, but instead murdered an American captain and half a dozen Iraqis.'

He looked at the photograph. 'Proof can be a difficult thing to come by in the middle of war,' he said.

'Your help might change that.'

He shook his head. 'I wasn't there.'

I took the blow-up of the photograph out and put it in his hands.

'Russell was, he set the bomb off,' I said.

Crawford stared at the picture for a moment, then handed it back to me. 'That could be anything.'

'So help me,' I said.

'Why?'

'Because sitting in this room waiting for someone to kill you or getting drunk enough to do it yourself is no way to die.'

He looked at me, his eyes focusing just long enough to see through the haze of alcohol and amphetamines.

'You an expert on death, are you, Lieutenant? You cap a lot of bad guys, have you?'

I shook my head. 'No.'

He walked over to the wall covered with photographs and stared at them. 'The problem is that they don't know that they're dead. I've tried to explain it to them, but they just won't . . . listen.'

His focus retreated back into the dull, pain-filled gaze. I walked over to him.

'Come back with me,' I said.

He smiled. 'Do the right thing?'

I nodded. 'Cathy Salem said you and Jack were friends.'

He closed his eyes as if he was looking inward, trying

to find a memory in the mess inside his head.

'I was such a good friend I didn't tell him that if he went to that café, he would never make it home.'

'It's not too late.'

He laughed. 'Do you see anything in this room that suggests I've ever done the right thing?'

'I need your help.'

'Don't push me.'

'Who ordered the use of children?'

He shook his head.

'Did it go beyond ISC?'

In one swift motion he slipped the revolver out from under his shirt and pointed it at my face.

'What happened to your wrists, Lieutenant? And if it's the wrong answer I'm going to blow your fucking brains out.'

I looked into his eyes, which were wild with intensity, as if every ounce of adrenalin in his body had just been let loose. I stepped forward until the dull cold metal of the revolver was pressing against my forehead.

'If I've been taught correctly, you press the gun against the head when you stretch them out in the dirt to interrogate.'

The muscles in his hand began to relax.

'Sometimes you even pull the trigger on an empty chamber,' I said. 'Sometimes more than once.'

Crawford held the gun for a moment longer then pulled it away.

'Sometimes the chambers aren't empty,' he said.

'Does the name Havoc mean anything to you?'

From the reaction in his eyes I knew it did.

'The American captain who was killed at the café. He was with that unit?'

'There is no unit, not that you would find on paper,' Crawford said.

'There are records of what they sent to Iraq.'

'Not everything.'

'There are bicycles on that list.'

He turned and looked toward me.

'Was ISC working with them, for them? What was going on?' I asked.

He flipped the gun in his hand and held it out to me. 'If I tell you what I know, you're as dead as I am.'

'We can protect you,' I said.

He closed his eyes and took a deep breath.

'No, you can't,' he said and grabbed one of my wrists. 'You can't even protect yourself.'

I tentatively reached out and took the gun from him. For an instant I thought I recognized relief in his eyes, but it didn't last.

'When I die, Lieutenant, I'll choose my own ground. You understand?'

'I still need an answer.'

Crawford stared at the pictures and shook his head. 'You're not even asking the right questions, Lieutenant.'

'Enlighten me.'

'Do you really believe this is about the deaths of a child or two? You're thinking like a civilian.' He looked at me, shook his head and began to pace about the room. 'I bet you even believe in democracy.'

Crawford walked over to the kitchen counter and found a pack of cigarettes amongst the bottles and lit one.

'You want a fucking history lesson. Why do we fight, Lieutenant? Why do you think we've armed ourselves to the teeth since our lowly ancestors started piling up rocks in a cave. And please don't say freedom or I'm going to have to start drinking very heavily again. Think real hard.'

'Power.'

He nodded. 'You're getting closer.'

'Tell me about Havoc.'

'Havoc existed for a single purpose, to win the hearts and minds of a nation that had been blown to hell and back and was pissed off. Actually, it was just to win a few minds, I'm not sure they actually believe in the existence of the heart.'

He smiled sardonically, tapped the cigarette out and immediately lit another. His movement and speech began to speed up as if a spring had been let loose inside.

'The opening offensive started small – blenders, microwaves, TVs, nice big HD flat screen, satellite dishes, washer-dryers, they could have opened a god-damned Target store, even your bicycles, which only later were adapted to more conventional weaponry when certain individuals' loyalty to the cause became questionable.'

'Bribes,' I said.

He nodded. 'Now you're thinking like a Jeffersonian democrat.'

'What was the relationship to ISC?'

'They started using us because of our special relationship with what is euphemistically called the Iraqi National Police. An organization that with our guidance has a sense of justice that makes the Mafia look like Quakers.'

He took another beer out of the fridge and began alternating drags on the cigarette and hits on the bottle as he moved about the room, the spring uncoiling faster and faster.

'At some point the geniuses in Havoc figured out that a toaster oven only bought so much loyalty. They started to deal in cash.'

'How much?'

'Started with a stack of bills here and there, those stacks became briefcases full, progressed to suitcases, bags, car trunks. Whatever it took. You getting the picture, Lieutenant?'

I nodded.

'Havoc was thinking like Americans, that you could fix anything by just spending more money. The Iraqis were thinking like Arabs, taking us for all they could. Hell, they had lost everything else, why not? As fast as the money flowed in, it went just as quickly back out of the country into numbered accounts in banks that didn't mind dealing in large amounts of cash. And if it wasn't going there, it was going right into the pockets of the insurgency. AKs, IEDs, RPGs and suicide bombers brought to you by the American taxpayer. Are you familiar with the term chaos theory?'

'I've heard it.'

'It's the idea that all systems, human or otherwise, have rules, and are so sensitive that even small changes will create unexpected consequences that appear random, but aren't. Welcome to Havoc's world. Someone eventually figured out that since there was no accounting going on, and that the money was just as likely going to be used to kill some Sunni day laborer standing in line to get a job or a nineteen-year-old private from Grand Rapids, Michigan, the only decent thing to do was to make sure it went to a better place.'

'How much did ISC steal?'

He drained the rest of the beer, shook his head and lit another cigarette.

'How high can you count? It was beautiful. A goddamn candy store and the best part was that Havoc didn't have a clue. People were buying condos in Cancun while Havoc believed they were fighting the good fight.'

The stale dead air inside the room and the pictures on the wall were more than I could bear and I walked over to the French doors and took a deep breath.

'You saying Albert Torres was murdered because of money?' I asked.

'Torres was killed because he got greedy and stole from the wrong people.'

'ISC killed him.'

173

'He tried to take too big a slice of the pie. Russell didn't like that.'

Crawford walked over to the doors and tossed the cigarette out into the yard.

'Everyone over there dies because of money, Lieutenant, even the lucky ones who are under the illusion that they're sacrificing for the guy or woman standing next to them.'

'And what about Salem?' I asked.

Crawford's wasted eyes looked out toward the ocean. 'He was a good cop. I don't think it took him too long to figure out what was really going on.'

'So they tried to kill him.'

He shook his finger in the air. 'No. First they tried to buy him. Who would have thought an honest cop would show up in Baghdad?'

'He went to high school with Torres.'

He turned and looked at me. 'A friend?'

He said it as if the concept was alien to him. I looked at Crawford for a moment then turned and looked back inside at the wall of pictures as rage began to rise inside me.

'Why did they use a child to try and kill him?'

Crawford continued to stare out at the ocean. 'Everyone who steps on that soil is used one way or the other.'

I shook my head, trying to keep the anger inside from taking over and pulling my weapon and pointing it at him.

'That's not a reason,' I said.

He turned and looked at the wall of pictures. 'You want a reason? All right. Because it worked. And in a place where very little works, the things that do, you use.'

'Even children?'

'The preferred term is asset.'

'Go to hell,' I said angrily.

He looked at me. 'You want that drink now, Lieutenant?'

'No.'

He walked over and took out another for himself.

'How many other children were killed?'

'I didn't count.'

'I want a number.'

'Three, six, ten, twenty . . . I don't know.'

'Did Havoc know about it?'

'Most of the targets we took out were at their request. No one asks how the mission went, they ask if it was successful.'

'That's not an answer.'

'There are no straight answers there.'

Crawford stared at the wall, then drank most of the beer and tossed it on to the floor.

'Did they know about the money?' I asked.

'Well, somebody put a bullet in Burns's head. Maybe it was them, maybe it was Russell. Then again, maybe it was a boy scout. You're the cop, you tell me.'

He walked over to the door to the bedroom. Having let go of what had been bottled up inside, he seemed barely able to stay on his feet.

175

'I'm very tired, Lieutenant.'

'I bet you are.'

Crawford turned and looked at me. 'There's a ferry just before dusk. I'll go with you then and tell what I know to whoever you want.'

'How much money did you take, Crawford?' I asked.

He tilted his neck to the side until I heard a faint pop of bone and muscle. 'Not enough.'

He looked into the dark bedroom as if sleep were something to fear, then turned and looked out the open doors.

'You have to watch the boats while I rest. Every ferry, sailboat, dinghy. The sailboats and motor launches will anchor in the harbor, you have to watch for that. Do you know what to look for?'

'Yeah, I know,' I said, though I didn't want any piece of his world.

'Every face,' he said. 'You have to watch them all, it could be anyone, a man, a woman, a child. Look at their eyes and their hands, the packages they're carrying. If you miss something . . .'

He stopped himself and his lost eyes found mine, and I realized why he had put the pictures on the wall. There was no past or present for him any longer, it had all become one. He was on an island a world away from Iraq, but he was talking as if he was standing on the streets of Baghdad. It was only with the dead that he now felt safe. Only the dead could be trusted, the living were the threat. Only the living could kill you.

Crawford had stepped so far over the line that he no longer knew how to find his way back.

'You can't miss anything,' he said.

'Did you know about the children from the beginning?' I asked.

For just an instant his eyes seemed to exist in the present, with all the understanding of who and what he had become, but it was fleeting, and didn't last.

'What do you want, Lieutenant? You want me to say that I patted little Hassan on the head and sent him on his way to fight the good fight. Where do you think we learned tactics like this? They don't teach it at Fort Bragg.' He stared at me for a moment, his eyes full of the battle being waged inside what was left of his soul. 'Everyone reaches a point over there when the only thing that matters is that you come home.'

'You think Salem would agree with that?'

'Salem wasn't there to fight a war.'

'And you were?'

'In the beginning.'

'And now you're home,' I said.

He looked past me toward the ocean and the dark blue water surrounding Catalina and shook his head. 'I was misinformed about that . . . Home doesn't exist any more.'

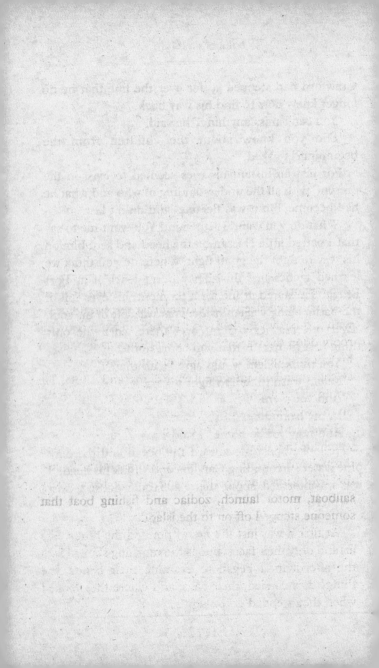

sixteen

Crawford lay down on the bed and fell into an exhausted sleep. Any illusion that rest would come with it quickly vanished. As I looked on from the bedroom door, the war appeared to rage just as brutally in his unconscious as in the light of day. He would flinch at the sound of imagined explosions and shots. He would shake his head as one after another of the faces on the walls called out from death.

I watched him until I couldn't any longer, then I watched the boats, counted them as they slipped through the curtain of fog several miles offshore into the light surrounding the island. Every ferry, every sailboat, motor launch, zodiac and fishing boat that someone stepped off on to the island.

At first it was just the men I pointed the binoculars at, and only their faces, but as the morning slipped into the afternoon, I began to examine their hands, the things they carried, their bags, and where they looked when they stepped on to land.

By early afternoon I was also watching every woman and when I found the glasses drifting toward a child I pulled them away as quickly as I could or put them down altogether and promised myself I wouldn't look at the next boat. But then it would come into view in the harbor and I would start again.

The boat that we would be taking back docked at four o'clock and I watched the twenty or so passengers step off. Couples and families mostly, the few individuals traveling alone were easily identified as tourists. A group of divers were the last ones off. I waited for another minute to be sure the boat had emptied then started to turn to go and wake Crawford when I saw a figure step on to the gangway and place his hand on the railing.

For just an instant the sun caught the surface of a ring and flared brightly. From this distance I couldn't make out any detail beyond that it was large and silver and appeared to be on the same finger I remembered it being. But most men wore rings on the same finger; there was nothing unusual about it, I told myself.

He stepped away from the boat and started walking down the pier. A Dodger cap shaded his face from view. His hair hung down just over the ear. He wore jeans and a baggy shirt with a floral pattern hanging loose over the belt.

As he reached the end of the pier, he turned as a gust of wind pressed his shirt against his back and I saw the bulge of something tucked in the belt against his skin. A back brace maybe. A paperback book he didn't want to hold in his hand, even a money belt, fanny pack, anything. A weapon. I didn't want to accept that as a reality because if that were true, then there was no separating myself from the tortured world Crawford existed in.

I focused the glasses on him, hoping to get a view of his face. He stopped on the street corner with half a dozen other tourists and looked left and right. He watched a young woman in a yellow skirt pass by. Then he took a step into the street and for just an instant glanced up into the hills toward me, and then vanished out of view behind a building.

Was it Salem I had seen, or someone else? I couldn't tell, it had been too quick. Was it even what I thought it was? Had I seen it, did he look this way? Or was it my imagination? He could have been looking at a piece of architecture, his home, a tree; he could have been glancing to watch a sea bird. To have stepped on to the island for the purpose of violence was surely the least likely.

But I had come here. And so had Crawford. And any reordering of reality that allowed for me to be standing where I was now must also have room for what I was trying not to think. And the more I tried to deny it, the closer I could feel him winding his way up through the narrow streets of the island toward me.

I glanced at the other side of the building, waiting for him to emerge back into view, but there was nothing. I moved the binoculars on to the surrounding buildings and streets but there was no sign of him. I caught the blur of movement in an alley as I swung the glasses, but by the time I was able to hold focus, whoever had stepped between the buildings had passed out of view.

Following the same path I had taken, I moved the glasses up the hill toward us, but there was no sight of him. If he was there, I would see him, I told myself. It was all right. A dog began barking off to the left. A chain-link fence began to rattle. I moved the binoculars and could just see the edge of a yard where the dog ran in and out of view, barking at something out of sight.

I stepped back from the edge of the patio and glanced into the house where Crawford slept. The dog fell silent and I took another step back and then turned and walked to the open French doors. Not a sound came from Crawford's room.

I pulled my Glock and crossed over to the front door and listened for any movement on the other side. There was nothing. I took a deep breath and looked about the room. The faces of the dead stared down from the walls. Would they want this man saved? Was he more than just a witness to their deaths? What had he traded for the money he had stolen? How much of their blood covered his hands and fueled his nightmares? Was it their voices that haunted him, a stack of dollar bills gathering dust, or just his own silence?

Something moved on one of the stone steps leading down to the front door, then on another and another, then stopped. I waited for the sound of another footfall, but it didn't come. I reached out, took hold of the handle and slowly turned it until I felt the latch come free, then raised the Glock and pulled the front door open.

A rolled-up newspaper lay near the door, where it had come to rest after being thrown down the steps. I went outside and looked round each corner of the house, but there was nothing. I stepped back inside. Crawford was standing at the door to the bedroom.

'What is it?' he said.

'Nothing, just the paper.'

Crawford's eyes focused on the door, then he walked over to the couch, picked up the shotgun and chambered a shell.

'Were you watching the boats?'

I nodded. 'I saw someone step off the ferry, I was just being careful.'

'What did he look like?'

'I never saw his face.'

'Which direction did he go?'

'He went into a building and never came out.'

'Are you sure?'

I shook my head. 'No.'

'Was he carrying anything?'

'There could have been something under his shirt, but his hands were empty.'

Crawford looked out into the patio then walked over and flipped the deadbolt shut on the front door.

'What is it?' I asked.

Somewhere close a dog began barking again. He listened for a moment, and then turned to me.

'I don't get the paper.'

seventeen

Outside, the sound of the dog barking abruptly stopped. Crawford stepped over to the mattress covering the side window and raised the shotgun. Something moved outside.

'When I say so, pull it away,' he said softly.

I walked over next to him then reached out and placed my hand on the stock of the shotgun.

'You want to add another picture to this wall?' I said.

He turned to me, his eyes lit up as if he had been jolted with electricity.

'Put the shotgun down and you pull the mattress back,' I said.

His hands tightened on the stock.

'Do it,' I said.

His hands began to relax, then he nodded, set the gun down and stepped over next to the mattress. I raised my Glock to the window.

'Now.'

Crawford yanked the mattress away. A starling

rustling in the ivy took flight, nearly hitting the glass of the window.

'Is there another way down to the boat where we won't be seen?' I said.

'There's a path down the hill out back to the street below,' Crawford said. 'It's steep.'

We moved to the French doors and looked out toward the corners of the house. He motioned toward some worn grass just off the left of the patio; his hand was trembling, his breathing taking on the clipped cadence of stress.

'Twenty-five, thirty feet at most,' Crawford said, staring toward the brown patch of dirt. 'Piece of cake.'

'I'll follow you,' I said.

'Drop anything you don't need.'

I turned and looked at him. His eyes looked right past me out into the open ground.

'If I'm hit, they'll try and draw you out,' he said. 'Watch your exposures, don't come after me until you have them covered, an armored vehicle would be best if they have anything other than small arms . . .'

He began to hear his own words and fell silent. He was back in Baghdad. 'It'll be all right,' I said.

A bead of sweat ran down his temple. His eyes moved about like an animal's searching for a way out of a cage.

'You want me to go first?' I asked.

He looked at me and then glanced into the house as if seeing it for the first time, and then he remembered.

'You're a cop,' he said.

I nodded. 'We have to get to the boat.'

'The boat.' He exhaled heavily and his breathing began to slow, then he nodded. 'I'm all right, I'll go.'

He turned and sprinted across the small open space and disappeared over the edge of the yard, then his head popped back up and he nodded. I took off in a run across the yard. Thirty steps at most. The dog began barking wildly again.

Twenty more steps.

I heard what sounded like the crack of wood splintering inside the house. Crawford reached out his hand toward me. He was mouthing something but I couldn't hear what. My legs felt sluggish as if I was running through knee-high grass.

Ten steps.

'Come on,' he said.

I crossed the patio and hit the small patch of worn earth where the trail began. The ground fell out from under me as I stepped over the edge. I hit the hard-packed soil and started to tumble into the ivy-covered slope that fell away when Crawford's hand grabbed my arm and held me in place.

'Just follow it now,' he said, motioning with his hand.

We began to slide down a narrow trail winding through spiked clusters of pale green agaves and bunches of wild rosemary that spread across the hill-side in dense bushes. For the last ten feet the trail vanished into an almost vertical drop covered with thick ivy. I slipped my gun into the holster and eased into the slope and began to slide toward the street below. I tried to grab hold of handfuls of the vines to slow me down, but they either broke or slipped uselessly through my fingers. The dark shape of a lizard skittered across my arm, trying to avoid being taken along toward the bottom of the hill.

I hit the hard-packed dirt next to the pavement of the road with a jolt and buckled to my knees. A Mexican gardener was standing in the yard across the street staring at me, then looked away when his eyes found the gun on my waist. Crawford came sliding next to me a moment later. I glanced once over my shoulder back up the hill, saw nothing, and then we started winding our way down the road to the harbor.

'Did you see anything?' asked Crawford.

I shook my head. 'I heard something in the house when I was running.'

'What?'

'Could have been a door frame.'

Crawford glanced at me. 'Then they know we're going for the boat.'

I could see that behind his eyes he was trying to work through it as if looking for a hole in a fence he could slip through undetected.

'This isn't going to work,' Crawford said. 'They'll be waiting on the mainland. We do this another way.'

I shook my head. 'I can have the entire Pasadena PD waiting for us when we land.'

Crawford looked at me, trying to find a reason to disagree. We rounded a corner and stepped out from

the empty residential streets on to the busy waterfront
that was now filled with crowds of tourists. There was
a mariachi band playing. The sense of being part of the
ocean, which becomes lost the higher you rise on the
island, now returned. Gulls circled overhead and
pranced about the edges of the street, picking up
scraps of food. The smell of the salt and kelp both dead
and living mixed with the aroma of grilling fish and
lime and peppers from a sidewalk café. Small groups of
people were riding along the boulevard on bicycles.
Couples carried shopping bags. Two children ran in
and out of the crowd playing tag. People chatted on
cell phones.

I began to scan the crowd for the man I had seen
step off the boat earlier. The blue of a Dodger cap
slipped out of a storefront and turned toward us
behind a group of people. My hand began to reach
toward my weapon when a woman in a pale yellow
skirt and long black hair jumped into her boyfriend's
arms and placed the cap on his head.

I turned to Crawford. He was frozen, his eyes
moving frantically through the crowd.

'No,' he whispered.

'This is the only way,' I said. 'The boat's right out
there, you can see it.'

He shook his head. A tray of glasses slipped from a
waiter's hand and shattered on the sidewalk. All heads
turned, and for just an instant everything stopped as if
frozen in a photograph, and then just as quickly
resumed as if nothing had happened.

Except for Crawford.

I reached out and touched his arm and he turned and looked at me. Sweat was beading on his forehead. His panicked eyes quickly returned to following the motion of every individual within a hundred feet, analyzing every bag, hand gesture and casual glance.

'We walk across the road and we're on the pier,' I said.

A kid on a bike leapt the curb on to the sidewalk and started pedaling hard, right toward us. Crawford began to reach for the M-16 that he carried on his shoulder like a phantom limb and realizing it wasn't there he took a step back, straining against my grip as the kid flew back off the sidewalk ten feet from us and pedaled off down the road. He watched the kid until he turned a corner, then glanced over his shoulder into the hills rising up behind Avalon.

'Maybe you were wrong about hearing something,' he said.

I nodded even as I once more looked over the people moving through the street for the man I had seen step on to the island.

'Probably was,' I said.

He searched the distance between where we stood and the pier and nodded. His breathing began to slow. His eyes settled on the ferry gently rocking against its moorings.

'You weren't wrong,' he whispered, and stepped into the street.

eighteen

He moved like a man walking across a sheet of glass who expected each step to be his last. He hesitated once when his eyes spotted a paper bag sitting next to a trash container, but as he passed it without the flash of light and blast of heat, his hand gripping my arm began to relax.

We crossed the street and started walking past a sidewalk café toward the pier and Crawford began to laugh.

'Nothing,' he whispered to himself, and then said it again and again with each new step.

A group of women wearing bright red hats stepped out of a shop and turned in our direction. Crawford stopped in his tracks, watching them approach.

'Terrorists, insurgents,' said Crawford, then he quietly stretched out his hand as they passed, and when his fingers brushed the fabric of a jacket or sweater or shopping bag, his laughter grew in intensity and we started to move again.

We reached the waterfront and joined a line of people already formed at the pier to board the ferry. A dark curtain of fog lay several miles offshore but where we stood the sky was cloudless and the sunlight lit up the water. Golden garibaldis darting in and around the pier's pilings flashed like struck matches.

Crawford was no longer looking at any of the faces of the surrounding people or the things they carried. His laughter had stopped, replaced by a dull joyless smile, as we stepped on to the pier and began to walk toward the boat. For the first time in weeks he was among people again, but he wasn't a part of what was going on around him. He looked like the lost tourist who didn't speak the language and couldn't ask for directions. And the harder he tried to blend in, the clearer it became that the world he inhabited would always be separate from those around him. On the best of days he would be little more than a visitor, and on the worst the lines would blur and he would see the faces of the dead in passing cars, the woman standing on the corner, the child on the park swing.

The line inched forward toward the boat and every few steps I turned and scanned the waterfront for the man who had stepped on to the island, but I saw nothing that suggested I had been correct about who he was.

I followed Crawford on to the ferry where he took one look inside the confines of the cabin and then walked out to the foredeck and picked a spot on the rail. We watched the last people board for the passage and when they pulled in the gangplank and shut the gate, I took what felt like the first breath since I had left Crawford's hiding place.

'I was wrong,' I said. 'You're safe.'

The engines rumbled into life, the lines were pulled in and the boat drifted away from the pier. Crawford stared down into the water, shook his head and looked back at land.

'Am I?' he said.

A kid on the opposite rail pointed back toward the island and said something to his father.

'I'm already a ghost,' said Crawford, staring up into the hills above Avalon.

A thin column of white smoke was rising straight up in the air. At the base of the column the smoke was darker and inside it you could just see the bright orange flames that were beginning to consume his house.

'They're making me invisible,' Crawford said.

The sound of sirens became audible and I could see the strobe of emergency lights moving through the narrow streets. The column of smoke turned from white to black and the fire began to send bright fingers of flame up into the sky. Crawford stood staring at the smoke, the knuckles on his fingers turning white from gripping the rail.

The ferry turned its bow toward the mainland and began to motor past the sailboats and sport fishers toward the channel and fog bank lying offshore. I took a last look toward the island. The sun had dipped below it and the pale orange sky that framed Catalina was streaked with dark lines of smoke that began to spread over the top of the island in long dark ribbons.

We cleared the harbor and the boat rose up on its planes and sped toward the mainland. We slipped into the layer of fog and the island vanished from view as if a door had been closed behind us. The temperature dropped and tiny beads of moisture began to hit my face. A few flickering rays of sunlight pierced the clouds briefly, streaking across the dark water, but within a few hundred yards the marine layer thickened and everything was colorless grey.

The other passengers retreated inside the cabin but we remained outside. Crawford moved back and forth along the rail, shaking his head, trying to work something out.

'How were you followed?' he said.

'I wasn't,' I said.

I looked back through the fog to where the island was and knew what I had said was foolish. That someone else had found Crawford the same day I did could not be coincidence.

'I don't know,' I said.

'How did you find me?'

'An LAPD captain traced the cell you called Cathy Salem with.'

'Has she given the number to anyone else?'

'No, she's gone into hiding.'

'What about her husband?'

'She hasn't seen or talked to him.'

'According to her.'

'I believe her.'

'That will pass.'

'She has no reason to lie to me.'

'You sure about that?' He looked at me for a moment.

I shook my head, I wasn't sure about anything.

'What about the LAPD officer?' Crawford asked

'He was the one who sent Salem overseas. He wants an arrest not another killing.'

'So what are you missing?'

I tried to work back through it but found nothing.

'Think!' he said fiercely.

I came up with nothing.

'People die because of the smallest things, Lieutenant. It only takes a word, or a glance in the wrong direction, and it's over. You must have said something to someone.'

If he was correct, I didn't see it. Crawford walked over to me and grabbed hold of both my wrists, exposing the dark bruising.

'Tell me about this!'

I hesitated.

'Come on, Lieutenant, you didn't get those at the health club lifting weights.'

'That happened before.'

'Before what?'

'Before I knew about you.'

He looked into my eyes. 'But you talked, didn't you? You said something to them.'

I shook my head.

'How many were there?'

'Four, I think.'

'But you're not sure?'

'You tell me. This is your line of work, not mine. What's the usual number?'

'What did you say?'

'Nothing.'

'Think.'

My knees began to shake.

'You talked. You told them something.'

I pulled my hands free and stepped back away from him.

'What did you say?' Crawford yelled.

'I begged for my life, is that what you want to hear? You want the little details? You want to know how they held me down and shoved their fingers inside of me, and how I tried to cover myself as I lay in the sand when they drove away?'

I took another step away.

'I would have told them anything, I would have given you up, I would have given anyone up, but I didn't because I didn't know anything. Does that bring it all back to you? Was that one of the lessons you taught the Iraqi police? How many of the faces on that wall of yours said they told you everything? How many pulls on the empty chamber did you give them before they posed for their pictures?'

He looked into my eyes for a moment, then turned and walked back to the rail and looked out into the fog. I followed him and turned him round. Crawford's eyes drifted down to my hand. I hadn't realized I was holding the handle of the Glock. He stared at it for a moment then looked back into my eyes.

'Have you ever shot anyone, Lieutenant?'

I shook my head.

'It's surprisingly easy to learn, that's the problem. It becomes easier to pull the trigger than not to.'

'I don't believe that.'

'You'll come to it.'

'I don't think so.'

'And if I told you I was one of the men who held you down in the desert, and put the gun to your head, and put my hands on you, what would you say then?'

My entire body was beginning to tremble.

'Tell me you deserve saving,' I said.

'No,' he whispered then walked over to the other side of the bow and stared out at the water.

I took my hand away from the Glock and slipped the cell out of my pocket and started to dial.

'I'm going to have people waiting for us when we get there,' I said.

Crawford looked across the deck toward me. 'What did you say?'

'I'll have people waiting for us. You'll be safe, you're going to be saved whether you deserve it or not.'

'Wait,' said Crawford.

'Why?'

He walked over to me.

'Did they touch your phone?' he said.

I stopped dialing and looked at the phone. 'No.'

'You're certain?'

I started to nod, but stopped myself.

'Does the name Taylor or Miller mean anything to you?' I said.

Crawford shook his head. I thought back to Taylor reaching over and taking the cell phone from my lap.

'Who is he?' Crawford asked.

'The most dangerous man in the room,' I said. 'He took my cell before they drove me off the road in Trona.'

'Trona?' Crawford said.

I nodded.

'I got it back the next day.'

'And you didn't check it?'

I shook my head, realizing I had made a mistake.

He quickly reached out, took the cell from my hand and threw it out into the fog.

'Now it's checked,' he said.

We both stood silently for a moment, staring out into the grey.

'Taylor drove a pickup full of weapons and surveillance equipment,' I said, and then turned to him. 'I led them right to you,' I said. 'I'm sorry.'

Crawford shook his head. 'Doesn't matter.'

Neither of us said a word for a moment. In the distance I thought I heard the sound of another boat, but then it was gone.

'Tell me about the men in the desert,' he said.

'The one who did the talking had a naval academy ring on. Does that mean anything to you?'

He closed his eyes for a moment as if trying to stem a spasm of pain.

'It wasn't ISC who was following you,' he said.

'How do you know that?'

'Russell and Burns were army Rangers, not navy. Henkel's a South African. Everyone they hired came from the army or overseas.'

He turned and looked at me.

'The captain killed at the café instead of Salem was navy. Havoc was a naval intelligence operation.'

'China Lake,' I said.

'Yeah.'

'What was his name?'

'Winslow.' Crawford looked down into the water rushing past the bow of the boat. 'It's a grey world over there, Lieutenant. It's only here that things are black and white. ISC and Havoc made a mess of things, and now China Lake is going to clean it up. And Salem is the perfect fall guy.' Crawford smiled. 'I don't think he's going to make it to trial. Game over . . . beautiful.'

'Salem found what he was looking for over there,' I said. 'I think he can prove what happened.'

Crawford shook his head. 'No one finds what they're looking for over there.'

Somewhere above the clouds the heavy thump of a helicopter's blades passed overhead. Crawford looked up into the mist and listened until the sound had vanished.

'The children were orphans, street kids who wouldn't be missed. One day I watched one of those kids kill an Iraqi policeman who had been funneling money to insurgents. If we had arrested or assassinated the policeman, the operative who gave him up would have been compromised and killed. That boy dying saved other lives, but it's not what I remember. What I remember is the way the bike wobbled when he first got on it because the explosives packed in it threw the balance off. And I remember how he looked at me and smiled because he thought for the first time in his short miserable fucking life something good had happened.'

Crawford turned and looked at me.

'That's the face I see every day.'

I looked into his eyes but there was only a dark emptiness. Whatever had been alive, whatever had once loved another human being had retreated so deep inside no light could touch it.

'I'll have the ferry pilot radio in and have some units there when we arrive,' I said.

'Maybe you should go home, Lieutenant.'

'How?' I said and shook my head.

'You're asking the wrong man.'

'Russell and Henkel. How do I find them?'

He shrugged. I turned and started toward the cabin.

'The money,' Crawford said.

I stopped and turned.

'Go back to the beginning.'

'What do you mean?'

'You'll figure it out.'

'I don't need to, I have you.'

He shook his head. 'I can't help you.'

His eyes focused and for an instant there was a spark of something alive to them.

'Crawford?' I said.

'I'm just a ghost, remember.'

I started to take a step but he was already sitting up on the rail.

'No,' I yelled.

He took a shallow breath and leaned back as if he was settling into a comfortable chair, and disappeared over the bow toward the dark water.

nineteen

The boat lurched heavily as the engines were cut. I held myself in place against the rail, trying not to fall, and then looked into the water. Crawford's faint outline slipped along the hull like a dolphin surfing the boat's wake and then he vanished.

The ferry began to swing round and I ran along the side trying to keep focusing on the spot where I last saw him. Crew members were rushing to the rail and were excitedly asking each other what had happened and staring into the water. I heard snippets of the voices. 'Jumped . . . a man . . . I think . . . No, he fell . . . Did you see?'

Someone said, 'There,' and pointed but it was only a piece of flotsam with some kelp wrapped around it. I ran to the stern, following what I thought would be his position, but it was now little more than a guess.

'What's that?' someone yelled.

A single dark shoe was floating in the water, moving gently up and down in the swell. The position didn't seem right. A crew member threw a flotation ring. In the failing light the line separating the sky from the water had merged and the ring appeared to be drifting in the air as it floated on the glassy surface of the water. What was up or down lost all meaning as soon as you looked away from the boat as a point of reference. Several people began to be overcome by nausea as the boat rose and fell. A man ran past me, rushing back inside toward the restroom.

I stepped away from the stern and stopped. Standing alone at the rail midship was a teenage girl with her hands on her face, staring at a point in the grey. Her mouth was moving but I couldn't hear the words. I pressed past two people staring out at the water, complaining that they were now going to be late.

The girl was trying to yell, but could only manage a whisper.

'Do something,' she said. 'Someone do something, do something.'

She turned and looked at me. Her face was flushed. She was hyperventilating. She tried to say something again but her voice failed altogether and she began shaking her head.

'What?' I said.

'Face,' she said. 'I saw his face under the water,' she said haltingly.

I turned and looked into the water but saw nothing.

'Where?' I said.

All she could do was point. The boat rose up on a swell and as we settled back down into the trough

I saw the faint outline of a figure hanging under the surface. I climbed up on the rail and jumped as another swell passed and the water rose to meet me. I hit the water with a sharp crack, and then a rush of air bubbles and then all sound was gone as I sank below the surface.

The cold went through me like an electrical current jolting every muscle in my body. Bright green specks of phosphorescence swirled about me in the darkness like star after star in the night sky, spinning into tiny pinwheels of galaxies. It was absolutely silent, not even the sound of a thought in my head.

Then the faint beating of a heart seemed to come from all around me as if I was drifting on the current of a human pulse. I tried to move my arms but the cold gripped me tighter and tighter and I felt myself beginning to sink, the faint light of the surface growing dimmer like a flickering bulb.

It would be so easy, I thought, just to let go. There would be no past, no present. No pain. I tried to fight it, not to be seduced by it, but the cold wouldn't release its grip and my body wouldn't react. I was nothing more than an observer. The water shimmered like curtains gently blowing in a breeze. A tiny orange sea star traveling in the current drifted past, its tiny arms folding and unfolding like wings.

This is how you die, I thought. Taken in an embrace with all the promise of new love.

Something brushed against me and then I felt the warmth of fingers close around my ankle and I looked down. In the dark water Crawford's face and hands were as white as stone. His eyes found mine and I saw that against the paleness of his skin they were little more than two empty black holes, as cold and lifeless as the abyss below him. His hair swept back and forth in the current. His mouth moved as if he was speaking but there was only silence. He looked below him and then he pushed me toward the surface and his hand slipped from my ankle. Crawford began to fall backward, slowly tumbling toward the blackness below, a trail of tiny green universes marking his path until he disappeared in the darkness.

The cold of the water hit my ankle where his fingers had closed around it and I screamed in pain and began kicking toward the dull window of the surface. The water tried to pull me down but I continued to kick and claw at it with my hands until it released its grip and I broke through the surface.

Air rushed back into my lungs and sound returned as if I had stepped through a door into a crowded room. There were voices all around and the rumble of the boat's engines, even the squawk of gulls as their long wings cut through the air above where I floated. I tried to yell but began to cough up bitter salty water. The shape of the boat rose above me on a swell and I could see a line of people against the rail pointing toward me. The mix of their shouts all merged into one until their voices were little more than a single note.

A flotation ring landed on a swell above me and then dropped down and I reached out and wrapped both arms around it. The sense of being weightless vanished as I gripped it as tightly as I could. The cold returned with a rush. I could feel the five thousand feet of water falling away below me as if I was suspended in nothing more than air.

'The line,' someone yelled.

'Take it,' said another.

The bright yellow rope slapped the water a foot from my face. I reached out and took hold, wrapping it around my hands, and then they began to pull me over the chasm where Crawford was still slowly falling alone in the darkness.

We circled on the gentle swell until the coastguard arrived and took over the search. The crew gave me some dry sweatpants and a shirt to wear and a blanket to wrap myself in. Night had fallen by the time the young lieutenant had finished questioning me. That I was a cop assured her that every word I told her was the truth. I was precise in detail, using the kind of language I had filled thousands of crime-scene reports with. I had just done what any policeman would do when a stranger needed help, which was the first lie I told her.

I had never seen him before I stepped on to the boat, I said. I didn't know his name, where he was from. We had had an innocuous conversation about the ocean while standing on the bow, the usual kind of things two strangers talk about, nothing more. I gave her an estimated age, height and weight. His eyes were dark brown. His hair was auburn, cut at the top of the ear. I described his clothes, the sound and demeanor of his voice. Whether he had fallen or jumped I couldn't say. That the last act of Crawford's life was to guide me back toward the surface before he vanished into the abyss remained my own burden to shoulder.

It was near nine o'clock when I stepped off the ferry back on to the mainland. A news crew looking for a shot of a hero rushed toward a young scuba diver with broad shoulders and took no notice of me as I hurried past.

I walked alone into the sparsely lit parking lot, waiting for the sound of a footstep or a car engine coming out of the shadows, but none came. If Havoc was waiting at the terminal, they remained hidden. Maybe it was because Crawford hadn't walked off the boat with me, or maybe it was because they already knew that halfway across the channel he had stepped off into oblivion, solving both of their problems. I drove a block and pulled over, watching the headlights of other cars pass, but they all appeared to be families returning from the island.

How long had it taken to turn the man Crawford had once been into the man I watched die? Was it measured in days, weeks, or was that kind of transformation measured in flashes of light? I didn't want to believe Crawford's words. I didn't want to believe that at the heart of so much pain was nothing more than money, but the cop inside me knew it was true.

I also didn't want to believe that such a man's last act on this earth was to save my life by guiding me back to the surface. Was he still tumbling through the darkness? How long does it take to fall a mile? An hour? Two, three? Was that his answer when I asked him how to walk away? Is that what he had done? And when he finally comes to rest on that empty sea floor, will it be dark enough to hide the faces of his nightmares, or will they follow him to where not even the faint glow of spinning phosphorescent galaxies will light his long sleep?

twenty

Go to the beginning, Crawford had said. But how do you find the first step taken in a reality that has been replaced by a fever dream, where the touch of a dead man's hand clung to my ankle and I could still feel the rise and fall of the ocean swell?

I drove into the basin on a ribbon of concrete. I badly needed sleep but there was no closing my eyes; every minute that passed pushed Salem one step closer to the same grave Crawford now lay in. He was being hunted down not for what he had done but for what he had seen, and knew. In a battle where the rules of engagement had lost all meaning, he possessed the most dangerous weapon of all: he knew too much, he could point a finger.

I drove through the fog not knowing where I was going or why but when I stopped the car, I recognized the small cedar house on a rise looking toward the ocean. A light burned in the front window. The house's simple Japanese lines stood like a door back to the world I had left behind; all I had to do was step in and I would be home. My daughter was in that world, my job; the man who, when I allowed myself dreams, filled them with his touch. It would be so simple, just to walk through the door. But I knew that if I went in I might not be strong enough to step back out, or if I did, it wouldn't be the same because I had changed.

I slipped silently out of the car and into the fenced yard on the side of the house, stopping just beyond the circle of light that illuminated the door. Through the thin fabric of the shades I could see Harrison standing at the stove in the kitchen, cooking. The air held the scent of ginger and lemon. He moved back and forth between the stove and the cutting board in short graceful movements, then stopped, turned to the window and quickly stepped over to the door and opened it.

I took a step forward, stopping just short of the line of light arching across the grass. Harrison stared into the night, uncertain whether he had seen anything. I took another step and the light touched my face.

'Alex?' Harrison said, rushing over to me.

The familiarity of his voice was startling. I tried to speak but words failed.

'Are you all right?'

As I nodded I realized why I had come here. I was following Crawford's words back to the beginning.

'The Torres case file, did you get it?'

His eyes looked me over for a moment then he nodded. 'I got it.'

'Is it here?'

'Yes.' He reached out and touched my hair and smelled the salt on it. 'You've been in the ocean.'

'Just to the bottom of it,' I said.

He gently took my arm in his hand. 'Come inside.'

The warm light of the kitchen and the scent of his cooking tugged at me like a whisper and I shook my head.

'I can't. I just need the file and I'll go,' I said.

'What's happened?'

How to start? Where? The wall of the dead, but that was ashes. And Crawford, he had stopped falling by now, a cloud of silt would have risen as he landed and then settled over him, giving him the appearance of the dust he would slowly become.

'They're going to kill Salem,' I said.

'Who is?'

'His own memories. ISC. China Lake. The grey men in their oak-paneled offices. They're going to do it for us.'

Harrison shook his head, not understanding.

'Did you know that the worst thing in a war for those who start them isn't the killing, or the wounding, or the broken minds? It's bad publicity.'

'Please come inside,' Harrison said.

'No. If I do that, I might not leave.'

'Let me help you,' he said.

I shook my head. 'They tapped my cell phone, they were following every word I spoke, every place I went. I won't put anyone else at risk.'

213

'I'll take that chance,' Harrison said.

'That's not your decision.'

I looked into the warm light of the kitchen. It would be so easy just to step through the door.

'I watched a man die today. He saved my life and then I lied about it because it was the only thing I could do for him. You can't be a part of this. They don't know where I am now, otherwise I wouldn't be here.'

Harrison shook his head.

'You have to trust me on this,' I said.

'Lacy's been calling. She hasn't heard from you.'

The sound of her name shook me. I looked at Harrison and wanted him to pull me inside, into the light, and not let me go. I had broken my rule that there would be no secrets between my daughter and me, but I knew if I talked to her, there would be no turning away from the sound of her voice, and that would be condemning Salem to death.

'I can't—'

'Alex.'

'You call her,' I said.

He started to protest.

'Do this for me, please.'

'What do you want me to tell her?' Harrison asked.

I could think of nothing. Anything would be a lie.

'Tell her I'll be home soon.'

He closed his eyes and took a deep breath. 'This is wrong.'

I nodded. 'Yes . . . from the very beginning. You have no idea.'

He hesitated then turned, walked inside and returned with the file and handed it to me.

'Thank you.'

'Do you have another phone?'

I shook my head.

'You'll need this too,' he said, slipping a cell phone into the pocket of the sweatshirt. I reached out and touched the crescent-shaped scar at the corner of his left eye.

'You're a good man.'

Harrison leaned in and placed his lips on mine and kissed me. I closed my eyes and my entire body shuddered as his tongue lightly slipped across mine.

'Stay,' he whispered.

The faint taste of lemon and ginger was spreading across the surface of my lips.

'No,' I said weakly.

He kissed me on the cheek, the line of my jaw and then down to the base of my neck.

'Stay.'

I leaned back and looked into his pale green eyes.

'Don't,' I whispered.

'Stay. Let me seduce you.'

His lips brushed against me again.

'You did that long ago,' I said, trying and failing not to look into his eyes.

'Then stay for me,' Harrison said.

'You're trying to keep me from leaving.'

'I'm trying to tell you that I love you.'

I started to shake my head and Harrison slipped his

hand around the back of my neck and began to run his fingers gently over me. I closed my eyes and for a moment I was floating again, tiny pinwheels of light spinning past me in the darkness.

'Please,' I said.

I could feel the warmth of his breath on the side of my face. I leaned into his hair and deeply took in his scent.

'Don't,' I whispered.

His hand slipped across the base of my neck and I heard the sound – the sharp metallic click of the hammer being pulled back, and then the cold touch of steel on the side of my face.

'Please stop,' I whispered.

He slipped his hands under the sweatshirt on to my back. I closed my eyes and heard the faint whisper of the voice from the desert.

'You're nothing.'

I dropped the file and pulled Harrison into me and kissed his neck and whispered into his ear.

'I'm lost.'

'Not here, not with me.'

'Hurry.'

He looked into my eyes and shook his head. 'I don't want to hurry.'

I heard another click of the trigger behind my head and I pressed myself harder into his arms.

'Please,' I whispered.

He took my sweatshirt and pulled it up over my head and tossed it on to the grass. His fingers moved gently down my neck and over my breasts. I heard another click of the trigger coming from behind my head, and I closed my eyes and pulled at his shirt until it fell off his shoulders.

His hand moved down over my stomach and on to the waistband of the sweatpants. Harrison's lips moved across my chest, down my stomach and I heard another whisper from the desert, fainter, but still there.

'Shoot her.'

I reached back and took hold of the grip of the Glock in the waistband against the small of my back as Harrison slid the pants over my hips and they fell to my ankles.

His hands moved down my legs and then lifted each foot out of the sweatpants, and then carefully rolled each sock off as if he was placing the last piece into a puzzle. The cool moist grass felt electric against my skin and I began to tremble as he moved his hands and mouth up my legs.

'Are you cold?'

I shook my head.

'Do you want to go inside?'

I looked over to the warm glow of the lights spilling out of the windows.

'No,' I said.

Harrison's hand closed around mine holding the Glock and tried to release my hold on the grip but my fingers wouldn't relax.

'We're alone,' said Harrison. 'It's all right.'

I looked out into the darkness, waiting for the click

of the gun's hammer or the voice in my ear.

'They are there,' I said.

He slid his fingers between the grip of the Glock and my fingers and eased the weapon out of my hand.

'Don't look at the darkness, look at me.'

I moved my fingers through his hair and looked into his face. His eyes held the light as surely as the spinning phosphorescence of the ocean.

'Hurry,' I whispered.

He set the gun down in the grass and then his hands moved up the inside of my thighs, gently parted my legs and he took me into his mouth. A heavy layer of fog moving in from the ocean closed around us, muting the light from the house and pushing the darkness further away. Thousands of tiny drops of salty moisture began to gather across my body and face and lips. I closed my eyes and I could feel each drop. I couldn't tell if I was standing any longer. The ground under my feet seemed to fall away. With each movement of his tongue I began to drift weightless again in the ocean swell.

I lowered myself down on to Harrison's thighs and he took my face in his hands, moving his fingers gently across my lips, and slowly entered me. I wrapped my arms around him and held on tighter and tighter until I could no longer feel what was mine and what was his.

'Don't move,' he whispered.

Our fingers laced around each other's. My hand became his, his mine.

'I want to move,' I said.

218

'Not yet,' he whispered, his voice breaking.

A single bead of moisture slid down the length of my spine and then another and another and then I realized we were beginning to move. I tried to take a breath but couldn't. We rolled on to the moist grass as if a wave had swept us up and was moving us back and forth suspended just above the sand. I couldn't hold him tight enough. I wanted to lose myself completely, but it couldn't last and the harder I tried to disappear into him, the closer the darkness seemed to creep back.

I felt him stiffen and then a shudder moved through him into me and I felt a cascade of warmth and light, and then memory, regret, and when I was finished I was lying on the grass on my back, and I felt something in my hand. I looked over and I was holding the Glock, and then the grass began to feel like sand against my skin, and my eyes filled with tears.

I rolled on to my knees and looked around us, my hand tightening around the weapon. Then I stood up and walked to the edge of the yard and looked out toward the street.

'You're trembling,' Harrison said. His hand touched my back. 'Come inside.'

I shook my head. I didn't want him to see the tears in my eyes. I didn't want all that I knew and carried inside to get anywhere close to him.

'Come in,' Harrison said.

'I have to go.'

I turned and walked past him over to where our clothes were spread out on the grass. I started to reach for them, but stopped when I noticed the pages of the Torres file had fallen out of the folder when I dropped it.

I knelt down and began quickly to gather them up, but stopped. On one of the pages a crime-scene photograph was attached of Albert Torres' face in death. His eyes were half open as if in order to see he had to squint. His jaw was cocked awkwardly from either the fall or the force of the bullet.

Harrison walked up behind me and draped the sweatshirt over my shoulders, then knelt next to me and touched my hand. I turned to him and I saw in his eyes that he had seen the tears in mine.

He reached over and wiped one away with his thumb and placed his hand against the side of my face.

'Stop before it's too late, please.'

I reached down and picked up the photograph and stared into Torres' dull eyes.

'What is it?' Harrison asked.

'I've seen him before,' I said.

'Where?' Harrison asked.

I stared at the image for a moment longer then shoved it and the rest of the papers back into the file. We don't really look at the dead, not when they begin to pile up one after the other; we glance and then turn away because we really don't want to know who they were. They all become the same face, and when there are enough of them, that face becomes little more than a blur, and that way we don't have to feel anything.

I turned and looked at Harrison.

'I saw his face on a wall,' I whispered. 'With his dark skin I assumed he was an Iraqi, so I looked no closer.'

Out in the fog the heavy horn of a fire engine split the stillness.

'I have to go,' I said, standing up and pulling the sweatshirt over my head. I put on the rest of my clothes as fast as I could, trying to avoid looking at Harrison standing naked next to me.

'Where?' Harrison said.

I fumbled with a sock and then just stuck it in a pocket and picked up my shoes and started walking toward the fence gate.

'Alex.'

I stopped and turned, looking over his body, trying to place in my memory every curve, every line, the way his leg slid around mine, the touch of his fingers, and how for just an instant there had been no past, no future, just the two of us wrapped around each other suspended in time.

'You are beautiful,' I said softly.

'What can't wait until morning?' Harrison asked.

I looked at the file in my hand and then past Harrison toward the darkness.

'The dead,' I said.

twenty-one

I could still feel the movement of our bodies together as I drove away in the fog. I should have stayed. I should have held on to Harrison and let him pull me out of the current that was taking me along, but it was too strong. So I drove away with the faint scent of ginger on my lips, and the touch of his hands fading with each passing mile.

If Crawford was correct about my phone, every step I had taken since Trona had been watched. And that meant I had drawn a line right to Cathy Salem and the widow of Albert Torres.

I took an hour to cross the basin and arrive at the single-lane dirt track and the ramshackle bungalow at the base of the San Gabriels. The fog had thinned as I drove beyond Pomona. A few raindrops fell as I turned off the 210 and headed north toward the mountains. I turned out my lights as I approached and came to a stop across the street. Through the breaks in the overcast I could see the bright specks of stars. The scent of damp eucalyptus hung in the air.

The sign for Rancho del Sol that promised a bright new future had two holes that appeared to be the work of gunshots. There were no lights on in the house, no cars parked outside. Was this the beginning that Crawford had told me to find?

When I had stepped to that door before and Maya Torres opened it, she had lied to me when I asked her about what her husband had told her about Iraq. But why? Was it as simple as protecting the memory of the man she loved? Or was it the money she was trying to keep secret?

I stepped out of the car and started across the street. Several bats dipped down out of the darkness and criss-crossed the road before disappearing back up into the sky. I stopped at the broken gate of the fence surrounding the bare dirt front yard and pulled my Glock from my waist.

The front door stood ajar several inches. I pushed open the gate and quickly crossed the yard and stepped to the door. Inside a faint metallic sound repeated itself again and again with the precision of a metronome. The lock and the jamb appeared untouched. It hadn't been forced. I reached out with my free hand and pushed the door open into the living room and waited for a reaction.

The sound continued unchanged. There was no movement inside. I stepped into the living room and raised the Glock. In the darkness I could see the few pieces of furniture about the room just as it had been before. The sound was coming from beyond the living room in the kitchen.

I crossed the room and stopped at the swinging door to the kitchen. The sound coming from the other side of the door took on the qualities of a finger repeatedly tapping out a beat, one after another, keeping perfect time.

I placed my hand against the swinging door and took a breath, then pushed it open and stepped into the kitchen. The sound came from the sink where the faucet was dripping on to the back of an aluminum pan.

'Maya Torres,' I called out. 'Cathy Salem?'

There wasn't another sound anywhere in the house. A half-eaten plate of food sat on the kitchen table. A serving for another person remained untouched on the opposite side. I stepped over to the table and held my hand over the food. A barely detectable touch of heat still rose from the plate. A fork sat on the edge of the plate, holding a small piece of chicken. On the kitchen counter a spilled bottle of beer had spread across the countertop and down the face of the counter.

Whoever had left the food uneaten couldn't have done so very long before I arrived, and when they did leave they had done so very quickly. I checked the back door for any sign that it had been tampered with but it was untouched, just as the front door was.

Down a short hallway on the other side of the kitchen were two small bedrooms and a bath. I eased down the hallway and stepped into the first bedroom. A suitcase lay on the floor, its contents spread about the room. All

225

the drawers on the small dresser had been opened and their contents also emptied. A small travel bag had been emptied on top of the dresser – some non-prescription drugs, toothpaste and a few other items, but none that was out of place. The closet door was open; two wire hangers were the only contents inside.

I stepped over to the bathroom. A few towels still hung from the racks. On the shelf above the sink a few toiletries and some prescriptions sat untouched. One of the meds was a prescription for Xanax with Maya Torres' name on it.

I crossed the hall into the other bedroom. Nothing had been touched in the room. The drawers to the dresser were all closed. A few clothes hung in the closet. A blouse lay neatly folded over the back of a chair, and a pair of shoes sat underneath it. I picked up the blouse and checked the size – a five. Maya Torres. Nothing of hers had been touched. Whoever had searched the inside of the house found whatever they were looking for in Cathy Salem's belongings.

I glanced around the room once more, and then stepped to the door. There was something else missing that I had remembered from my previous visit. I rechecked each of the other rooms and the closets but it wasn't to be found anywhere.

The shotgun was gone.

As I stepped back into the kitchen, the glow of headlights rose briefly in the windows and then went dark. A car door closed and then the sound of footsteps on gravel began to approach the house. I rushed into the living room and took a place beside the front door. The steps crossed the yard and then took the first step to the house. I closed my hand tightly around the door handle and then pulled it open and raised my weapon.

'Police officer, don't move.'

A set of keys fell to the ground.

'Oh, no,' said a woman's voice.

I held the weapon for another second and then lowered it. Her eyes stood out against the darkness.

'I'm sorry,' I said.

Cathy Salem was holding a small grocery bag. She stood motionless for a moment, taking several deep breaths. I knelt down and picked up her set of keys.

'I didn't know it was you,' I said.

She looked at me for a moment, trying to find her place back in the present.

'What are you . . .' she lost the words and just stared at me. 'Has something happened?' She rushed past me into the house. 'Maya! Maya!'

I followed Salem into the kitchen where she was standing looking down at the plate of food.

'Where's Maya?'

'I don't know. She was gone when I arrived.'

Salem set the bag of groceries on the table and then took a seat. She reached out and picked up the fork holding the food and shook her head.

'She said she would have dinner ready when I got back from the store. I was gone less than an hour.' Salem turned to me. 'Something's happened, that's why you're here. Is it Jack?'

227

I shook my head.

'They said on the news that he killed a man. I called LAPD but they wouldn't tell me anything. Is it true?'

'I don't think so.'

'Can you prove this?'

'I don't know. I found Crawford,' I said.

'Had he seen Jack?'

'No.'

'Are you sure?'

'Yes, I'm sure.'

'I want to talk to him, can you take me to him?'

'Crawford's dead,' I said.

She stiffened in the chair, staring at me for a moment though I got the impression she was seeing something beyond the walls of the room.

'Did you talk to him?' Salem asked.

'Yes.'

She started to ask another question, then hesitated. 'How did Crawford die?'

'He killed himself,' I said.

'Did he tell you anything that can help find my husband?'

I nodded. 'What has Maya told you about her husband and ISC?'

'I'm not sure what you mean.'

'Albert Torres was murdered because he had stolen money. Maybe a great deal of it.'

She shook her head in confusion. 'I don't understand.'

'Among the things Jack discovered was that ISC had been stealing money meant for Iraqis.'

'How much money?'

'I don't know a number, it doesn't really matter,' I said. 'It was enough to kill for.'

'And you're saying Al was part of this?' Salem asked.

'Whether he took money that ISC had already stolen or went off on his own I'm not sure. Either way ISC killed him because of it.'

Cathy Salem looked at me for a moment, trying to make sense of what I had told her.

'The Al that Jack knew wouldn't have done something like that, I don't believe it.'

'I think what people did over there bears little resemblance to who and what they were back home.'

Salem looked out the window. 'I thought this was about children having been killed. And now you're telling me I might lose my husband because of money?'

'The deaths of children had nothing to do with Torres' murder, except for one.'

Salem thought for a moment, then closed her eyes as if in pain. 'The boy in the picture with Jack?'

I nodded. 'ISC used him to try and kill your husband. He escaped, but an American captain and six Iraqis didn't. It was after that he vanished.'

Salem settled back in the chair and took a breath and wiped away some gathering tears.

'Jack saw that?'

'It happened right in front of him.'

'Do you know what the boy's name was?'

'No, Crawford said they gave him a nickname.'

Cathy nodded. 'Ace.'

'Did Maya ever say anything about money or her husband that might sound different knowing what I just told you.'

She looked at me for a moment as if she had misunderstood me, then I saw understanding rise in her eyes.

'Maya couldn't have known anything about this.'

'Are you certain of that?'

She looked at me and I knew she wasn't.

'It's been my experience that when people steal, they're rarely completely silent about it,' I said.

She started to shake her head then stopped. 'She mentioned something the other night about Albert's promise that when this was over they would be taken care of. I assumed she was just talking about the salary he was making compared to the army.'

'Did she ever mention a place that didn't fit with anything else?'

'No, and if this is true, I think she would have told me something.'

'Are you sure of that? Your husband's a policeman.'

'Maya wouldn't have anything to do with something like this, I've known her too long.'

'Like Jack knew her husband.'

Salem looked at me.

'When she left, she took the shotgun with her,' I said. 'Has she ever done that before?'

Salem stared at me in alarm. 'No.'

'And either she or someone else went through your room.'

She sat up and looked toward the hallway to the bedroom.

'Can you think why she would have done that?' I asked.

Cathy started to shake her head then quickly rushed out of the kitchen and down the hallway to her bedroom. I gave her a moment then followed. She was frantically going through the clothes scattered about the floor and then rechecking each of the empty dresser drawers.

'You still had your husband's envelope, didn't you?' I said.

Cathy pushed one of the drawers shut then turned toward me and nodded. 'I didn't know whether to believe you about your involvement with Jack . . . and then when they said he killed that man . . . I thought that if I held on to it . . . I wouldn't lose him.'

She began to move about the room, picking up the clothes strewn about the floor.

'Stupid,' she said softly.

'Is it gone?' I asked.

She lowered her head. 'Yes.'

'Did Maya know you had kept it?'

She nodded and then walked to the bed and sat down, clutching the clothes tightly across her chest. 'I told her after you left here yesterday.'

I walked over and knelt in front of her.

'I'm sorry,' she whispered. 'I've acted foolishly.'

'Can you think of anything else she may have said that could help me find her?'

231

She shook her head. 'Maya's in danger, isn't she?'

'If that envelope has anything to do with the money, yes.'

She leaned her head back and took an exhausted breath.

'There was a key inside the envelope, if that helps,' said Salem. 'I looked at it once after I left your house, then I sealed it back up. What it's to or for I don't know.'

'What is Maya driving?' I asked.

She thought for a moment. 'It's white . . . a minivan, I don't know the kind.'

'You need to leave here, tonight, right now. Pack up and don't come back. Find a cash machine, get enough for several days, then check into a motel room and stay there, don't use a credit card, your cell phone, don't talk to anyone tonight. Then tomorrow I want you to call Detective Dylan Harrison at the Pasadena PD and tell him where you are and that you're all right. Do you understand?'

She nodded.

'I'll call Detective Harrison.'

I picked up a shirt from the floor and began to fold it.

'How does something like this begin?' Salem asked.

I placed the shirt on the bed next to her and looked out the window into the darkness.

'The first lie went unchallenged,' I said.

twenty-two

I watched Cathy Salem's car drive into the night until the red of the tail lights vanished down the narrow road. If Crawford had been correct, then the beginning had to have been the last day Albert Torres spent on this earth.

I got back in the Volvo and opened the Torres file and began to go through the pages of the report on his death. There was the close-up of his face, a picture of a 9mm Beretta a few inches from his hand, the shell casing from the expended round, and a wide picture taking in the entire scene. Along with the photographs was a crude line drawing of the placement of his body, a single black dot on the side of the head where the bullet had entered and macerated his brain.

The understanding of what had happened on that street was summed up in a page and a half of typing amounting to a little over two hundred and fifty words, by my counting. Not much of a story about the end of a life – an interview with his wife that focused on her husband's level of depression about returning to Iraq in a few weeks, a few words tracing the weapon to ISC, which had issued it to Torres, and an empty time line that placed Torres at home at four in the afternoon, and then dead on a deserted downtown street sometime near midnight. He had made one phone call on his cell that night to his wife shortly after eleven o'clock. According to his wife, when she picked up the receiver there had been only silence.

There was nothing about how he loved being a father, or the sound of his laughter, or how the tours of duty in Iraq had made every previous moment in his life little more than a distant dream that grew fainter and fainter until the light went out completely with a single shot in the night.

How do you find a beginning in a house of mirrors? The sum total of what I could produce for evidence was a grainy photograph of a man holding a cell phone on a Baghdad street, a dead man lying at the bottom of the ocean, a wall of pictures that were in ashes, and a military operation whose existence was probably now little more than a pile of shredded documents.

Salem had come to me for help, and I had little more than the stuff of crackpot conspiracy theories to show for my supposed skills. For all I knew, my part in this had been orchestrated from the very beginning as if my role all along had been to lead Crawford to the one place where his secrets would forever be silenced.

I stared at the report for another moment then turned out the light. My hair was matted with the dried salts of the ocean, my skin heavy with the scent of Harrison and making love. If I closed my eyes, the images came like a flood. The dead staring from a wall, their silent faces asking a question of me that I can't understand. Crawford's falling toward the abyss below, his skin white as porcelain against the dark water until he is little more than a distant point of light as faint as a star. The curve of Harrison's shoulder and neck, his fingers becoming mine, his lips, his taste lingering in my mouth like an unidentified spice.

Was any of it real, or had all of it taken place in the brief moment between sleep and waking where the line separating dreams from reality flickers like a candle? I had made love to a man I was silently in love with, and when we finished, instead of holding him, I was clutching a gun in my hand.

I looked back down at the report.

'Why did he die where he did?' I whispered silently to myself.

Why in a city stretching hundreds of square miles did it come to an end on this street at this time right in the heart of skid row? There was nothing in the forensics that provided an answer. Did it lie somewhere in those eight unaccounted-for hours? Was that when the first step had been taken that led to everything that had followed?

I opened a Thomas guide to the map of downtown and located the crime scene on the eight hundred block of Kohler. Torres' Chevy Tahoe was parked on Merchant Street more than a block away from where

235

he died. It was unlikely that he had been pulled forcibly from the truck, there were no signs of a struggle on his body, no damage to his hands, no bruising anywhere. And Green Berets don't get pulled out of trucks without a fight. Why park a truck and go for a walk?

I stared at the map, looking for any possible explanation. Two blocks north was a post office. Four blocks east a bus station. If the key, or what I believed to have been a key, in the envelope from Salem was to a locker in that bus station, then why had Torres parked his truck and walked in the opposite direction? Was he going to the post office? But why go to a post office at midnight? If there was an answer to what had taken place on those streets, no symbol for it existed in the map's legend.

Was this really the beginning that Crawford had talked about? And if so, what was it the beginning of? His own madness and guilt? Had he taken part in the killing, watched it, or merely added the photograph to that wall because the dead were all he had left, because anything that had been alive inside of him had long ago been spent as if it were just another round being fired.

I had been working under the assumption that whatever Salem had found in Iraq was proof of a crime that had taken place there – the killing of innocents or the plundering of Havoc's money or maybe even both. But if he had also solved the murder of a friend on the streets of LA, then a line had been drawn directly from these streets all the way to Baghdad.

How do you solve a murder that took place thousands of miles away?

'The envelope,' I whispered.

If Salem had found his proof in Iraq, then Torres must have mailed it there because the closest he ever got to Baghdad again was the eight hundred block of Kohler – one block from a post office.

I paged through the report again. There were no answers except in what wasn't there.

'Eight hours,' I said to myself.

Four to midnight, Torres had been driving for eight hours. I could see the circle of the headlights cutting through the darkness of the high desert. Then the lights of the potash plant lighting up the darkness like a carnival ride.

'Trona,' I whispered.

Eight hours was about how long it would have taken to drive there and back. Had the money been there? Coming back down the pass into the basin, he could have become aware that he was being followed and instead of driving home to the Valley he headed for the labyrinth of downtown where he could more easily lose his pursuers.

He parked his Tahoe on a deserted street then quickly cut across an empty alley to where he saw the sign for the post office. There would be a drive-up box outside, it wouldn't matter that the building was closed. And when he was certain he had lost the tail, he stepped out of the shadows and mailed an envelope with a key inside to himself in Iraq because in two weeks he would be back there to pick it up.

I opened my eyes.

'And then Salem found it,' I said. An unclaimed piece of mail that had been lost in the shuffle of death, and like the cop he was he began to trace its meaning.

I glanced over to the abandoned house. If Maya had lied about that phone call from her husband, then there had been more than just silence on the other end. There had been an ending, but there had also been a beginning. I looked down at the map of downtown and slid the key in the Volvo's ignition.

twenty-three

Was I following Maya Torres as I drove back into
the fog creeping inland across the basin – a
housewife clutching an envelope in a minivan with its
floor littered with Legos, driving headlong toward the
same chasm where Crawford and Ace and the remains
of truth lay in unimaginable darkness?

Or was something else propelling that van forward?
Did she know about the money? Had the sickness that
had begun on a Baghdad street slipped quietly into her
suburban home when her husband returned and
infected her? Or was she innocent? Did she believe that
the key inside that envelope unlocked a fragment of her
husband's memory that death had stolen?

He was alive one afternoon and when darkness fell
he was dead. And there was no grateful nation's thanks
or a folded flag to dress her wounds. No after-action
report detailing the manner in which he sacrificed his
life. By slipping that key into whatever it unlocked, did
she hope to find his words inside, the touch of his

hand, a chance to say the goodbye that had been denied her?

I pulled off of the 5 freeway on the same exit Torres had probably taken and drove down into the heart of Chinatown heading south. It was after 11 p.m., about the time he would have passed through. The streets were still alive with life. Mexican street vendors worked corners trying to sell trinkets made in Hong Kong. Families emerged from restaurants carrying bags of food. An old woman shuffled along, dangling a live chicken in each hand. The air was thick with the scent of anise and incense. The bright colors of the storefronts' electric and neon signs reflected off the thick fog, giving each block its own particular hue.

I passed city hall and then Little Tokyo. The glow from the towers of downtown to the west illuminated the rest of the city like a lighted closet in a dark room with its door left ajar, and the further south I drove to where Albert Torres had been killed, the fainter the light grew.

I turned at seventh on to Merchant where he had left his truck. The street was lined with warehouses and the occasional small business barely clinging to life. There were no street lights and few parked cars. The shadowy figure of a transient slowly swayed back and forth in a recessed doorway. I looked up and down the length of the street. Maya's minivan was nowhere to be seen. I slowed where I guessed Torres had left the vehicle and continued on foot. Halfway up the block I stopped at a narrow alley that cut west between two brick buildings.

Torres would have been running by this time. I drove down the length of the alley and paused at the end, as he would have done. When he was certain no one was behind him, he would have stepped out on to Kohler. I pulled out of the alley and looked to the north and saw the faint lights of the post office in the fog.

He had a full block of running left. He wouldn't have left his truck if he had thought he was going to get back into it. And if he knew that, he also knew he was a dead man. But he had given himself enough time while his pursuers found the truck to make it to the post office and slip the envelope in the slot.

I drove halfway up Kohler and stopped where his run had ended. There had been no struggle, no fight. Why had a former Green Beret gone so quietly? The coroner had found traces of the gunshot on his right hand, but I didn't believe he had pressed the weapon hard enough against his head to cause the tissue burning. The residue on the hand could easily have been the result of the gun being placed in his hand after death and another shot being fired.

Somewhere in the fog the sound of a bottle shattering pierced the darkness, followed by a slurred shout that appeared to be cut short.

A gunshot or two would barely raise an eyebrow here. Two quick pops and then silence. I stared at the pavement where his body had been discovered and felt a shudder run through me as if I had been plunged back into the cold water.

'Crawford,' I whispered.

Torres would have been trying to make it back to the truck and seen the SUV approaching down the street, and then maybe a figure stepping out of the shadows behind him. He could have run or fought but he didn't because there was no fight left in him. Instead he made a phone call to his wife. And in place of saying goodbye, he told her enough about a future he had secured for her and their children to know that his work was finished. And when he hung up he handed over his weapon to his killers, and then leaned back over the bow just the way Crawford had. His fall into oblivion had lasted only a few feet but when he hit the pavement the faces of the dead that had followed him back from Baghdad had been silenced.

'She knows,' I whispered.

I sped the few blocks east, blowing through the intersection at Central, and turned right on to Terminal. The Greyhound station and yard took up most of the block. A bus heading for Fresno had just pulled out on to the street and passed me. An old Hispanic man wearing a white cowboy hat, his face heavily wrinkled, leaned against the glass of the window staring blankly ahead as I slowed to a stop.

A handful of spindly palm trees marked the entrance to the station halfway down the block. A few solitary figures sat or milled about on the edge of the light cast in a semicircle from the entrance.

I pulled to the curb across the street from the entrance and stepped out of the car. In the distance I heard the sound of a single police squad's siren. A young black male came running out the doors of the station and continued running until he disappeared down the street into the darkness. A moment later what sounded like a faint scream came from somewhere inside the station. ·

I started toward the station's entrance then stopped and looked back toward the parking lot across the street. A single light illuminated the center of the lot. The few cars parked there were clustered around the light pole except for one, which was just visible at the back of the lot – a white minivan.

I took a step toward the lot, staring at the windshield, then ran to the entrance and stopped. Just visible inside the van I could see the dark silhouette of a seated figure. The sliding side door was open a few inches. The distant sound of the police squad's siren was drawing nearer. My hand fell to my side and took hold of the Glock as I broke into a run toward the van.

Ten feet from the vehicle I slowed to a walk. The figure inside was not moving. On the side of the sliding door two streaks of crimson stained the white paint. I raised the weapon.

'Police, step out of the van,' I said.

There was no response, no movement, not a sound.

'Police officer, step out,' I said.

Nothing. I took a step, waited another moment for the smallest of movements from inside, but the dark figure remained frozen.

'Maya Torres?' I said.

The figure slowly turned toward me with the slow mechanical movement of a wind-up toy. I stepped to within a foot or two of the van. That close I could see that the streaks of blood on the door were made by fingers trying to open it. A single drop of blood had run down the edge of the door all the way to the bottom.

'Maya,' I repeated.

The faint sound of a breath, as if being drawn through heavy cloth, emerged from inside. I steadied the Glock, then reached out with my free hand and took hold of the door above the bloodstains. I slid it open. The dome light came on, casting a hard white light across the inside of the van, and Maya Torres began to scream.

twenty-four

Her scream ended as abruptly as it began. If she recognized me, I saw no indication of it in her eyes. Her face and the front of her shirt were speckled with small drops of blood. The fingers on her left hand were nearly covered in it. I quickly holstered my weapon and held my hands out to show they were empty.

'Look at my face,' I said. 'You know me, it's all right now.'

Her eyes continued to look through me, seeing only whatever horror she had just endured.

'Maya,' I said.

Her eyes focused for just an instant as they locked on me.

'You,' she whispered.

'Delillo,' I said.

She tentatively nodded, unsure of even the smallest of gestures.

'Where are you injured?' I asked.

She tried to say something but could only silently mouth words.

'I need to look to see if you're hurt.'

Her eyes began to retreat again. I gently took hold of her left arm and turned it over to examine her bloodstained hand. I could see no visible wound. I slowly eased into the van and looked over her chest and face and neck for any sign of injury, but there was none that I could find.

'Maya.'

She didn't respond. I reached out and took her face in my hands.

'Look at me, Maya.'

Her eyes settled on mine.

'You're going to be all right.'

She started to shake her head.

'Yes, it's OK.'

She drew a shallow breath.

'Delillo,' she said.

I nodded. 'Whose blood is this?' I asked.

Panic began to spread in her eyes.

'Whatever happened is over, do you understand? You're safe now.'

Her eyes began to calm and she looked past me toward the entrance of the station.

'Now tell me whose blood this is.'

'His,' she whispered.

On the seat next to her was a box of Kleenex. I pulled out a couple of tissues and began to wipe the spots of blood from her face.

'Where's the envelope you took from Cathy?'

She shook her head.

'It had a key to a locker inside it,' I said.

'It was mine,' she whispered.

I wiped the last spot of blood from just below her eye.

'I know. Your husband wanted you to have it,' I said.

Tears welled up in her eyes and she silently answered yes.

'Do you know where it is?'

She looked past me toward the entrance.

'Is it in the station?' I said.

Maya stared at me for a moment and nodded.

'He took it,' she said barely above a whisper.

'Who did? Did you see a face?'

'All I saw was blood.' She began to laugh sadly. 'For what? All this . . . for nothing.' She looked at me and shook her head. 'A piece of paper, that's all there was.'

'Inside the locker?' I asked.

She nodded. 'I thought there would be . . . Numbers, that's all it was.'

'Do you have it?'

The emotion began to drain from her face and she stared past me into the darkness.

'I have nothing.'

Her eyes drifted away and I knew there would be no more answers. I quickly looked the van over until I found the shotgun lying across the floor of the front seats. I pumped the chamber empty of three shells and placed them in the pocket of my sweatshirt, then set the gun back down under the seat.

'Stay in the car and lock the doors,' I said, but there was no reaction, she just stared straight ahead.

I left the van and ran toward the entrance of the station. Half a dozen people were gathered at the entrance. A black woman wearing a security guard uniform was standing in front of the door. The siren I had heard before was now only a block away at most.

'You don't want to go in there, the po-lice are coming,' said the woman with a heavy southern accent.

I took out my Glock. 'I am the police.'

Several of the bystanders who probably had outstanding warrants of one kind or another turned away so I wouldn't see their faces.

'I still wouldn't go in there,' said the woman.

'Did you get everyone out?'

She nodded.

'When the other officers arrive, tell them I'm inside and what I'm wearing.'

The automatic doors slid open and I stepped inside the terminal. Fluorescent lights lit the large space in an unnaturally bright white that drained all color, all life from everything inside. The only sound was a television hanging on the wall above the seats of the waiting area, an endless infomercial playing over and over. A bucket and mop sat on the floor in front of the ticket counter on the far right wall. The air held the heavy scent of ammonia and cleaning product. A sign at the back of the terminal directed passengers to baggage and all buses.

I crossed the waiting area to the passenger corridor and stopped. The wall to the left of the hallway was lined with lockers. Halfway down in a center row a single locker door hung open, the key in the door, a dark slash of liquid staining the floor in front of it. As I stepped up to the locker, the color of the liquid on the floor became evident and the faint but unmistakable odor of blood filled the air.

I swung the door of the locker open with the barrel of the Glock. It was empty. The blood trail moved off down the hallway toward the swinging doors that led to the buses. I replayed in my head what Maya had said, trying to understand what had taken place. She had opened the locker and found the piece of paper inside, and then someone had taken it from her before she had gone more than a step from the locker. I looked down at the blood across the floor. Maya hadn't done this. A third person had stepped up to this locker, and one of them was now bleeding to death.

I followed the blood to the swinging doors, raised the Glock and stepped through. Half a dozen buses sat in the dark loading terminal. The air smelled of diesel and the sweat of the thousands of lives that moved in and out of this space every day.

I clung to the doors for a moment, listening for any movement, any sound, but there was only silence broken by the occasional metallic tinkle of an engine cooling. The trail of blood disappeared between two of the buses.

Numbers, Maya had said.

What kind of numbers? Telephone? An address? Bank account?

I began to follow the trail away from the light of the terminal. Whose blood was I following? I passed the first bus and when I reached the front of the second one I stopped. A smeared handprint stained the silver metal of the front just beyond the headlights.

The door of the bus was partly open. Blood stained the first step, and on each of the others the amount of blood increased. I pushed the door open the rest of the way and eased up the steps.

There was almost no light inside, and from out of the darkness at the other end of the bus came a horrible sound. It was breathing, but not just breathing. It was the sound of someone drowning in his own blood, gasping for breath.

I raised the weapon and stepped into the center aisle.

'I'm a police officer,' I said, holding on the point in the darkness where the sound appeared to originate.

With each breath the desperate cadence of the breathing slowed. I stepped past the first row of seats and then the second. As my eyes adjusted to the light, the dark shape of a figure lying in the aisle at the other end began to emerge out of the darkness.

I held the gun on the body and moved slowly toward the figure. He lay on his back, arms at his side. I held still, training the weapon on the figure, waiting for any movement, but other than the rise and fall of his chest there was none. I reached up above the seat next to me and turned on the reading light. The small circle of light spilled just enough into the aisle to see the features of his face.

His eyes were moving back and forth as if trying to find one last thing to focus on as he died. Blood covered his lips and gathered in the spaces between his teeth. A dark V-shaped wound sliced through the middle of his neck, exposing tendon and muscle. A 9mm pistol was stuck snugly in the waistband of his pants, its presence all but useless to him. By the time he had realized his killer had stepped up behind him, it was already too late, the knife had cut him before he had even touched his weapon, and then he had run in panic like a wounded animal seeking shelter.

I recognized him from the photograph Smith had shown me.

'Henkel,' I said.

There was no point in asking him if he had seen his attacker, there would be no reply given the nature of the wound. If I was right about what was happening, then it was Taylor who had walked up behind him and planted the knife in his neck. And if I was wrong and it had been Salem, I didn't want to know.

His eyes settled on me and I felt a chill. There was no panic in them, no plea, there seemed to be nothing that even remotely connected him to any other living thing. My fingers tightened around the handle of the Glock as I kept it pointed at his face.

'Were you there?' I said, knowing there would be no reply.

In the instant before the bomb had exploded, did the little boy understand what was about to happen? Had he seen it in Salem's eyes when he saw him moving toward him on the wobbly bike? And in that instant of understanding what had he wished for? Another life, another day, minute, maybe for his flash of light to be the one that would end all others; a child's dream of peace. And maybe there was just enough time for him to be frightened.

'How many bicycles does it take to win a war?' I said.

Henkel's eyes held on mine and for an instant I saw the reflection of a human being inside him, and in that moment I sensed the presence of all of Crawford's faces looking down on me and I felt ashamed for what we were capable of doing to each other.

Henkel took a heavy breath and a small bubble of blood and saliva formed on his lips and then burst. I sat on the armrest of the seat and looked down at him. I held the weapon for a moment longer and then lowered it.

'I'm not going to be your witness,' I said. 'You're never going to take from another human being again. You have to die alone.'

His eyes held on mine and I stood back up and started to walk out of the bus. The sound of his breathing started again then faltered and then struggled to begin, gasping for air. I stopped.

'Don't,' said a voice in my head. 'Please.'

It was a child's voice. It sounded like my daughter's,

and then like a boy's, and then like every child I had ever heard. I turned around and looked back down the aisle at Henkel. His chest rose, straining against an enormous weight, and then fell as if every bone, every muscle inside of him had collapsed.

'No,' I whispered.

I tried to take another step toward the exit, but couldn't. I walked back down the aisle and knelt next to him. His eyes were again moving back and forth, searching for something to focus on.

'You bastard,' I whispered to myself.

I reached down and took his hand in mine; it was cold and nearly lifeless.

'Look at me,' I said.

His eyes stopped moving and found me.

'Ace wanted me to do this. You remember him? He was just a boy who thought he had been given a gift.'

His eyes opened wide.

'It's his hand you're holding,' I said. 'Can you feel it?'

Henkel looked into my eyes.

'Tell me you remember him. Tell me you remember how he laughed and the sound of his voice . . . Tell him you're sorry.'

For an instant I saw fear in his eyes and they blinked and his chest rose violently, straining for a breath, and then silently fell until the last bit of air had escaped back into the world he had taken so much from.

I laid his cold hand down next to his body and looked at his now empty eyes. I wanted to believe his death brought some form of peace to those he had killed, but wanting belief was a poor substitute for having it.

I stood up and started to walk away when I saw the reflection of movement on the shiny surface of the bus to my right, heading toward the terminal's exit to the street. There was nothing definable, barely a shifting of the light across the surface, and a sense that I was no longer alone.

I reached down and took the Glock in my hand. The reflection stopped, and then was gone. I rushed to the front of the bus and down the stairs to the pavement. Footsteps resonated in the cavernous space, echoing off the high ceiling, coming from all directions.

I stepped to the end of the bus and stopped. The footsteps fell silent. I closed both hands tightly around the handle of the weapon and stepped into the open. In the terminal's exit half a football field away I could see the flashing lights of patrol cars reflecting faintly off the fog. I took a step toward the exit when I heard movement coming from behind me.

I started to swing round, raising the Glock, expecting the feel of a blade to hit me before I could turn completely. The muscles in my shoulders tightened as a footstep slid across the pavement. I drew my arms in protectively to my side as the figure came into view out of the shadow of the bus.

'Police officer,' I yelled.

The figure froze.

'Drop what you have in your hands.'

An object fell from his hand, hit the pavement and rolled a few feet from me – a dark plastic spray bottle. I stared at it for a moment.

'Who are you?' I said.

'Janitor,' the man said with a heavy Hispanic accent.

'Where did you come from?'

'Office,' he said, his voice cracking.

'Did you see anyone?'

He shook his head.

'Go back there and lock the door.'

'*Si*,' he said and took off the way he had come.

I turned and ran to the terminal's exit and stopped. The lights of two patrol cars now illuminated the bus-station entrance half a block away. I took a few tentative steps, listening for footsteps, looking into the fog up and down the street. Nothing.

The engine of a car came to life and I raced through the yard's exit on to the street. The squeal of tires cut through the heavy air. The faint outline of a vehicle was moving at the limits of sight and then disappeared into the darkness. I raised the gun and held on it, then lowered it as the tail lights disappeared into the darkness.

Two of ISC's partners were now dead. Russell was the only one left alive and I could feel the clock ticking on his life. I started toward the parking lot but stopped and looked back into the dark terminal.

'Salem,' I whispered to myself.

Evidence would have been planted in that bus linking Salem to the murder and I hadn't looked. I

255

glanced over to the entrance to the station. Officers had already entered the lobby. They would be at the lockers and in another minute would follow the blood trail to the bus. I stared into the darkness of the terminal. I could slip back in, or re-enter the front, it would be awhile before detectives arrived . . . No.

Another nail was being driven into Salem's coffin and I had missed my chance to help him. I ran back toward the front of the bus station and stopped next to my Volvo. The back corner of the parking lot, where I had left Maya Torres, was empty; her minivan had gone.

'It doesn't matter now,' I said silently to myself. Whatever Havoc had wanted from her, they had got it from inside that locker; she would be safe now, at least from them. All the pieces of the puzzle were being neatly picked up and tucked away where the light of truth would never touch them. What dangers remained for her would exist only in her memory of what she had lost.

I got in the Volvo and sat for a moment listening to the sound of more sirens approaching, then drove away, another piece of the puzzle disappearing in the rear-view mirror.

twenty-five

I needed sleep, but how to slow down the images and thoughts racing through my head? The empty touch of a dead man's hand, a lover's leg curled around mine, the smell of sage, and blood, and the taste of the ocean. I would be drifting in the water one moment, then watching the wobbling wheels and shaking handlebars as my daughter's first bike ride became Ace's last.

It's 'all true', the voice would say, even the lies. There was no separating the past and present, it was all part of the same current, moments of time spinning on the drift until they touched each other and became one. Maya Torres knew all about that, I had seen it in her eyes as I wiped the blood from her face. And Salem knew it, and Crawford, as did all the dead. And I felt powerless to change any of it.

Twice on the drive home I began to change directions and drive toward Harrison's, thinking I would find solace in his arms, and each time I turned away when I remembered his eyes looking at the gun in my hand after we had made love. My world had changed, and if I accomplished nothing else, I would at least keep the people I cared about separate from this. Until this was over, at best I would only be a visitor in what had been my life.

I parked on the street outside my house for several minutes, studying the surrounding darkness and then every window, every door, until I was satisfied I was alone. Once inside I checked each room, each closet, each corner of shadow.

This was my world now, and with the paranoia came a kind of strange comfort that I didn't understand.

I laid the Torres file out on the kitchen table. It was the only record of the moment in time when the violence of Baghdad first reached into a street in LA. But it couldn't replace actual memory, and Russell's was the only one that remained. If Havoc found him before I understood all that had happened on Torres' last day, then it would probably be lost forever.

I stared at the file, wondering if I had missed something, until the words on the pages began to run together and lose all meaning.

I ran a shower, stripped off the coastguard sweats and stood under the water, washing away the salt of the ocean from my hair and the faint scent of ginger that clung to where Harrison's lips had caressed my lips and skin. I leaned into the shower tiles and closed my eyes until I had exhausted the hot water.

'Walk away,' I said silently.

Why hadn't I listened? What price was worth this? I

stepped out of the shower into a robe, too exhausted to dry off. It would be better in the light of day, I thought to myself. Let it go, if only for a few hours. Lie down and get some sleep.

The dreams seemed to come as soon as I closed my eyes. I was looking up at the surface lens of the ocean, the hull of the ship visible, a line of people standing at the rail pointing toward me. I swung my arms, trying to reach the surface, but it did no good. The boat was growing smaller, the water colder. A hand closed round my ankle and I screamed but there was no sound. I bolted out of bed and stood there until the movement of the water from the dream stopped under my feet. My robe was damp with sweat.

I looked at the clock; barely an hour had passed. I stepped into the bathroom, ran cold water into the sink, soaked a washcloth and slipped it round my neck. As I started back to the bedroom, I passed the window and saw the dark shape of an SUV parked on the street in the fog. I froze. I tried to take a breath, but couldn't. The tiny muscles in my hands began to quiver.

Do something, move, the voice in my head began but my body refused to cooperate.

Take a step, just one, and then another.

I stepped back from the window and pressed myself against the wall.

Think. Do something.

A floorboard creaked under the weight of a step somewhere in the house. They were already inside.

Move.

A rush of air filled my lungs and I ran to the night-stand next to the bed to retrieve my Glock but it wasn't there. I had left it on the kitchen table.

The voice in my head changed, as if a switch had been flipped. *No, no, no. Get on your knees, don't fight it, beg. You're nothing.*

I could smell sage in the air. My hands were shaking as I clung to the wall next to the door into the hallway. This is how they win their wars. You listen to the voices. They shoot a bullet of fear into you.

I clenched my fists, digging my nails into the palms of my hands until the trembling stopped. Don't give in. I started to slow my breathing, one breath and then another.

Fight it, think, work it out.

A floorboard creaked somewhere beyond the hallway. I looked at the window. I could slip out, disappear into the fog, and run until I found a place to hide.

I could taste the sand on my lips, and feel the barrel of the gun pressed against my ear.

'Go to hell,' I said silently.

I looked around the bedroom. I needed a weapon, anything would do, but there was nothing. I rushed across into the bathroom and began opening drawers in the vanity. Cotton balls, mascara, lipstick. I pulled out a plastic bag. I could fight them off with Tampax; they wouldn't be expecting that. The laughter of fear began to rise inside, and that voice in my head began to grow fainter.

In the darkness my hand closed around the shape of a pair of scissors and I rushed back to the door of the bedroom. I pressed in close to the opening of the door and listened for movement. Nothing.

I had left the Glock on the kitchen table next to the Torres file. If I could get across the living room to it, I would have a chance. I stepped into the hallway, holding the scissors with both hands, and eased along with my back against the wall.

A few feet from the end of the hall I stopped. I could see most of the living room, and the dining room, but the kitchen was out of sight. I stepped to the edge and looked round the corner. The rest of the living room was empty. Maybe I was wrong, maybe what I had heard was outside. I could make a run across the room for the gun.

I leaned into the wall and took a deep breath and then started to move across the living room. As I passed the couch, I smelled the scent of perspiration and deodorant hanging in the air. They weren't outside, they were right here, maybe only a few feet away. I stopped. The kitchen table creaked as if someone had put weight on it.

I took a step and then another and the figure came into view. He was leaning over the kitchen table staring at the Torres file ten feet away. In his right hand I could see the dark shape of a 9mm. His left hand was on the table a few inches from my Glock.

The voice in my head came back.

You're nothing . . . run.

261

I leaned back on the heels of my feet. The grip I had on the scissors seemed to slip involuntarily. I lifted the scissors up to where I could see them and closed my hand around them but I still couldn't feel them. I took a breath and settled back on to the balls of my feet.

Over the collar of his jacket the side of his neck was exposed. Hit him there, as hard as you can. If he turns, hit him in the face, the eyes. The surprise might be enough. The gun would fall from his hand as he reached for his neck. By then I would have the Glock. The feeling in my hand returned, I was sweating, the steel of the scissors was cool against the heat of my skin.

I didn't take a breath, or think. I had halved the distance between us before I realized I was moving.

Grab his hair; hit the neck as hard as you can.

My left hand started to reach out toward him, the hand holding the weapon felt as if it was going to explode. I was screaming inside my head, a kind of primal wail.

Faster, faster, faster, do it, hit him.

He began to turn as I brought the scissors up and started to strike. I saw the weapon come up, and then his other hand rose with his palm open. The screaming in my head stopped and I froze.

'Jesus Christ,' he said.

twenty-six

Neither of us moved. The only sound in the room was my breathing. I lowered the scissors to my side and let them fall from my hand to the floor. I stared at the gun for a moment and then he lowered it.

'You,' I said.

'Jesus,' he said again and then slipped the gun into his waist holster.

He looked down at the scissors on the floor.

'Jesus, I almost . . .' He let the rest go.

'Smith,' I said.

He took a deep breath and steadied himself on the edge of the table.

'Christ, I thought you were dead,' he said. 'I've been trying to call you for hours.'

'My phone isn't working at the moment.' I picked up the Glock and slipped it into the pocket of my robe and took a seat on the opposite side of the table.

'How did you get inside?'

'I forced the garage door.' Smith studied me in silence for a moment. 'Where's Crawford?'

'You knew about him?'

He nodded. 'He's with ISC. Worked with Jack.'

'Was . . . did. He jumped off the ferry on the way back from Catalina. He's lying on the bottom of the channel about a mile down.'

Smith's eyes looked about the room as if he might find some meaning for Crawford's death hidden behind the couch.

'Why?'

'Too many voices in his head.'

Smith looked at me, waiting for another answer.

'I think it was his best option,' I said.

Smith picked up the page of the report with the photograph of Torres then leaned heavily on the edge of the table and shook his head.

'I think it's time we help each other, Lieutenant,' Smith said.

I settled back into the chair, the rush from the adrenalin was fading. Everything felt heavy, every movement, breath, even trying to form a question in my head seemed to take effort.

'Are you all right?' Smith asked.

I nodded unconvincingly.

Smith shook his head, took a seat. 'Henkel is dead, someone put a knife through his neck.'

I gave no indication that I already knew. He looked at me for a moment, pressed himself back in the chair.

'But you already know that, don't you? That was you

at the bus station, the woman officer who identified herself to the security guard.'

I hesitated.

'You left a crime scene, Lieutenant.'

'Did I?'

'I can prove it if I have to, but I'd rather let it go.'

Something had changed in his demeanor, but I couldn't put a finger on it.

'Why were you there?' he asked.

'I was following Maya Torres,' I said.

He looked at me for a moment, piecing something together in his head.

'The lockers?'

I nodded. 'Her husband had put something there the night he died.'

'Did she see what it was?'

'A piece of paper with numbers on it.'

'Numbers? What the hell is that? It could be anything.'

'Or something specific enough to kill for.'

'Did Salem know about it?' Smith asked.

'If you're here thinking I'll help you hunt him down, you've wasted a trip,' I said.

'I'm not here to hunt him down. I'm a cop, Lieutenant, not an assassin.'

'Yesterday you thought Salem killed a man. What's changed?'

He drew a breath. 'I've been removed from the case.' He made brief eye contact then looked out the window toward the darkness.

'Why?' I asked.

'The official reason is that I'm too close to the investigation . . . The real reason? You tell me.'

'You don't want to know what I think,' I said.

'Yes I do. Who is Salem such a threat to?'

'The men in grey suits,' I said.

'What the hell does that mean?'

'If I knew the answer, I would be lying dead in the sand.'

He set the page of the report back down, ran a hand through his hair, his eyes searching the room, looking at nothing at all. Inside the exhaustion in his eyes, there was something else, embarrassment maybe.

'Tell me what you know, and I'll help you,' Smith said.

For an LAPD cop to make that offer was no small thing. He could be risking his career and pension, and if he was risking more than that then we were both in more trouble than I wanted to think about.

'Why?' I asked.

'I sent Salem there. I should have known better, but I did it anyway because the worst I could imagine didn't have any of this as part of the scenario.' He leaned back and looked toward the ceiling. 'I'm not sure I imagined failure as part of the equation at all.'

'You don't think Salem killed Henkel, do you?'

'It was no cop who put that knife in his neck,' Smith said.

I nodded in agreement. 'How many agencies are looking for him?'

266

'Every state, local and federal agency has his picture. And he's considered armed and extremely dangerous.'

'I think he has more worries that that.'

He leaned on the table, clenching his fists. 'The print on the door of Burns's truck, Salem's print, it was perfect, every contour, scar, every line. And that was all there was. No other partials, no smudges, nothing but that one perfect print.'

'That doesn't happen,' I said.

'Not in our world, but this isn't our world any more, is it, Lieutenant?'

'No,' I said.

'Let me help you.'

Trusting an LAPD captain was like asking me to enter a beauty contest. But then I still believed in democracy, didn't I, though the rule of law was being severely tested. How far did my willing suspension of disbelief extend? I looked across the table and wondered.

'Does the name Havoc mean anything to you?' I said.

Smith shook his head.

I removed the photograph of Russell on the Baghdad street from the jacket hanging on the back of the chair and held it out to Smith.

'What is it?'

'A photograph of a murderer.'

He stared at the picture, trying to make sense of it. 'Russell?'

'Yes. He had just tried to kill Salem, but instead

murdered an American captain and half a dozen Iraqis. He's holding the weapon in his hand.'

Smith looked more closely at the picture. 'A cell phone.'

'The weapon of choice these days,' I said.

Smith leaned back in the chair, holding the picture. 'I think you better start at the beginning.'

I looked down at the table and shook my head. 'I've been trying to do just that.'

I laid out the story of what Salem had walked into as Crawford had told me, the whole sad thing. The money meant to win hearts and minds that managed to corrupt everyone it touched. The dead faces lining a wall that turned paradise into just another dark corner of a nightmare. The way a bike will wobble when packed with explosives. The way truth becomes a threat when everything else is based on lies. The envelope. Trona. China Lake. The way the world looks when every passing face, every car, every sound, holds the same potential as a weapon.

When I was finished, Smith sat in silence, his eyes focused internally on some private place of retreat. I walked over to the cabinet in the dining room and poured us both a shot of bourbon.

'And I can't prove a word of it,' I said.

He held the glass in his hand, rolling it slowly back and forth in his fingers for a moment.

'Son of a bitch,' he whispered.

'I think LAPD is the least of Salem's worries,' I said.

He took a deep breath and shook his head.

'The men in the desert, you're sure they're the ones who followed you to Catalina?'

I shook my head. 'Crawford was sure. According to him, ISC didn't possess that kind of surveillance ability.'

'And you think they're the ones who murdered Burns and Henkel?'

I nodded. 'Havoc is trying to erase from memory everything they and ISC did over there. And what's left will be blamed on a dead cop.'

'Salem.'

'Yes.'

Smith stared into his drink. 'How many children were killed?'

'Once you count past one, does it matter,' I said.

He shook his head. 'Every time you think you can imagine the worst, you discover how little imagination you truly have.'

Smith emptied the glass in one gulp and then carefully placed it back on the table as if even the smallest of acts now held a gravity that hadn't existed before. He looked down at the Torres file spread out before him.

'You think somewhere in here is the beginning Crawford told you to find?'

'If it's not there I don't know where else to look.'

Smith picked up a page of the file. 'It's also possible that he had lost his mind and was pointing you in the wrong direction.'

I shook my head. 'Whatever Crawford had lost, he had enough left at the end to save my life.'

269

Smith turned to me. 'You went in the water after him?'

I nodded and took a sip of bourbon. 'I don't think he drowned in the end. I think what killed him was that he had run out of lies.'

Smith stared at the pages spread out in front of him. 'And what if this all ends with that locker at the bus station?'

'I don't think it does.'

'I've been over these reports dozens of times. If there's any answers in them, I never saw it.'

'What about the time line?' I said.

'It's empty.'

'Only on paper. Something happened in those eight hours.'

'You have an idea?'

'I think he went to Trona to either collect or hide the money. The timing would be about right,' I said.

'ISC is there.'

I nodded.

'Why would he go anywhere near ISC if he knew they were looking for him?'

'That's the problem, he wouldn't.'

'And that leaves what?' Smith said.

I emptied the glass of bourbon, shivering as it slid down the back of my throat.

'How do you move money illegally into the country from outside?' I said.

'You hide it so it won't be detected, or you bring it across the border where there's no control at all.'

We both sat in silence for a moment and then I realized what I had been missing. I stepped over to the bookshelf and grabbed the road atlas and opened it to California.

I laid it down in front of Smith. 'A place where money could have been brought into the country with no authorities to stop you.'

He stared at the map for a moment.

'China Lake,' he said.

I nodded. 'No customs, no inspections. The same base Havoc was shipping money out of, Torres was sending it back through.'

'The beginning,' said Smith. I nodded.

'That's why Salem mailed the envelope from Trona,' Smith said. 'He had gone looking for answers in China Lake.'

I stared at the map for a moment and shook my head. 'No, he went there looking for someone.'

'Who?'

'A partner inside the base,' I said. 'Someone had to be there to receive the money when it came back. And who knows what the numbers on that piece of paper meant.'

Smith stared at the map for a moment, shook his head. 'Do you have any idea how many people work on that base?'

I nodded. 'Thousands.'

'That doesn't narrow it down very much.'

I started working back through the last forty-eight hours until a piece of the puzzle that I had thought fitted seemed to slip out of place.

'Maybe,' I said.

He studied me for a moment. 'You know something?'

'A young officer showed up at my house after the deputy in Trona was killed. He was the one who told me about the existence of Havoc. He said he was a supply officer.'

'Someone who could move shipments of money from Iraq without anyone taking notice. You think he could have been working with Torres?'

'He was frightened. I assumed it was because of the deputy's death, but maybe it was more than that.'

Smith walked over to the cabinet and poured himself more bourbon. He took a drink and then stared into the dark smoky liquid as he swirled it in the glass.

'Why come to a cop if you're involved in stealing money?'

Out the window a thick layer of ground fog was moving like a current of water flowing up the street.

'You can't spend the money if you're dead,' I said. 'He gave me just enough information to point me toward who he was afraid of.'

'Havoc?'

I nodded.

'You have his name?'

'He said it was Lowenstein, but I doubt it was real.'

Smith picked up the map and stared at China Lake. 'Thousands of personnel. A needle in a stack of needles.' He paused. 'You mentioned a name yesterday.'

'Taylor. Maya Torres gave me the name. I met him in Trona and described him to her, and she remembered a man who could be him. He was in Delta, and when this is over I doubt there'll be a single piece of paper confirming his existence.'

'I don't believe in phantoms, Lieutenant.'

'You haven't spent time like I have in the desert.'

'You're going to have to go back. Can you do that?'

The thought alone was enough to let the panic loose inside of me. I glanced out the window so he wouldn't see it in my eyes.

'I don't really have a choice, do I?'

Smith stood up and walked over to the front door. 'He'll be looking for Russell now.'

'That would be my guess.'

'You find Lowenstein, leave Russell and your ghost to me,' Smith said.

I walked over to the door. 'I think the point, Captain, is for him not to find you.'

twenty-seven

Dawn came in dull shades of grey as I drove across the San Fernando Valley and began the climb toward the high desert and China Lake. Smith may not have believed in ghosts, living or dead, but I did. I knew what they could do. I knew that they could follow you across a globe, to the bottom of the ocean, or inhabit a space as confined as the human heart. And I knew that Salem had understood the same thing.

If his life could still be saved, the answer was to be found in the washed-out desert light and dust on the road to Death Valley. Whether truth would play any part in it remained to be seen, but as I drove up out of the fog covering the basin and into the sun rising above the endless car dealerships of Palmdale, and the dry lake beds and extinct volcanoes of the high desert, I realized it wouldn't matter. There was only one truth for those who had already died, and that was that their lives had been given for a lie.

When I reached the southern tip of the spine of the

Sierras I turned east into a series of broad valleys and the company town of Ridgecrest that supported the sprawling complex of China Lake Weapons Center. Hundreds of square miles of dry mountain ranges and arroyos spread out further than the eye could see.

Nothing ever appeared permanent to me in the desert, and the more strip malls and subdivisions were built, the more easily it seemed a strong wind could blow it all to dust.

I pulled off at the top of a small rise that looked toward the base. There was nothing remarkable about its appearance. If not for the security checkpoints at the gate, China Lake would look like any other industrial park. But it wasn't, and never had been.

Early man had once come to these same hills and valleys in search of obsidian to fashion spear points and arrowheads. And now instead of spears we built missiles and named our weapons after some of the same animals they had carved elegant pictures of in rocks.

The Shore Patrol on the base confirmed that there was nobody stationed at China Lake by the name of Lowenstein. Smith was right; I was looking for a needle in a stack of needles.

My only link to the man who had called himself Lowenstein was a dead deputy, which meant my only chance of finding him was to return to the one place I never wanted to see again. Trona.

The dead don't always take their secrets with them. If I was lucky, Deputy Gilley had left behind one or two that no one in the sheriff's department would understand, and one that whoever murdered him knew nothing about. But I would have to go back there.

It was afternoon when I drove in past the painted football field and the hulking potash plant of Trona. A cold wind was blowing down out of the snow-covered mountains to the north. What darkness had hidden of this town, the light of day exposed in all its bleakness. More houses than I realized had been abandoned. The ashes and rubble of the burned-out bus station were now covered with a thin layer of dust, the lingering odor of burned timbers the only reminder that the fire wasn't a part of the same slow death the rest of the town was succumbing to.

The sheriff's substation was a small single-story cinder-block structure half a block off the highway. An American and California flag flew at half-mast on the pole at the entrance where a small garden of freshly painted white rocks adorned the dead grass. Two empty storefronts were the only other buildings on the street. A chain-link fence surrounded an empty lot next to the station; the only vehicle parked inside was the battered remains of Gilley's cruiser.

I stopped and walked through the open gate and over to the damaged car. The collapsed roof had been cut away and was lying on the ground next to the car.

The deployed air bag hung from the steering wheel, bloodstains were visible in the folds of fabric. Discarded scraps of plastic and tape from the paramedics' work littered the vehicle's floor. A few coins that must have been in Gilley's pockets lay scattered around the seats and on the dash. The entire interior was covered in a fine layer of dust except for where Gilley's body had rested on the seat. A faint outline of his arm stretched out across the seat.

The front end was heavily damaged. Much of the paint on the left side had been scraped off, dried pieces of plant remained lodged in the door and window seams. I walked round to the back of the vehicle. The top of the trunk was crushed, the entire back end pushed in. The car must have tumbled end over end before coming to a rest on the roof.

I knelt down and examined the bumper. Amid all the damage a single vertical crease of about four inches was visible on the driver's side. I ran my fingers along its length. The indentation was smooth, unlike the uneven damage done by rocks across the rest of the cruiser.

'You're trespassing, you'll have to leave,' said a voice behind me.

I turned round. A woman in her mid-thirties was standing behind me. She wore a sheriff's department shirt with badge emblem but carried no weapon. Her face was set with anger and her right fist clenched a cell phone.

'This car should be in a secure area,' I said, then pulled back my jacket and showed her my badge.

The anger in her eyes softened.

'It was. Someone cut the lock last night.'

'Was something taken from it?'

'Who knows? A new deputy won't arrive here until tomorrow, so there's not much I can do. All calls are being handled out of Barstow for now.'

'Did an accident investigation team examine the car?'

'Yes. Highway Patrol.'

I looked down at the small vertical crease in the bumper.

'Did they find anything?'

'There were skid marks on the pavement, they think he may have begun a pursuit and lost control on the curve.'

'Did he call in a pursuit?'

'No,' she said.

'Is that unusual?' I asked.

'Yes. Deputies work alone out here, the radio is the only partner they've got sometimes, so they always use it.' She looked at the car for a moment, and then turned to me. 'Is your name Delillo?'

I nodded. 'How did you know that?'

'Deputy Gilley left an envelope on his desk with your name and number on it. When I found it yesterday I tried calling but never got through.'

'May I see it?'

'If you can find it.'

'I don't understand,' I said.

She looked at the car again. 'Is there a reason you're asking about this? Because it isn't really Pasadena business.'

'I met Deputy Gilley the morning he died. He was going to look into something for me.'

She looked at me in silence for a long moment.

'At China Lake?' she said softly.

I nodded. 'Did he tell you the name of the person he was meeting there?'

'No.'

'How about his call logs for that day?'

'Investigators took all his things.' She started to say something else, then hesitated. 'What kind of a detective are you, Lieutenant?'

'Homicide.'

She looked back toward the station. 'Is this important?'

'It is if Deputy Gilley's death wasn't an accident,' I said.

Her face flushed with color.

I pulled out the photograph of Salem and handed it to her.

'Have you ever seen this man before?' I asked.

She looked at it for a moment and then nodded. 'He came to the station about two weeks ago; talked with Deputy Gilley.'

She looked at it again, recognizing something else.

'I know him, he's the missing LAPD cop who's wanted for murder, isn't he?' she said.

I nodded.

'Are these related?' she asked.

'Not in the way you're probably thinking.'

She took a deep breath. 'I made copies of his logs before investigators removed them.'

'Why did you do that?'

She looked around up and down the street where the only occupant was a black dog lying in the middle of the dusty road.

'In case you showed up,' she said.

'What about that envelope?' I asked.

'Let me show you something,' she said.

She introduced herself as Carol Ennis and then walked me over to where the back door had been forced with what appeared to be a ramming device or a sledgehammer. At least two or three blows had been needed to break the lock. The inside of the station had been vandalized. Every filing cabinet had its contents spread across the floor. Pictures and posters from the walls had been pulled down and trashed. Desk drawers had been pulled out and thrown across the room, spreading paper and records everywhere. She explained that she had managed the substation for the last six years, handling calls and paperwork. As she looked over the mess I could see moisture gathering in her eyes.

'Goddamn,' she whispered to herself. 'If your envelope is here, I haven't found it.'

'Could you show me the logs?'

She nodded and walked over to a shoulder bag, pulled out a manila folder and handed it to me.

'The received calls have an R next to them, the rest are telephone calls he made from here, and from his cell phone when he was out.'

There were about a dozen calls on the list.

'Are these in chronological order?' I asked.

She nodded. 'Do you recognize something?'

I shook my head. 'Do you know what some of these are?'

She began to go through the calls. 'The first few were about the fire at the bus station. This one is a call to the Wagon Wheel.'

'The motel where I met him.'

'Yes. Most of the rest were local calls, a stolen bike, domestic dispute, normal stuff.'

'You said most of the rest?'

She nodded and pointed to three numbers. 'This call he made from here before he left for China Lake. It's a base number. And the last two he made from his cell phone. I don't know what this one is. The other one is a bar in Ridgecrest called the Blue Hanger.'

'Which desk was his?'

She motioned to the desk at the back of the room. The only item on the desktop was a small photograph in a frame. I picked it up. The glass had been cracked and the frame broken in one of the corners. The faint outline of a boot or shoe tread was visible on the surface of the cracked glass.

'I was going to send it to his folks back in Wisconsin,' she said. 'I'll have to get it fixed first now.'

The photograph was of Gilley in combat gear, with a Shore Patrol insignia on his shoulder, standing next to a Humvee in Iraq with two other soldiers. I started to place it back on the desk but stopped and looked at it again. Through the fractured glass the image was difficult to make out clearly enough to distinguish who was who, but there was something familiar there.

'Do you mind if I remove the picture?'

She shook her head. The frame came apart easily. I slipped the photograph out and the glass fell into half a dozen pieces on the desk.

'Did Deputy Gilley ever tell you anything about this picture?'

'I know the one on the left was killed. The other was his lieutenant, I think. I don't know if he was killed or not. He didn't really like talking about it.'

I looked around at the station. There was something that wasn't quite right about it. Given the amount of mess, there was little destruction. It wasn't teenage rage that had torn the room apart; I knew a thing or two about that. This was something else. What had gone on inside these walls had been a methodical search; the damage that had been done was window dressing.

I looked back at the photograph and my heart began to beat a little faster and the hairs on the back of my neck rose.

'Did he ever tell you the lieutenant's name?' I asked.

She shook her head. 'No, why?'

'Because he's the man Gilley went to see at China Lake.'

I looked more closely at the photo. Gilley's name was visible on his uniform above his breast pocket; a fold of fabric blurred the lieutenant's name. I handed the picture to Ennis.

'Can you make out the name on his uniform?'

She stared at it for a moment and then walked over to her bag and retrieved a pair of reading glasses and looked at it again.

'It might be Lowery.' She shrugged. 'Best I can do.'

She glanced around the office. 'This is because of what was inside that envelope he left for you, isn't it?'

I nodded, pulled the phone Harrison had put in my pocket out and began to dial the number on the base that Gilley had called before leaving for China Lake. On the second ring the line was picked up and a female voice answered.

'Bravo Company.'

'Lieutenant Lowery, please.'

'One moment.'

I was put on hold for a moment and I glanced over toward Ennis.

'If you need anything else, I'll be outside,' she said, then stepped out the door as a male voice came on the line.

'This is Lieutenant Lowery.'

I closed my eyes and I was pressing my gun against the side of his face on my front steps. I could hear him pleading for me not to shoot.

'Don't hang up,' I said.

He hesitated.

'Do you recognize my voice?' I said.

There was dead silence on the other end.

'I think you have the wrong person,' said Lowery.

'I'm a cop, Lieutenant. If you're going to hide, you'll have to do a lot better than this.'

I heard his breath catch and he cleared his throat.

'Would you like to start this conversation over?' I asked.

'What do you want?'

'I want to help you stay alive.'

'I don't know what you're talking—'

'Burns and Crawford and Henkel are all dead. Do you want to join them?'

'Jesus,' he whispered.

'Henkel had a knife driven through his throat, he died in the bus station where Torres had hidden information about the money. Were the figures on that paper an account number?'

Lowery's breathing became faster. 'I don't know what you're talking about.'

'Both Russell and Havoc are looking for you. If I found you, how much longer will it be before they do?'

'Christ,' he whispered.

'Deputy Gilley knew something. He had figured it out before he ever saw you that day, hadn't he?'

'No,' he whispered.

'Or did he know even back in Baghdad? Did you offer him a piece of the pie?'

'I met Gilley in my first tour during the invasion. Before—'

'Before what?'

'Before so many friends died.'

'You're a thief, Lieutenant.'

'Do you really think the first and last shot over there will have been fired for freedom, Delillo?' Lowery said. 'Because if you believe that, you're living in a dream world.'

'Gilley talked to Salem, that's how he knew,' I said.

Lowery hesitated. 'I'm not a murderer.'

'How much money did Torres ship back to you?'

He was silent.

'How many lives has it cost?'

'No one was supposed to get hurt, the money wasn't supposed to be missed.'

'Did Gilley know about the money?' I asked.

'He was asking about ISC, but he didn't know specifics.'

'He may have known more than that,' I said.

'Why?'

'Because last night the Trona substation was broken into. If Gilley had something here, your secret's out, and you're being hunted.'

Only silence came back.

'Does the Blue Hanger mean anything to you?'

He hesitated before answering.

'It's just a bar. I met Gilley there the day he died.'

'You mean the day he was murdered.'

'Yeah,' he said softly.

'I can take you to a safe place,' I said.

Lowery began to laugh. 'It's too late for that.'

'I'll come and get you right now.'

'You can't get on the base.'

'Then meet me at the gate.'

He took several deep breaths.

'You have two choices,' I said. 'Living or dying.'

He exhaled heavily.

'Which is it?' I asked.

'I'm on duty until seven. I'll be in a white Mustang. If you're not alone, you'll never see me again.'

I glanced at my watch. It was almost three o'clock.

'Can you stay alive for four hours?' I asked.

Lowery forced another laugh.

'There's always a catch, isn't there, Lieutenant?' he said, and then the line was dead.

twenty-eight

It took me nearly an hour to retrace my steps back to China Lake. The clear desert sky had given way to dark storm clouds sweeping down out of the Sierras. In the distant valleys that spread out toward the weapons center, white curtains of rain were falling halfway to the ground and then vanishing into vapor.

Lowery had lied to me on the phone. But why? Was he already running? Or had his run ended? If the only thing a soul retains when the heart stops is its last conscious thought, then I doubted that Lowery would be carrying anything but fear into the next life.

I parked across from the base's gate well before seven in case Lowery had a change of heart or someone had changed it for him. There was no white Mustang at six-fifteen, or six-thirty or six-forty-five. Seven o'clock came and went and at seven-fifteen I placed a call to the number I had reached him at earlier.

A male voice answered this time.

'Bravo Company Shore Patrol,' he said.

I ran his words back through my head to make sure I had heard them correctly.

'Did you say Shore Patrol?' I asked.

'Yes. Can I help you?'

Lowery was a cop, not a supply officer. I began to replay his words from the phone conversation. Was he on the job, or just a cop gone bad? Or maybe both.

'Lieutenant Lowery,' I said.

'The lieutenant's off duty.'

'Do you know when he left?' I asked.

'He was gone when I came on station at four.'

I had missed him by three hours.

'Do you want to leave a name? Is this the number he can reach you at?'

I hung up and pulled out the list of phone numbers Gilley had dialed the day he died. There were two numbers I hadn't dialed yet; one was the Blue Hanger, the other unknown. I punched in the unknown number. On the fourth ring it was picked up.

'Yes.'

The voice was deep and carried a faint memory of a southern accent. The hairs on my arm began to rise. I instinctively knew the voice, even though I had never heard it in my life. And I knew what I hadn't before: it wasn't Havoc who had killed Deputy Gilley.

'What do you want?' he asked.

'Russell,' I said.

He paused, but it wasn't silent, it was as if I could hear a thought being formed.

'The policewoman. How did you find . . . The deputy, of course.'

'Turn yourself in, and I'll guarantee you'll live.'

'I was just discussing that very thing with a colleague of yours. He's been very helpful.'

My heart began to pound against my chest.

'What did you say?'

'Tomorrow is promised to no one. Don't bother trying to trace this phone, it no longer exists,' Russell said, and then the line went dead.

A colleague. Who was he talking about? Had he already found Lowery? I looked at the phone in my hands and then dialed Smith's number. It rang half a dozen times before he picked up.

'Yes.'

'It's Delillo. Lowenstein's name is Lowery, he's a cop, Shore Patrol. I'm afraid Russell may have already found him.'

He didn't reply.

'Smith, did you hear that? I found him, his name's Lowery—' I stopped and listened to the silence on the other end. The screen on the phone said I was still connected.

'Smith?' I said.

The connection ended. I started to hit redial when I saw movement in the rear-view mirror. I reached for the handle but before I got the door more than an inch open a gun was sticking through the window, pointed at my head.

'Empty your hands.'

291

I slowly put the phone on the passenger seat as two white Shore Patrol squad cars came to a stop, blocking the front and rear of my car.

'Step out of the car and raise your hands now.'

'I'm a police officer,' I said.

Two other officers stepped out of the squads and trained their weapons on me.

'Step out of the car now,' the officer repeated.

I opened the door and slowly stepped out, holding my hands in the air.

'I'm a police officer,' I said again.

'Now put your hands on the roof of the car.'

I put my hands on the car.

'I have a weapon,' I said.

One of the other officers patted me down and removed the Glock from my waist.

'I got the weapon,' he said, and then one of the others put my arms behind my back and cuffed me.

Without saying another word they put me in the back of one of the squads and then drove me into the base's security building and placed me in an interrogation room. Fifteen minutes later a black officer stepped inside.

'I'm Sergeant Lawson. Would you like to tell me why you were outside the base for over two hours?'

'I was waiting for someone.'

'With a weapon.'

'I'm a police officer. You can check that with a phone call.'

He continued as if he hadn't heard a word I had said.

'What were you planning on doing with this weapon?'

'I always carry a weapon, it's my job, I arrest bad guys with it.'

'Were you planning on attacking the base?'

I had dealt with military police a few times over the years and had always been astonished at their adherence to protocol regardless of how it flew in the face of the reality they were staring at.

'How many others are you working with?'

'I'm not working with anyone,' I said.

'You admit to carrying a weapon and staking out a secure military facility.'

I looked at him for a moment; he appeared to be in his early thirties and was built not that differently from a large refrigerator.

'How many others are you working with?'

I suspected he had just returned from a homeland security workshop.

'There are several hundred,' I said.

His eyes brightened. 'In the cell?'

I shook my head. 'Pasadena PD. Last I checked they weren't on a watch list, but that may have changed.'

'You phoned asking for Lieutenant Lowery. What is your relationship?'

'There is no relationship. He asked me to meet him at seven when he was off duty.'

'The lieutenant's duty shift ended at four, not seven. Now why don't you tell me the truth?'

I realized I had been set up, and every minute longer I sat here, Lowery was slipping further away, or his grave was being dug another foot deeper.

'Let me guess, Sergeant. You received an anonymous call that there was a woman in a car outside the gate with a weapon.'

From his silence I assumed I had struck a chord.

'Sergeant, you know as well as I do that I'm not here to attack the base. Why don't you tell me what you think is going on?' I said.

He considered my words for a moment, and then nodded.

'I think the two of you are involved in some kind of domestic problem and I'm being jerked around.'

'Try again, Sergeant,' I said.

'I think you've been dumped by a younger man and are pissed off.'

'I'm humbled by the level of your detecting skills,' I said.

'Threatening a naval officer is a serious matter. You're in a great deal of trouble, Lieutenant,' he said.

'Does the name Havoc mean anything to you, Sergeant?'

Whatever else he had been planning on saying he immediately let go of. He stood across the table from me in silence for a moment, then turned and left the room without saying a word.

There was no clock on the wall and with my hands

cuffed I couldn't see my watch but I guessed nearly an hour had passed when the door finally opened again. Another officer whom I had not seen before stepped into the room. He carried nothing that identified him as Shore Patrol, and there was no name tag on his uniform and nothing that identified his rank, though I assumed it to be higher than the previous officer.

He pulled out the chair on the other side of the table and took a seat across from me.

'Lieutenant Delillo, is that correct?'

I nodded.

'We've checked with your people, you're free to go.'

'Good. Would you undo the cuffs?'

He made no move to do so.

'Do you know the whereabouts of Lieutenant Lowery?' he asked.

'Don't you?'

'We're trying to cooperate with you, Lieutenant.'

'That would explain the handcuffs.'

'We were assured that you would cooperate.'

'Do you have a name and rank?' I asked.

He shifted in the chair, his face betraying no reaction at all to my words.

'You mentioned the name Havoc. Would you like to explain that, Lieutenant?'

'I think it would be better if you did,' I said.

'There never has been a unit with that name on this or any base.'

'Which explains your need to deny it,' I said.

'Your insistence on the presence of a unit is only

295

going to result in a great deal of wasted energy and time.'

'Whose?' I asked.

He stood up. 'Where's Lieutenant Lowery?'

'I've been inside this room. You tell me.'

He walked over to the door and opened it. A young officer in fatigues standing outside the door looked in, making eye contact for a moment, then turned away.

'I never used the word unit, I just asked you about a name,' I said.

The officer looked at me for a moment, his eyes focused with anger.

'Have you been out in the desert north of Trona in the last few days?' I asked.

He shook his head. 'No.'

I think that was the first thing he had said that was truthful. He studied me for a moment as if he wanted to ask a question, but he didn't.

'You really don't have a clue why you were sent here, do you?' I asked. 'What are you, a public information officer?'

From the look in his eyes I guessed I wasn't far off the mark.

'You still refuse to answer any questions about the whereabouts of Lieutenant Lowery?' he asked.

'I already answered your question.'

'Stay away from China Lake, Lieutenant,' he said. 'Any further attempts on your part to enter the base, you will be arrested and prosecuted.'

'Did they tell you why they want to find Lowery?'

He didn't shake his head, but he didn't have to. He was curious now, or at least as curious as a junior officer could allow himself to be when following orders.

'You're free to go.'

'Where?' I said.

'I suggest home,' he said.

He looked at me for a moment longer then turned and walked out.

twenty-nine

It was dark when two Shore Patrol officers drove me out to the base's gate and dropped me off. As I walked the half block to my Volvo, the distant horizon was briefly lit up with a flash of lightning and a moment later the deep rumble of thunder echoed far out in the desert night.

My phone was still on the passenger seat where I had left it, but the rest of the car had been searched. Sitting in the interrogation room I had thought it was the work of Lowery giving himself more time to escape. But the second officer's questions had changed that.

I went through the car to see what was missing. The phone numbers from the sheriff's station were gone; the photographs of Russell after the explosion and of Gilley and Lowery together had been taken.

I picked up the phone. The battery still had power, but all numbers dialed within the last day had been deleted. Havoc now had whatever they wanted to know without my answering a single question. And I assumed the phone and maybe even the car were now bugged.

I looked around the surrounding streets. I saw no obvious tails, but it didn't matter. The one thing I did know that Havoc didn't was that on the other end of my last call was Russell, and if Lowery's run wasn't already over, it would be soon.

I picked up the phone and dialed Smith again but only got his service. I left a message for him to call and then started the car. As I began to pull away, a figure stepped out of the darkness into the beam of the headlights and I stepped on the brakes. My hand slipped down to the handle of the Glock and I checked the mirrors for any other movement around me, but there was none. Before I had my weapon out of the holster the figure had stepped to the passenger side of the car and was opening the door.

'You don't need that, Lieutenant,' he said, looking down at my gun coming up from my side.

I held it for a moment and then slipped it back into place as the officer wearing fatigues I had seen outside the door to the interrogation room got inside and closed the door. He had changed out of his uniform and was wearing jeans and a loosely buttoned shirt. If a weapon was concealed under it I saw no indication of its presence.

'This is not a good place to talk,' he said, his eyes quickly taking in the surroundings.

'The car or here?' I asked.

'Both.'

He motioned with his hand toward the corner.

'Drive,' he said.

We drove away from the base through Ridgecrest until we reached an empty street that dead-ended on the edge of the desert. He stepped out of the Volvo and walked ten feet away from the car then turned and looked back toward town. I got out of the car.

'Are you sure we weren't followed?' he asked.

I nodded. 'You want to tell me why we're here?'

He looked toward the glow of Ridgecrest and the base until he was satisfied we were alone.

'You shouldn't be here.' He made eye contact for a moment then looked back toward town.

'Do I know you?' I asked.

He spoke without looking at me. 'I know you.'

'How?'

He took a deep breath, shaking his head at some private thought.

'You have a name?' I asked.

'My name isn't important,' he said.

'We can play twenty questions or you can tell me what you came here to say,' I said.

'Your life is in danger if you stay here.'

'How do you know that?'

He hesitated. 'You hear things.'

I looked at him for a moment. 'What is it you're not telling me?'

'A few days ago I was ordered to take part in an exercise.'

'What kind?'

'Insurgent capture and interrogation.' His eyes found me for a moment and then he looked away again. 'It was a night-time operation.'

My heart began beating heavily against my chest, and my hand slipped down to the handle of the Glock.

'You were there?' I said.

He nodded and my hand closed tightly around the handle of the weapon.

'Go on,' I said.

'I was told it was part of a training exercise in unit fragmentation in battle. No one taking part had worked with any of the others.'

'Which part of me did you get to hold down?' I asked.

He shook his head and the fear inside me began to turn to anger.

'Did you get one of my hands or legs?' I said.

'I wasn't—'

'Which was it?' I yelled and began to raise the Glock.

'My assignment was to maintain the perimeter. I don't think I was supposed to see anything, but when things started to go so far—'

'You got curious,' I said.

He took a deep breath.

'I realized it wasn't a training exercise,' he said.

I slipped the Glock back in its place.

'Can you identify the others involved that night?'

'We were instructed to wear balaclavas when we

mustered for the operation to further enhance the sense of unit disintegration. It was on the way back to base afterward that I realized why we were really wearing them.'

'If no one can identify anyone else there's no way to prove it ever happened,' I said.

He nodded. 'We came and went from the base by an unmanned remote gate. No record of us leaving or coming.'

'How did you get your orders?'

'Verbally over the phone. Usual chain of command an hour or so before it began. The orders were very specific, no communication within the unit during the exercise, all talking would be done by the officer in command.'

'So you brought me out here to clear your conscience?'

He looked back toward the lights to the north and shook his head. 'I don't know what's going on between you and Lowery, but what was done shouldn't have happened.'

'There's nothing going on between me and the lieutenant.'

He nodded, unconvinced. I walked over next to him.

'You don't have any idea what's going on, do you, and what's probably going to happen out here tonight?'

He shook his head.

'If it hasn't happened already, a man is going to put a bullet in Lowery's head.'

The officer turned and looked at me.

'Then either later tonight or tomorrow or next week

the man who pulled that trigger will be sitting in his car or stepping out of a bar at night or lying in bed, and someone will step up, maybe call out his name as if they're old friends and then place a nine millimeter against his ear and shoot him. After an exhaustive and thorough investigation, no charges will be filed but the blame will be put on an innocent man who will either have vanished from the face of the earth or eventually be found dead of a self-inflicted gunshot.'

He stood in silence for a moment. 'Why?'

I looked out beyond the lights of town at the surrounding darkness. High above the desert a flash of lightning briefly lit the clouds with a white glow.

'A little boy wanted to go for a bike ride,' I said.

The officer looked at me, not understanding. If the words existed to explain the events, I hadn't stumbled on them yet.

'Money was stolen,' I said. 'And people have been murdered because of it.'

'Can you prove this?'

'I don't know. Do you know who the officer was who came in and questioned me?' I asked.

He shook his head. 'He just showed up, flashed some credentials and asked to see you.'

'How well do you know Lowery?'

'Not well.'

'Do you have any idea where he may have gone when he left the base?'

'When I came on duty, I saw him running to his car. He looked at me but didn't say anything.'

'Does he live on base or off?'

'Off. We called there after you showed up but there was no answer.'

'No one was sent there?'

He shook his head. 'We had no reason.'

'Can you take me there?'

He glanced at his watch.

'I need to see inside,' I said.

'Maybe it would be better if you just got out of here.'

I shook my head. 'I'm a cop, I can't do that.'

He sighed. 'This doesn't sound like a civilian problem.'

'Murder is murder,' I said. 'If you want to keep him alive, I need your help. And we need to do it now.'

He swore silently to himself as a bolt of lightning dropped from the clouds and touched the cone of an extinct volcano in the darkness west of the base.

'Are you carrying a weapon?'

He shook his head. 'I shouldn't be involved with this,' he whispered.

'You were involved the moment you put that mask over your face,' I said.

'I was just following orders that night.'

I looked at him. 'Is that why you came out here? Orders?'

He looked at me as the thunder from the distant strike rumbled past us into the empty desert to the south.

thirty

We drove to the western edge of town toward where a series of housing developments were in various stages of completion. Lowery's street was tucked in a shallow canyon amongst a few Joshua trees. We passed two houses as we entered the street but the rest of the lots were either empty or had not gone beyond the pouring of a concrete slab. We rounded a series of large boulders and Lowery's house became visible at the end of the empty cul-de-sac. I turned out my headlights and pulled to a stop.

'What is it?' the officer said.

A single light illuminated the front door but the rest of the house was dark.

'Lowery drives a white Mustang, is that right?'

He nodded. There was no car visible outside the house.

'Maybe it's in the garage,' he said.

'Maybe.'

I turned off the ignition, then reached into my

pocket and removed the photograph of Salem and the boy and handed it to him.

'Have you ever seen this man?'

I watched him study the photograph, his young eyes seeming to see far more than what was in this single picture.

'Baghdad,' he said softy.

'You've been there?' I asked.

'Two tours,' he said. 'We're going back in sixty days.'

He didn't say two months, but the number of days, as if they were being scratched into his heart the way a prisoner marks off time on the wall of his cell.

'There's always kids like that around. You know when something is about to go down because they vanish. They're like that thing with the birds in a mine.'

'Canaries,' I said.

'Yeah.'

A flash of lightning lit his face, which looked young enough to still be in high school, but his eyes belied that youth. He handed the photograph back to me.

'I've never seen him,' he said.

'How old are you?'

'Twenty-seven.'

'I need you to do one more thing,' I said.

He nodded.

'Can you get back to the base from here?'

'Yes.'

'I want you to go home and forget that you ever saw me tonight.'

I opened the door and stepped out into the night

and the officer followed a moment later. The air had begun to warm with the approaching storm.

'Maybe it's not too late for you to walk away from this,' he said.

'That bridge was burned a long time ago,' I answered.

'You could let the Shore Patrol handle this.'

'Go home,' I said.

He started to protest, but I interrupted him.

'I'm not stepping away from this car until I see you disappear around that corner,' I said, motioning back down the street where we had come from.

'That an order, Lieutenant?' he asked.

'Yeah, that's what it is.'

He thought about it for a second. 'The guy in that picture, does this have something to do with him?'

'Something,' I said.

'He make it home?'

I shook my head. 'Not yet.'

The officer looked at Lowery's house and then started to walk away but stopped after a few steps.

'You know it doesn't work, Lieutenant,' he said.

'What doesn't?'

'Forgetting things that happen, and things you did.'

He looked at me for a moment. Not even the darkness could mask the sadness in his eyes.

'They don't go away, ever.'

'I know,' I said.

His eyes found mine for a moment and he nodded. 'Yeah, I guess maybe you do.'

He turned and walked away down the street. I watched him until he was out of sight and there was only the sound of his footsteps on the pavement, then I started toward Lowery's house.

On the bare house slabs lining the street, lizards soaking up the remaining heat of the day skittered off into the dark as I passed. The faint wisp of air moving above my head gave away the presence of bats on their night-time hunt. A hundred feet from Lowery's house a flash of dry lightning lit up the clouds overhead and I saw the shape on the far side of his house that I hadn't from my car – the back of a large SUV – and then just as quickly it disappeared back into the darkness.

I froze and looked around for cover but there was nothing in the two hundred feet to the house but bare pavement and more empty lots. My hand slipped down to the Glock as the ground shook from the thunder and I broke into a run, trying to reach the house before the next flash lit me up like a spotlight.

One hundred feet, then fifty, with each step I could feel the static electricity in the air increase. I started to whisper to myself as I kept my eyes focused on the dark windows at the front of the house. *Faster, run, you're too slow, too old, run.*

The hair on the back of my neck began to rise and a strong bitter taste filled the air. *Faster.* A flash of white light split the darkness and all sound, all movement stopped. I tried to look toward the house but it had disappeared in the light. I couldn't tell if I was running

310

any more or standing or even if I was still touching the ground. I looked down at my hand holding the Glock and for an instant thought the skin had been stripped from my hand and there were only the bones of my fingers closed around the weapon.

A rush of warm air began to stream past me and the sky erupted with an explosion of sound as the white light disappeared into the sky and everything was plunged back into darkness.

How many seconds had passed I couldn't tell. I was on my knees on the pavement, my hands covering my ears. The lightning had struck very close. I took a breath and could taste the scent of electricity, acrid like burning hair. Lowery's house was in front of me. I suddenly felt the presence of a rifle's cross hairs on my chest as if a hand had touched me. I stared at the windows of the house, black and empty like a set of eyes. My Glock was on the pavement in front of me.

Pick it up.

I reached out and took it in my hand.

Now run.

I got to my feet and sprinted toward the closed garage door, waiting for the tiny flash of a muzzle blast to appear from the window, sending the bullet spiraling through me. I reached the garage and pressed myself hard against it, as if I could slip into the wood and disappear from sight.

I looked back down the street hoping to see the officer emerge out of the darkness but the next flash of lightning revealed only the empty street.

One voice in my head was telling me not to move a muscle and the other was screaming at me to get moving, to do something. I wrapped both hands around the handle of the Glock and slowed my breathing until I could get enough air to feel I wasn't suffocating.

You've done this before, take a step, the next will be easier . . . Don't listen to that voice, stay here, it's safe here.

I took a tentative step and then another until I had moved across the front of the garage to where I could look toward the front door. As I eased my head around the corner to steal a glance, another flash in the sky lit everything in its cool white light and I saw through the front windows into the darkness of the house. There was something there. A figure.

I pressed myself back out of sight again. Had I seen what I thought I had? Someone standing in front of the window, their arms held out from their sides as if in a gesture of communal prayer. Was that what it was? Or had the light played a trick, turned a lamp or a jacket on a hanger into a man?

I took another glance around the corner but with each new flash of lightning the storm moved further away into the desert and the windows gave away no more secrets. I backed away from the front to the other side of the garage and the corner of the house.

The windows on the SUV were tinted, masking the interior. I started around the corner but stopped. The door on the side of the garage a few feet from the truck was ajar. *Had they seen me at the front? Had they slipped out?*

In the stillness between the rumbles of thunder I listened for movement, the snap of a twig or the slip of gravel. Nothing moved. I crossed over to the truck and tested the rear door – it was locked. I moved around the other side and up to the passenger doors and tried them each with the same result.

Was the garage door open as an invitation?

I stepped over to it and reached out with my free hand, pushed it open and then pressed myself against the vehicle, waiting for a response. The only sound coming from inside was the door hitting the wall.

The garage was empty – a few boxes, golf clubs, a shovel. No white Mustang. The door on the far wall into the house was also open. I took a step into the garage and then stopped as the voice in my head began to yell *no, no, no, this is what they want, find another way in.*

I backed out and then moved to the far corner of the house and looked down its length. The spidery tentacles of lightning spreading across the sky reflected off the surface of a sliding glass door. I crossed under two windows to the door and waited for the next flash of lightning to illuminate the room. The flash was dull and lasted only an instant but it was enough to see the empty bed.

I tested the handle and the door slid open. The stale air inside the room rushed past me, carrying all the scents a house contains when shuttered – the smell of sweat and dust and garbage and aftershave and stale food, but there was something else present, a strong pungent presence. It was familiar, but I couldn't place it.

There were two doors visible in the bedroom, one open, one closed. I stepped into the house, holding my weapon toward the closed door that led into the rest of the house. The bed had been slept in, but whether it was the previous day or week I couldn't tell. A pair of shoes and slippers sat neatly under the bed, a set of fatigues was thrown over the back of a chair next to the open closet.

I stepped past the bed to the door of the bathroom and pushed it the rest of the way open. The odor of soap filled the space. I began to step back out, but stopped. Why was I smelling soap? It wasn't stale; it was as if someone had washed his or her hands not more than a few minutes before.

I glanced back over my shoulder one more time into the corners of the bedroom then took a step into the bathroom and stopped at the sink. Dark spots specked the porcelain of the sink's bowl and dotted the tile of the vanity and surface of the mirror.

Blood.

A towel streaked with bloodstains hung over the edge of the tub. I turned and rushed over to the bedroom door and listened for any movement or sound on the other side. I heard no movement but there was a sound, faint but distinct. Like a child's voice, singing a nursery rhyme.

I turned the door handle until the latch cleared and then slowly opened it until I had a view of the hallway.

The music was coming out of the darkness at the end where the hall opened into the living room. I could hear the words now. I didn't recognize them, but it wasn't the kind of music a twenty-something sailor would be listening to for relaxation. The lyrics repeated over and over with a kind of manic energy.

The good baby laughs, the good baby cries, the good baby pees, the good baby poops . . . and on and on. A potty training song?

It ended and then began again and with each word the sense of something gone horribly wrong inside these walls began to spin out of control inside me.

The good baby laughs, the good baby cries . . .

'Jesus,' I whispered.

I pressed myself against the wall and held on to the Glock with both hands as hard as I could. The good baby started laughing . . . the good baby had done something very, very bad.

thirty-one

There were two doors between where I stood and the living room and the figure I had seen in the flash of light. I moved along the wall with my weapon held on the darkness at the end and stopped at the first door. I pushed it open with my foot – nothing but a linen closet, all but empty.

I moved to the second door and pushed it open – a small office, sparsely furnished, something on the wall, a desk and some boxes on the floor. It could wait to be looked at.

From the darkness at the end of the hallway the song kept coming, again and again. I took a step and then another and when I stopped at the opening to the rest of the house, I began to mouth the words – *The good baby pees, the good baby poops* . . .

The kitchen and dining room were off to the left, the living room to the right. The strong odor I had detected when I had opened the glass doors was stronger here – solvents of some kind, ammonia maybe.

From the edge of the hallway I could see past the dining room to the corner of the kitchen. The song was coming from the right in the living room. I began to take a step toward the music but hesitated. My hand holding the weapon began to shake. *The good baby laughs* . . .

I looked back down the hallway where I had come from. I could back out, walk away. *The good baby cries* . . .

The air held another scent, not one you would find described in a textbook, but I knew it just the same, and it was just as palpable and real as the scent an orange leaves behind as it is slowly peeled – fear. I closed my eyes and eased the hammer on the Glock back until it clicked in place and then looked ahead. The darkness had a weight to it, it appeared to move the way a curtain does in a gentle breeze.

'The good baby,' I whispered and took a step around the corner into the living room and raised the weapon.

The space at first appeared empty, but then shapes began to appear. The furniture had been pushed against the far wall into a pile except for a single folding chair left in the middle of the floor. On the floor behind the folding chair the dark shape of a boom box and its red and green LED lights glowed faintly.

I took a step toward the stereo to turn the song off when the shape I'd seen through the window was briefly lit by another flash of lightning. Against the wall facing the front window a figure sat limply on another folding chair placed on top of a box, his bare feet hanging loosely a few inches above the floor. The arms were stretched out and above the head as if in a swan dive. A dark bag covered the head. White briefs were the only clothing he wore.

I swung back for a moment, holding the gun on the direction I had come from until I was certain no one was behind me, then turned back to the figure.

'Can you hear me?' I said. 'Lowery, can you hear me?'

If there was any reaction I couldn't hear it over the sound of the good baby song going on and on like the nightmare that refuses to end. I crossed into the living room toward the stereo then knelt and began pressing buttons until the song finally stopped. The silence that followed was jarring in the way the sound of an airplane's engine falling silent during the middle of take-off would be.

The odor I had detected was strongest here, it smelt like a janitor's closet, and then I saw that the carpet around the chair where the victim sat was dark with fluid. I took a step toward the victim and then heard a sound in the room – a breath. I quickly spun, raising the Glock back toward the kitchen, and then heard the sound again.

There was no one behind me. It had come from under the hood on the victim's head. It was heavy and labored – a breath taken half submerged in water. I rushed over to the figure in the chair, holstered my weapon. The bag he wore was soaked with a mixture of water and cleaning fluids. His chest was dotted with small raised welts. A piece of wire was wrapped round several of his toes. I took hold of the bottom of the bag loosely lying on his shoulders and raised it up over his head.

'Lowery—' I began to say and stopped.

The features of his face became recognizable and I felt the pit of my stomach turn.

'Smith,' I whispered.

Cord was wrapped round each of his wrists and tied to a nail on the wall, stretching his arms out and up.

'Can you hear me?' I said.

He opened his mouth and his entire body shuddered as he gasped heavily for a breath. I placed my hand on his neck to feel his pulse; the rise of his pumping heart pressed strongly against my fingers.

'It's Delillo,' I said. 'You're all right now.'

He took another breath and then another and then slowly raised his head and opened his swollen eyes.

'It's Delillo,' I said. 'Can you hear me?'

I saw the brief flash of recognition in his eyes then he closed them and lowered his head. His lips moved as if trying to speak but I heard nothing.

'I'll free your arms,' I said and started to reach up to where the cord was wrapped round the nail in the wall.

'Don't,' he whispered.

I stopped. A tear slipped out of the corner of his eye and fell to the floor.

'What?' I asked.

He tried to speak again but his chest heaved with a

sob and he shook his head. Saliva began to drip from his mouth and I gently reached down and wiped it away with my hand. He slowly shook his head.

'What do you want me to do?' I asked.

His head sank and turned away from me.

'Don't look at me,' he said softly. 'Please.'

I started to reach out to touch his head, but the smell of sage and sand and the violent touch of hands tearing at my clothes and the click of a gun's hammer came rushing back and I pulled my hand away.

'It's OK,' I said. 'I understand.'

I stepped to the side of the chair so I was no longer in front of him and then knelt down and looked away as I spoke.

'I'm not looking, it's dark.'

The hinges of the chair began to creak from the rise and fall of his silent sobs.

'No one will ever know,' I whispered and then closed my eyes. 'I promise.'

But that was hardly true. He had a secret now that he would never forget, and the only person he could ever truly share it with was the one who had done this to him. Smith tried to say something but could manage little more than a whimper.

'I'm going to go get a blanket and then I'll free your hands.'

If he heard me there was no indication. I stepped away from him and rushed back into the hallway to the bedroom and pulled the blanket off the bed.

At first I thought Smith was unconscious when I

stepped up to him. His chin rested on his chest and his body hung forward against the cords around his wrists.

I began to drape the blanket over his legs and he shook his head.

'No.'

'It's just a blanket,' I said.

He shook his head again and spoke in a whisper.

'He'll see.'

'We're alone, it's all right,' I said.

He shook his head ever so slightly. 'The front window.'

I turned and looked toward the picture window out on to the street. Nothing moved in the darkness, I saw no one watching. I turned back to Smith.

'There's no one there, I'm going to cover you—'

A flash of lightning lit the sky outside, throwing light into the room, and for just an instant cast a faint shadow of a figure outside on to the wall where Smith's hands were bound. It lasted but a second and then we were thrown back into the dark.

I froze, staring at the wall where the shadow had been, and tried to calculate the time it would take me to clear the Glock from the holster and turn. Adding luck into the equation I figured I might get the gun in hand but would never make the turn before he got off his first round.

I set the blanket over Smith's legs.

'I have to go outside through the back of the house,' I said in a near whisper.

He shook his head. 'No, no.'

322

'I'll be back, I'm not leaving you.'

He began to shake his head and began to repeat over and over, 'Hands, hands.'

I reached up to where the cord was wrapped round his wrists. Dark lines of hemorrhaging marked his skin where the line had begun to cut into his flesh. I pulled at the knots binding him but they were stretched beyond my ability to loosen them. Where the cord was connected to the nails driven in the walls the results were the same.

'I need to get a knife,' I said.

I reached down and pulled the blanket up around his neck and over his shoulders and then he looked up at me. The eyes that had belonged to the captain in Robbery Homicide were gone; what were left in their place were those of a traumatized child, pleading for me not to leave him alone.

'He won't come back inside, I promise.'

He looked at me again, his eyes beginning to dart about the room in panic. I started to reach out to touch him.

'Don't,' he whispered.

'I won't touch you, and I'll be right back, you don't have to be afraid.'

I retraced my steps back down the dark hallway to the bedroom door and pulled the Glock. I wouldn't have much time before whoever was outside realized I hadn't gone to the kitchen to retrieve a knife to cut Smith's rope.

I pushed the door open, raised the gun, crossed the

room to the sliding glass door and stepped back into the night. A single bolt of lightning soundlessly split the distant horizon.

There wasn't time to be cautious, I was running along the back of the house, training the gun on a point in the darkness that was roughly the height of a man's chest. I hesitated briefly at the far corner, then slipped round and started moving along the side toward the front. The gravel under my feet popped with each step. He would hear that, hear my breathing. He was waiting there in the darkness for me to step into the open. He was a professional at this game of shadows. I wouldn't even hear him. I would be in mid-step, maybe I would catch his scent, but I wouldn't see him, I wouldn't even finish the breath I was taking. This was what Salem had been running from.

Have you ever shot anyone? Crawford asked.

I stopped short of the front corner and pressed myself against the side of the house. Moisture began gathering in the palm of my hand gripping the Glock.

It's surprisingly easy to learn, that's the problem.

I edged up the last few feet and stopped.

It becomes easier to pull the trigger than not to.

A bead of sweat slid past the corner of my eye and on to my cheek. My finger began to tighten round the trigger, and I swung round, raising the Glock. In the darkness the yard in front of the window appeared empty. I held on the spot where I thought I had seen the figure, took a step and then another. There was nothing there, not in the yard or the street.

Maybe I had imagined it; maybe the shadow had been my own. I started toward the other side of the house and stopped as I passed the front door. It was halfway open. The door had been closed before. I looked into the darkness beyond the window but could see nothing.

'Smith,' I whispered to myself then ran toward the door, hitting it with my shoulder, and raised the weapon as I stepped into the living room. The chair where Smith had been sitting was empty.

thirty-two

Pieces of the cords that had held Smith to the wall still dangled from the nails pounded into the wall. I swung the Glock back and forth across the darkness of the room, but it was empty.

I walked over to the edge of the hallway and stopped.

'Smith,' I yelled.

From the darkness of the kitchen a door slowly swung open or closed, creaking on its hinges. I rushed through the dining room and raised the gun. The kitchen was empty, but the door on the other side that led to the garage was open.

'Smith,' I said and took a step.

Nothing came back.

The kitchen sink was filled with empty cleaning fluid bottles. The air was still heavy with the odor. I crossed the kitchen to the garage door and pushed it open. It was even darker than the rest of the house. The door on the other side that led out had been closed, keeping even the faintest hint of light from entering. I stepped down on to the concrete and took a step toward the far side and stopped. The cleaning fluid scent was here too.

'Smith,' I said softly.

I thought I heard the sound of a breath.

'Can you hear me?' I said. 'Tell me where you are and I'll come to you.'

Another breath came out of the darkness as if the room had exhaled.

With one hand I held the gun, and with the other I reached out into the darkness and took a step and then another.

'Smith?'

A faint line of light under the door on the far side of the garage became visible.

'Don't move, I'll find you,' I said.

I took a step toward the pencil-thin line of light and then another and then I stopped. The air seemed to move, just brushing the side of my face like a spent breeze.

'Smith?'

No response. I closed my hand even tighter on the handle of the weapon and raised it toward the darkness from where I had felt the movement come.

'I have a weapon,' I said.

My finger began to close round the trigger and I reached out with my other hand.

'Smith!'

I swept the darkness, but there was nothing there. I

pulled in my free hand, took a step back toward the line of light under the door when fingers touched the back of my neck.

I swung round, raising the gun.

'I can't see,' came a voice.

I held the gun on the darkness where the hand had come from.

'I'm lost,' Smith said barely above a whisper.

I held the gun at the point of darkness for another moment then lowered it and reached out with my free hand.

'Take my hand,' I said.

Fingers brushed the side of my face and I reached up and closed my hand around them.

'I'll take you outside,' I said.

He hesitated then took a small step and then another and I slowly led him to the door and pulled it open. In the faint light of the night sky I could see that Smith's hair was still damp from the water and cleaning products. With his right hand he held the blanket tightly around his shoulders. A foot of cord dangled from his wrist.

'Can you see now?' I asked.

He nodded without looking up, keeping his eyes focused on the ground and avoiding contact with me. I walked him over to the black SUV and sat him down on the running board, and then I stepped out from behind the truck to make sure we were alone. In the distance I could hear the faint sound of a vehicle moving away across the desert, but it could be coming from anywhere and be nothing. I holstered the Glock, walked back and knelt down in front of Smith.

The blanket had partially slipped from his shoulders and he was uselessly pawing at the cords, trying to free them. I reached out to help him and he jerked his arms away.

'Let me help,' I said softly.

He leaned away from me, shaking his head. In what light there was I could see that the skin of his face was swollen and irritated.

'I need to get you to a doctor,' I said.

Smith shook his head and continued to pull at the cords. I reached out and gently touched his wrist.

'Stop,' I said softly.

His eyes stayed focused on his wrists and he continued pulling at the cords.

'Let me do that.'

'No,' Smith whispered.

'You need help with those.'

I took hold of his hand and slowly, one by one, his fingers closed round mine, and then he raised his head and his eyes filled with tears. What had happened to this man inside the house was something I could perhaps begin to imagine, but to do so from the standpoint of a captain of Robbery Homicide was something else, even after my experience in the desert of Trona.

A captain of Robbery Homicide doesn't cry. Doubt doesn't even exist in his vocabulary. What had been taken from him was what had made him who he was.

All that was left behind were the broken parts of what he used to be. His eyes held the same empty light that Crawford's had once he had taken that step past the point of no return.

'No doctor . . . no one,' Smith whispered.

I nodded. 'No one has to know.'

His grip tightened as if he was trying stop from slipping further into the darkness he had been plunged into, then he leaned against my chest and his shoulders shook as he tried to fight off more tears.

I set his hand on my knee, uncurling his fingers from mine, and then gently pried open the knots of the cord. The raised lines of hemorrhaging around his wrists appeared like dark tattoos as I unwound the cord and tossed it away. When I had freed both hands, he pulled the blanket tight around his shoulders and slowly rocked back and forth, his gaze never leaving the ground.

'I need to take the wire off your foot,' I said.

He continued his rocking as I began to remove the copper wire that had been wrapped round several of his toes. The skin it had been in contact with was raised and bright red where the tissue had been burned.

'You need a doctor,' I said again.

He reached down and took hold of my hand and pulled it toward him, exposing the bruising on my wrist where I had been held. He stared at it for a moment and then looked at me.

'No doctor.'

I took a seat next to him on the running board of the Suburban and waited for him to inch his way back to the present. Overhead the clouds that had rolled down out of the mountains began to break and points of starlight appeared in the moonless sky while faint rumbles of thunder still echoed to the south.

Forty minutes after peeling the cords from his wrists, Smith sat back against the door of the car and raised his head. He stared straight ahead at the door to the garage and took several labored breaths. The skin of his face was still irritated, but the swelling around his eyes had lessened a little.

'I need to know some things,' I said.

He looked straight ahead as if not hearing the words, then tentatively began to speak, his voice raw with the chemicals that had been soaking his face.

'We had a cell phone trace on Russell to this location,' he said.

'This is Lowery's house . . . Lowenstein,' I said. 'He must have been waiting for him.'

'It was just past dawn. I was stepping out of the truck . . .' His words trailed off and he closed his eyes. 'And then I was in that room.'

'Did you see him?' I asked.

He opened his eyes again but didn't look my way.

'I was hooded, there was only a voice.' He briefly fell silent. Tears again began to fill his eyes. 'He began with the water . . . then chemicals. I couldn't breathe.' He fell silent.

'You don't have to tell me any more.'

'The wire was . . .' The words trailed off and he glanced at me. 'I told him what he wanted.'

'What did you tell him?'

'The numbers.'

'What numbers? Maya Torres' numbers?'

He nodded.

'How did you know about her?'

He grimaced from a spasm of pain and his body tightened then relaxed.

'We found her a few blocks from the bus station.' He glanced toward me but avoided making eye contact.

'You were following me?'

He nodded. 'She remembered the numbers from the locker at the bus station.'

'Do you remember them?'

'Yes.'

I pulled a notepad and pen out of my pocket and held them out to him. He stared at them as if he didn't know what they were.

'Write them down for me,' I said.

He hesitated then slipped one of his hands out from under the blanket, took the pad and pencil and set it on his lap, but then just stared at the dark marks on his wrists from the cords and began pulling on the skin as if the cords were still attached to him.

'We took them off, it's gone,' I said.

He stopped pulling on his skin and then dropped to his knees on the ground and began picking up the pieces of cord. I knelt down next to him and held out my open hand.

'I'll take care of them.'

He gathered the pieces into a smaller and smaller

ball then looked down at his hands as if he didn't know what they were doing.

'Let me,' I said.

He held them in the palm of my hand.

'No one can see them,' Smith said.

I nodded and he released the cords. I helped him back on to the running board and handed him the pad and pencil again. He started to write, then stopped and just stared at the blank page.

'The numbers,' I said.

He gripped the pencil in his hands with the intensity of a grade-schooler learning to write for the first time, and then slowly wrote out a series of numbers, pausing between each one before moving on to the next. When he was finished, Smith stared at the paper for several moments as if wondering where it had come from and then handed the pad to me.

He had written the letter N, followed by seven numbers. There was no discernible order, grouping or pattern.

'Could this be a phone number?' I asked.

He shook his head. 'It's something else.'

'Did Russell know what it was?'

He didn't react to my question; he seemed to be retreating into himself as if seeking shelter.

'Smith.'

His slide inwards hesitated and he looked at me.

'The numbers?' I said. 'Did these mean something to Russell?'

He nodded. 'Yes.' Smith tried to work something

out in his head and then whispered, 'Did you cut me free?'

'No, there was someone else here.'

His lips silently mouthed something, and then for just an instant his eyes appeared to clear of trauma and he nodded as events began to resurface.

'A man.'

'Did you see a face?'

Smith shook his head. 'A voice, different voice.'

'What did he say?'

'The numbers.'

'Did you tell him?'

'No . . . he just wanted to know if Russell knew.'

'He said the name Russell?'

He nodded.

'Did he say or ask anything else?'

Smith took a deep, labored breath. His shoulders sank and he leaned back against the car door.

'He said go home, he would take care of everything.' His eyes began to retreat again, back into his private hell.

'Did you recognize the voice?'

'I don't know.'

I tried to work the logic out in my head. Lowery didn't fit, he was running, he wouldn't stop to set anyone free. I replayed what Smith had just said over in my head. There was something familiar about the words go home.

'Could it have been Salem?' I asked.

The name had the effect of cold water hitting his

face and Smith looked at me. He started to say something then lost the thought. For a moment he closed his eyes and his hands tightened around the blanket.

'It could have been him,' he said.

'Are you sure? Think about the voice.'

He began to shake his head. 'His face, I can't see his face . . . I don't remember his voice.'

The words go home kept swirling in my head.

'No, it was Salem, it had to be,' Smith said.

Then he slowly stood up and looked out toward the darkness and the desert.

'How do I go home, Lieutenant?'

I thought of Crawford tumbling into the darkness, and the grip of his cold fingers on my ankle.

'Someone helps you,' I said.

thirty-three

Smith's clothes were in a pile in a corner of the garage, along with the holsters containing his Beretta. I placed the gun inside the SUV then dressed him in silence as one would a sleepy child, carefully slipping each leg into his pants and then easing the shirt over his shoulders and the damaged skin of his chest. I didn't say a word and there wasn't a sound from him. His eyes never wavered from a point in space just over my shoulder, as if he was waiting for something to appear on the horizon.

I left him sitting on the running board and walked back inside the house to the room where he had been tortured and turned on the lights. The residue of violence leaves a mark on a place as clearly as it does on an individual and no amount of fresh paint or new carpet would ever erase what had happened here. I stared at the empty chair and the pieces of cord still hanging from the walls. This was no longer a tract house, any more than a bicycle was just a child's toy to me, any more.

I walked back down the hallway to the office I had seen and stepped in. Before, in the darkness, I hadn't noticed that sitting on the desk were several neatly cut pieces of plywood. I walked over and picked one of them up, then looked around the room. The contents of the drawers littered the floor. The room had been thoroughly searched.

If a connection existed to the numbers on the notepad, from what I could tell Russell hadn't found it either. There would have been no need to torture Smith if he had already found what he was looking for.

I walked quickly through the rest of the house, finding nothing, and then stepped back into the living room and stopped. Smith was standing a few feet from the chair where he had been tied, staring at it in silence, an utterly empty expression on his face as if he was incapable of holding on to the simplest of emotions. I started to take a step when I saw the Beretta in his hand at his side.

'Captain,' I said softly.

He didn't respond.

'Maybe you shouldn't be in here,' I said.

He stepped over to the chair, then reached out a hand and touched it as if to be certain it really existed.

'Where should I be?' Smith said softly.

I took a step. 'I think you should give me the gun.'

He pulled the hammer back with his thumb and shook his head.

I took another step and started to reach toward him.

'Don't,' Smith said.

I stopped.

'There's something I have to remember,' he said, then slowly stepped up to the chair and sat down on it again.

'What is it?' I said.

'There's something,' he repeated.

With his free hand he reached up and rubbed his eyes. The simple act of retrieving a memory seemed to cause him pain.

'You don't have to do this now,' I said.

He shook his head. 'Yes, I do.'

I took a step toward him and he raised his hand holding the weapon and set the gun on his lap. Smith looked at me, barely clinging on to what remained of the cop inside him.

'What did you say his name was?' he asked.

'Who?'

'The man who lives here.'

'Lowery.'

He thought about it for a moment then nodded. 'He took the money?'

'He and Torres, yes.'

'Is he alive?'

'He was a few hours ago. That's why Russell was here.'

Understanding seemed to come as if he was squeezing it from a sponge. 'He wasn't expecting me?'

'No.'

He stared blankly into the room for a moment, then shuddered and took the gun off his lap and looked at it.

'When the electricity goes through you, you feel it move through your veins. It's like you've been filled with boiling water.'

'Hand me the gun, Captain . . . please.'

Smith looked at me then quickly stepped off the chair and began to raise the Beretta. I started toward him and yelled.

'No!'

He shook his head.

'Smith!'

The shot shook the room like a crack of thunder, the walls amplifying the sound to a deafening level. I stood frozen as the discharge from the round hung in the air, carrying the sharp odor of gunpowder. Smith held the gun toward the back of the chair where he had just put the round through, then exhaled and lowered it to his side. A tear slipped out of the corner of his eye and down his cheek.

'I'm a policeman,' he said softly. 'I'm a . . .'

'Yes you are,' I answered.

He looked at me, trying to force a thought into recognizable order. 'Lowery?'

'He's a second lieutenant in the Shore Patrol, late twenties.'

'How much money?' Smith said.

'Hundreds of thousands, maybe more, I don't know.'

'They couldn't take that much money to a bank.'

'No.'

'So what would they do?'

I moved back down the hallway and into the office. I stepped to the desk and picked up the pieces of plywood. They were a little over a foot long and half as wide. A small notch was cut in the end of each. I stepped round the desk over to the wall. There was something wrong with the way the floor lay, an unevenness. I ran my fingers along the edge of the carpet against the baseboard until I found the break. The carpet came up easily and I peeled it back, exposing the hole where the boards had been removed. I reached my hand down into the crawl space and touched the cool damp ground. There was nothing there.

I turned to stand and Smith was behind me looking down at the hole in the floor.

'He dug a hole,' Smith said.

I nodded.

'Maybe more than one. Lowery's been panicking since the moment he opened up that bag from Baghdad and saw the stacks of money,' I said.

'Russell isn't panicking,' Smith said.

'No, and he wants the money,' I said.

Smith knelt down and ran his fingers across the edges of the cut in the floor.

'So where's the next hole?' I said. I took the notepad out of my pocket and looked down at the numbers. 'These numbers could be a code.'

Smith held out his hand and I gave him the notepad. He looked at it in silence and then shook his head.

'Not a code, they're coordinates.'

'Coordinates, like a map?'

Smith nodded.

'You knew this before?' I asked.

'We didn't know what they meant, it could have been anything. It's just a spot in the desert.'

I looked at him for a moment, then down at the numbers.

'Where in the desert?'

Smith shook his head, trying to remember through the haze of his ordeal. 'I don't . . . it was somewhere . . . I don't . . .'

I walked over to the map tacked on the far wall. It was a BLM map of the desert surrounding Ridgecrest, stretching all the way to Death Valley to the north.

'We can find it on here,' I said to Smith and held out the numbers to him.

He took the pad in his hand and stared at the numbers.

'Try to remember,' I said.

He walked over to the map and stared at it for a moment, then began slowly working the grid lines, trying to coax a distant logic out of his shattered psyche. Sweat was beading on his forehead and he was breathing as if he had just run a mile.

'I think this is it,' he whispered.

'Are you certain?' I asked.

Smith shook his head. 'Maybe . . . I think so. I don't know.' He looked at me, barely holding off the panic just under the surface. 'Russell told me to tell no one.'

'You can tell me.'

He shook his head.

'You can just show me, you don't have to say anything,' I said.

Smith nodded. I stepped over and he began to trace a line across the grids of the map from top to bottom. Halfway down the map, his finger stopped.

'Here,' he said.

'You're sure?'

Smith wiped some sweat from his brow as he looked at the map and then turned to me.

'Trona,' I said.

Smith nodded.

'Where in Trona? There's hundreds of miles of desert around it. Can you be more specific?'

I started to turn toward him when I saw his hand coming up from his side and heard him make an anguished sound that seemed to come from some primal place hidden deep inside where it was never meant to be found.

I tried to raise my hand to block the blow but I was too late.

'I'm sorry,' said Smith as I saw the blur of his fist just before the room went black.

thirty-four

A voice was calling. I couldn't tell where it was coming from. I was on the floor, could feel the fibers of the carpet against my face, but it moved under me as if I was back in the ocean, drifting on the swells.

'Lieutenant.'

I was caught in a current.

'Can you hear me, Lieutenant?'

The side of my face burned with a piercing heat where I had been struck.

'Lieutenant.'

It was Salem's voice, then Crawford's, and then Gilley's. I felt fingers slip under the back of my neck. I reached for my Glock, but found only the empty holster, then held my hands up to stop another blow. The hand on the back of my neck pulled me up and his face came into focus.

'You,' I said softly as my head began to spin and I fought to stay conscious.

'Try to take a few slow breaths.'

It was the young SP officer I had told to go back to the base. I tried to nod but the movement sent pain through the side of my face.

'I waited at the end of the block to see if you came out. When the other vehicle did and you didn't, I came back,' he said.

His words sped past me before I could find their meaning. Every other breath I seemed to slip back into the ocean swell and begin to drift. I closed my eyes and slowly the movement of the floor under me began to diminish.

I opened my eyes; he was kneeling in front of me a few feet away.

'How long have I been unconscious?'

'Ten minutes since I arrived.'

'Do you see my weapon anywhere?' I asked.

He motioned across the room. 'It's over on the floor.' He leaned in close and looked at my face. 'Are you hurt anywhere else?'

I started to shake my head but even that small movement made me dizzy. 'I don't think so.'

'Do you know where he was going?'

'Smith?'

He nodded.

'I think he's going to kill a man . . . or end his own life.' I looked at the officer squatting in front of me. 'He's going to Trona.'

I tried to get to my feet but my head began to spin and I sat back down.

'I think it's time for you to go home, Lieutenant,' said the officer.

I reached out a hand to him. 'Can you help me to my feet?'

He took my hand. 'Hold on to me and I'll get you up.'

I slipped my hands round his back and as he lifted me up, my hand brushed the shape of a weapon tucked in the waist of his pants against the small of his back.

'Can you stand?' he asked.

I nodded and glanced into his eyes. He had told me before that he didn't have a weapon, and then he had told me to go home; the same words Smith had been told by the man who cut him free. Had I been played the entire evening from the moment I was taken into the base? Was this all just another piece of theater put on by Havoc?

'How did you know about Smith?'

He shook his head. 'I didn't, you just mentioned it.'

I looked down at his hand on my arm and my heart began to beat against my chest. I glanced across the room to where my Glock lay on the floor.

'Home?' I said.

He nodded. 'Sounds like a plan.'

His hand still held my forearm.

'I don't know your name,' I said.

'I never gave it to you.' He looked at me for a moment. 'Johnson.'

There wasn't a hint of the lie he had just told in his eyes.

'Thank you, Johnson.'

He nodded.

'I think I'm all right now,' I said, trying to calculate how many steps it would take for me to reach my gun.

'You sure?' he asked, his fingers tightening ever so slightly on my arm.

I nodded, certain that he could hear my heart pounding against my chest. I looked again over to my gun across the room. Had he felt my hand discover his weapon, or had he seen it in my eyes? The smallest 'tell' that any good gambler would bet the house on. The Glock was half a dozen steps away, and even if my head wasn't balancing on a stick I wouldn't get closer than two before his weapon would be against the back of my head. I turned to him but his eyes gave away nothing.

'I think I'm all right,' I said again.

He held my arm just a second longer than was natural, then released me.

'Take it slow, Lieutenant.'

The hand he had been holding me with dropped to his waist, his thumb hooking on the belt just a few inches from the gun in the small of his back.

'Good advice,' I said.

I took a cautious step toward my weapon and then another, then reached out and steadied myself on the corner of the desk.

'If I bend over I think I'll pass out. Can you get me my weapon?' I asked.

He looked at me, registering no reaction to my words.

'Did Smith tell you anything about Russell?' he asked.

I shook my head. 'No.'

'Too bad,' said Johnson.

I motioned toward the Glock. 'Would you hand me it?'

Johnson looked at me for a moment longer then walked across the room and picked up my Glock by the grip and turned to me.

'They're light, aren't they?' he said.

I noticed his index finger slip inside the trigger guard.

'A good weapon for women,' he said.

'Yes,' I said.

He moved it in his hand as if testing its weight and then walked over and stopped just out of reach of me.

'It's a long drive back to LA, you going to be all right?'

'I'll take it slow,' I said, and then reached out for the Glock.

Johnson, or whatever his name was, looked down at my hand and then into my eyes.

'Drive safe, Lieutenant.'

He held the gun out to me, the barrel pointed at the center of my chest, then spun it in his hand with the ease of someone who had been born holding a weapon, and placed the grip of the Glock gently in the palm of my hand. I've never been a particular expert when it comes to weapons, but Johnson was right, it was a good woman's gun, and I knew this one well enough to know that he had just handed me a weapon with no bullets in the magazine.

I slipped it back into the holster and took a step

toward the door and stumbled, falling to one knee. Johnson bent down and put an arm around my shoulders.

'I think I overestimated my abilities,' I said.

'I'll help you to the car,' he said.

As he lifted me back up, my right hand came up under the back of his shirt and slipped his automatic from its place tucked in against the small of his back. As I placed the barrel against the base of his neck, he froze, and I stepped out from under his arm.

'What are you doing, Lieutenant?'

'You knew the name Russell,' I said.

He shook his head. 'Did I?'

'How?'

'You must have mentioned it.'

'Who are you?'

'I told—'

I pressed the gun harder against his neck.

'I'm tired of being lied to!'

'You should go home.'

I moved the barrel up to his head, pressing it forward, forcing him to look down at the floor.

'You don't want to shoot me, Lieutenant.'

'What I want you can't give back to me.'

'You're making a mistake.'

'Get down on your knees and cross your ankles behind you.'

He shook his head. 'I won't do that.'

My hand holding the weapon was moving and I watched it as if someone else was holding the gun as it hit the side of his head. He cringed from the blow but stayed on his feet.

'Get down,' I yelled, but he still shook his head.

The next blow made the sound of a limp stalk of celery snapping in my hand as the gun struck his cheekbone. His knees buckled and a trickle of blood slid down his neck from his ear.

'What are you doing?' he yelled.

I pulled the hammer back on the Beretta and pressed it against his head.

'Don't, Lieutenant,' he said.

I pulled the weapon back from his head, pointed the gun toward the wall and pulled the trigger. The shot shook the room and the officer dropped to his knees.

'Lieutenant!' he yelled again.

I slipped the Glock silently out of my holster and placed it against his head just behind the ear where I had held his 9mm.

'What were your orders?' I asked.

'I can't tell you that.'

I pulled the hammer back on the Glock.

'What were your orders?'

He shook his head. My hand pressed the gun harder against his head.

'Answer the question.'

He started to shake his head and my finger closed around the trigger, firing the empty weapon. The hammer snapped next to his ear and he jerked away and began to cover his head with his hands before he realized there hadn't been a shot.

'Answer!' I yelled.

Again he started to shake his head and I pulled the trigger and he jerked involuntarily away from the hard hit of the hammer falling.

'Answer it!'

His hands covering his head began to shake.

'I can't.'

I pointed the Beretta at the wall and fired another round. He bent forward, covering his bleeding ear with his hand, and then I pressed the Glock to the back of his head.

'Can you tell the difference between an empty and a loaded barrel by the feel of it against your head?' I said. 'Because I can't, and I've had extensive training.'

'Don't—' he started to say and I pulled the trigger on the Glock and his head jerked away, and then I pulled it again and then again and each time he dropped closer to the floor until he was finally curled into a ball with his hands covering his head.

'Where's Lowery?' I asked.

He took a deep, shaky breath.

'How would I know?'

'Where's the money?'

'What money?'

I took the Beretta and then reached down and pressed it into the back of his head. His hand covering his ear had a slim silver wedding band on it. A bead of sweat slid down from his hairline and curled around the barrel of the weapon.

'Answer the question.'

'He's been moving it around,' yelled Johnson.

'Where?'

'Here, the bus station.'

'In Trona?'

He nodded.

'Was it destroyed?'

He shook his head. 'He moved it before the fire.'

'Where is it now?'

He started to shake his head and I felt my finger tightening on the trigger.

'Please,' he said.

I swung the Beretta away from his head and fired a round into the floor a foot from where he was curled up. His entire body began to shake.

'No,' he screamed.

'Where is it?' I yelled.

'I have a daughter,' he whispered.

'Answer me!' I yelled.

'We don't know.'

I pressed the gun back against his head. 'Where is it?'

'I don't—'

'Answer me!'

'It was recovered days ago,' he said.

'Where?'

'A hole in the desert.'

I stared at him in disbelief. 'Why didn't you arrest him?'

He shook his head.

'Why?'

'We're not cops.'

I pressed the gun into his head and then my hand began to shake and I saw that it wasn't someone else's hand holding the gun, but my own. And then he said it again.

'I want to see my daughter . . . please.'

I looked down to where the barrel of the gun was pressed against the soft skin at the base of his skull.

'What did you say?' I said.

'I have a daughter.'

My finger was still curled around the trigger and I felt a sickness rising in my stomach. I quickly pulled the weapon away from his head, lowered the hammer back into place and walked over to the desk and sat down. The sailor remained curled on the floor for a moment then slowly sat up, wiping moisture from his eyes. A small red welt was rising on the side of his face where I had hit him. A thin stream of blood streaked his neck. I couldn't look at his face, or didn't want him to look at mine.

'What's her name?' I asked.

He took several breaths, his gaze never leaving the floor.

'Your daughter, what's her name?'

'Amanda,' he said.

I looked at his face and I could see him on the sidewalk running alongside her pink bicycle as she wobbled back and forth on the training wheels. There were ribbons in her hair, tassels on the handlebars.

'I have a daughter,' I whispered.

thirty-five

Neither of us said a word for several minutes. The odor of the discharged weapon hung in the air with its sick, sweet scent. Outside, the flashes of another storm moving in occasionally lit the darkness. I had beaten a man with a weapon and then pressed it against his head and pulled the hammer back. I knew I had done it, because I had watched it like a spectator, but I had not felt anything until now, and now what filled me was the same shame I had felt when I had been held down in the sand on another dark night.

Johnson finally got up from the floor and walked across the room and sat against the wall without saying a word. His ear had swelled and blood slipped down his neck in several thin streams.

'Is Lowery alive?' I asked.

He put his face in his hands and shook his head.

'I don't know, he's running. The Shore Patrol will eventually find him. He's a thief and he's AWOL.'

'You're not Shore Patrol?' I asked.

He shook his head.

'What were you supposed to do with me?'

'Make sure you went home,' he said.

'That's all?'

He nodded.

I picked up his Beretta and walked across the room and held it out to him. He looked at it for a moment then up into my eyes and took the gun from my hand, setting it on the floor next to him.

'You're with Havoc,' I said.

'Havoc no longer exists. And any paperwork proving its former existence has been destroyed.'

'And Taylor?' I said.

He looked at me a moment, then out the window toward the darkness. 'I'm not aware of any individual by that name.'

'Murders have been committed. And an innocent man is going to be blamed for them.'

He shook his head. 'Not by us.'

'Who then?'

'We were an intelligence unit, we played games; buy a little good will, that's all we did.'

'It's not all you did, you looked the other way.'

He took a deep breath. 'Everyone looks the other way over there.'

'Salem didn't,' I said.

He looked at me. 'He didn't belong there.'

'Havoc made a mess of things and now Taylor's cleaning it up.'

Johnson didn't react.

'Isn't he?'

He nodded.

'Did you cut Smith free?'

He stared ahead without looking at me and nodded.

'Is there anything else you've said that wasn't a lie tonight?'

'Do you really believe there's just one truth, Lieutenant?'

'There was once,' I said.

He closed his eyes. 'Not in my world.'

He opened his eyes and looked at me for the first time since I had put the gun to his head and almost pulled the trigger.

'That night, what happened to you, it was like I told you,' he said.

The air went out of me. Connecting truth to what happened to me was never part of the equation.

'I could arrest you.'

'It's a long drive to Los Angeles,' he said.

He took a deep, exhausted breath and stared across the room at a point in space far beyond the confines of these walls, and then his eyes seemed to focus.

'How do I stop him?' I asked.

'You can't.'

I walked over and knelt in front of the man.

'You can help me,' I said.

He shook his head. 'Do you think Taylor would be here if they wanted it stopped? By dawn it will be over, he'll be on his way to another continent, and there will be no record of what happened here or in Iraq.'

'I'll know what has happened here, and so will you,' I said.

He shrugged. 'Memories fade.'

I shook my head. 'Yours won't, or mine.'

He turned to me, his eyes seeming to carry the record of the things he had done and seen that only he would ever know.

'Ours don't matter.'

'What happens to Salem?' I asked.

He shook his head. 'I have my orders.'

'I don't,' I said.

I reached into my pocket and took out the notepad with Torres' coordinates written on it and held it out to him.

'Tell me about these coordinates.'

He took the pad and glanced at it, then shook his head. 'They were never meant for Mrs Torres to find, that wasn't the plan.'

I heard him say the words but it took me a moment to fully understand what he had said.

'Plan?' I said.

He nodded.

'You planted them?'

He nodded again. 'The plan was good. It would all have worked.'

The whole pathetic thing fell into place, or at least enough to understand how I had got to here.

'It was a set-up,' I said. 'You knew the money had been stolen by ISC, you just didn't know by who.'

'We intercepted Torres' letter after he was murdered.'

'What was in it?'

'Instructions for his wife on how to find the money, but it had already been moved, so we came up with a different scenario.'

'You put your own coordinates in that locker and waited to see who would find the letter.'

He nodded. 'Then ISC killed one of our officers.'

'At the street café with Salem.'

'Yeah. We thought he was part of it. It would have worked—'

'It didn't.'

'It was a good plan.'

'The plan is over . . . it's over, all of it.' I grabbed the notepad from him. 'Where is this?'

He shook his head. 'It will be over before you can get there.'

I looked at him for a moment. 'You called Taylor and told him Russell had the coordinates.'

He nodded. 'You see the plan did, in the end, work.'

'Where is it?'

He closed his eyes and leaned his head back. 'What is it you think you're going to accomplish, Lieutenant?'

'Where?' I said.

He got up from the floor and walked over to the window. I picked up his Beretta, went over to him and held it out.

'What were you supposed to do with this if I didn't return to LA?'

He looked down at it and shook his head. 'I'm just an intelligence officer.'

'You play games.'

He stared at the gun.

'Go on, take it!' I yelled.

He glanced at me for a moment longer then looked back out the window as a flash of lightning lit the dark silhouette of a jagged ridge of distant hills.

'The ISC facility north of Trona,' he said.

'The combat town?'

He nodded, smiled the way the smartest kid in the class would after getting away with cheating on a test.

'We liked the irony.'

'Irony?' I said.

He continued to stare out the window.

'Salem was running for his life,' I said.

'We didn't know he was a cop, we only found that out after. There was nothing we could do by then.'

'So you used him.'

'It was a good plan, right from the start—'

'No,' I said. 'It was never a good plan, not any of it.'

He took a deep breath and shook his head. 'We thought we were doing some good over there.'

I tossed the gun on to the floor at his feet.

'That's irony,' I said and turned and walked out.

thirty-six

How do you know what the right thing to have done is if long before Ace or the American captain and the nameless Iraqis died, truth was the first casualty? Where does that leave every act, every death that had taken place since then? Is there such a thing as truth in a reality based on lies?

The only way Salem could prove that ISC had killed innocents and murdered his friend Torres was by connecting them to the stolen money. But Salem had been running for his life, following a piece of evidence that was meaningless from the moment he found it. And Havoc had known it from the very start. They had let him continue to run because without the money they knew Salem could prove nothing, and if Russell just happened to kill him, then not only was that one more loose end tied up, they also had the perfect fall guy on whom to blame the murders of Burns and Henkel.

A storm cell was moving over Trona as I drove back

into town. The air held the scent of rain, though none was falling here. The only thing the wind carried here was dust, blowing down the empty streets and swirling around the boarded-up homes, gas stations and the blue football field, covering it all in fine alkali dust.

Smith may have believed that it was Salem who had cut him free, but Smith needed belief more than truth. Salem dying was the only way it worked for the people who had let Taylor loose. His ultimate silence was necessary to assure the ending they wanted. A man going to trial for murders he didn't commit was too unpredictable. If Salem was still alive then this was where he would be, there was nowhere else to hide or run; every death, every lie, led right back here.

How I fitted into that was the only part I didn't understand yet. Had I been manipulated from my very first step? Was I being manipulated now? In returning to Trona was I somehow aiding in the final act of an operation that began the moment Russell had touched the button on the phone that transformed a little boy into a flash of light.

I pulled to a stop across the street from the sheriff's substation. There were no lights on. No new patrol car parked in the fenced lot next to Deputy Gilley's destroyed cruiser. Back-up, if it existed at all for a cop who had wandered so far from home, was an hour or two away at best. And by then it would all be over.

I continued on past the burned-out shell of the bus station and then the liquor store where I had briefly set eyes on the man I believed to be Taylor. I slowed the car and looked into the desert to the north where the walls of an imaginary town had risen out of the sand. He was out there. I didn't have to see or hear him to know Taylor was moving through the darkness, waiting to reach out and snatch all official memory of what had taken place half a world away and turn it into fiction.

I pressed my foot on the accelerator and drove past the sign north toward Death Valley and into the growing dust storm. How far I had driven on that previous night before I turned off the pavement I couldn't remember. The things that had been seared into my memory had nothing to do with distance traveled.

I passed one road and then another, each appearing out of the darkness and dust as little more than a faint line in the sand. The red glow of a coyote's eyes appeared for a moment at the edge of the headlights and then vanished. A single white shoe sat discarded on the road's shoulder, rocking back and forth in the wind on its worn sole as if it were taking phantom steps.

At another dirt track as unremarkable as the ones before it, I turned off the pavement and began to follow it into a series of rolling hills. I could see the tracks of other vehicles that had followed the same road, but how many and when they had passed was impossible to tell as the storm's dust began to gather like drifting snow where it could get purchase.

Nothing seemed right, or familiar. If I had taken the wrong road, by the time I had driven far enough to be certain, it would be too late – history would have been rewritten, and there would be more bodies in the sand.

Rocks and brush flew past as I pressed the car to the limits of its ability to hold the road. One curve and then another, nothing seemed right. Then I rounded a long sweeping bend and my lights illuminated the tracks of a car that had driven over the edge, knocking down a fence post.

The voice in my head began saying again and again *don't stop* but I ignored the voice, my tires skidding to a halt where the tracks left the road. I took a shallow breath. The lights lit the gash in the post and the deep tire tracks where the vehicle had come to a sudden stop. I had taken the right road. In the sand beyond it I could see that several deep indentations where I had been held down were beginning to fill with blowing dust.

I reached down and began to slip the Glock out of the holster, and then stopped. My breathing became shallow. The desert, like the human heart, is slow to heal from what we have done to it. The scrapings of miners and the wagon-wheel tracks of homesteaders could still be found a century or more after they had paused on this ground. But nothing of what had happened to me here would remain. The outline of my body was slowly turning to dust grain by grain.

I held on to the cool plastic of the gun for a moment longer and then stepped hard on the accelerator. With each turn, each boulder and dry stream bed the road began to slip back into memory. But what was clearest was that the person who had driven this road that other night no longer existed. That life was now little more than a collection of snapshots pasted in an album. I might visit it occasionally, page through its memories. But I could never return completely, too much had happened. Crawford's hand would always be there around my ankle, reminding me how deep the abyss is. It's no wonder he chose to take his last breath by filling his lungs with the chilled water of the Pacific. No dust, no sand, nothing to remind him of Iraq. His death would be as close as he would ever come to who he was at the very beginning, before he opened his eyes on this world.

I reached a fork in the road, stopped and stepped out of the car, shielding my eyes with my hand. Tracks headed both to the right and left. I reached back in, turned off the engine and listened for the vehicles that had preceded me. There wasn't a sound. Not a car, an insect, a bird, nothing, not even the thunder from flashes of distant lightning seemed able to escape the wind's grip.

The road to the right was the one I had taken before that led to the abandoned tank and windmill. The left fork I guessed led directly to the town. In the dust beyond the limits of the headlights, a faint glow appeared to rise up above the horizon.

I turned off the headlights, uncertain of what I was seeing. The light was barely discernible, little more than the light of an ember, but it was there. Whatever was going to happen must have already begun.

I got back in the Volvo and started down the left fork of the road without turning on my lights. What a moment before had appeared to be an empty lifeless landscape in the headlights now seemed to come alive in the dark. In the swirling sand, dull shapes appeared and vanished as if I was being tracked along the road. Something bumped the windshield with a dull thud. I heard a brief clatter of hooves on rock and then nothing as a gate came into view, a broken chain lying across the road.

I crossed the chain and passed a series of warning signs – NO TRESPASSING, DANGER, LIVE FIRE ZONE. The road dipped into a narrow canyon with steep rock walls on either side and then opened up.

A flash of lightning lit the sky, illuminating the pale shape of a dust devil spinning madly as it moved across the road ahead. The sky plunged back into darkness and the little twister drifted off into the night. In the middle of the road, the shape of an SUV began to emerge from the dust.

I eased my foot on to the gas and halved the distance. The driver's side door was open. I could see no movement inside.

'Smith,' I whispered.

I stopped and started to reach for my Glock. The voice in my head let loose.

No, no, no, turn around, get out, get out get out.

My foot was on the brake.

What are you doing? Do it now, turn around.

'Oh, God,' I whispered.

I was holding an empty weapon. I had walked out of Lowery's unarmed.

Think it through, figure it out.

I had no back-up clip.

Do something . . . Maybe if you . . . come on, work it, there's nothing . . . think, think.

I pushed the door open and was running. Twenty yards. I couldn't stop. No turning around. I reached the back of the SUV and pressed myself against it. The engine was still running; faint wisps of exhaust rose from the tail pipe.

The Glock was still in my hand. The more useless it was, the tighter my fingers closed around it. I eased over to the corner of the truck and then up along the side to the open door.

It was empty. Smith wasn't there. There was no blood anywhere, no signs of violence. A fine layer of dust and sand covered everything, forming little piles in the corners of the dash.

I started searching, opening anything that would open, checking a leather bag, glove compartment, everywhere – he was Robbery Homicide, it had to be here. I began pounding on the steering wheel. There was no back-up weapon stashed under the seat, no extra clip hidden above the visor. No secure lockbox in the back. Nothing. All I had was an empty Glock in my hand.

I stepped out of the truck and looked back toward the Volvo – twenty yards, maybe thirty steps. I could go back, but it wasn't the way home.

Another bolt of lightning flashed overhead, followed by a rumble of thunder that moved across the ground in a wave, bringing with it another sound, the single sharp pop of a gunshot. I backed away from the truck as a gust of wind blew the door shut. Ahead the shapes of the combat town appeared to rise out of the dust and darkness and I started to run.

thirty-seven

When I reached the edge of the pavement, I stopped at the corner of the first building. The glow I had seen came from the center of the street fifty feet away. I stared at it for a moment then stepped back against the cool cinder blocks of the building, gripping my empty weapon.

Maybe it wasn't what I thought it was, maybe I was wrong. I glanced around the corner again, my eyes fixed on the flames. I wasn't wrong. I could see an arm bent awkwardly at the elbow; a hand pointing straight up in the air, engulfed in flame.

I stepped around the corner and ran toward the burning figures and stopped a few feet short. The flames looked like blowing strips of ribbon winding tighter and tighter around each other as they swirled above a head, up into the air. The eyes were open, staring into the sky. A knee had separated from the rest of the leg and lay several inches away, charred black like a piece of coal.

'Mannequins,' I whispered.

There were dozens of them, some burned beyond recognition, others only beginning to be consumed. On some of the figures bullet holes were still visible, on others the fabric that had dressed some like Iraqi civilians and others like soldiers. The evidence of what ISC had used these for was being erased.

A flash of light in a window followed by the sound of a gunshot came from one of the buildings down the street. I ran into the nearest doorway and waited for another shot, another flash of light, but there was nothing. And then I heard the faintest of sounds from down the street – a breath maybe, or a sigh of pain.

Out of habit I slid the chamber open on my Glock as if there was a round in the clip. The smell of burning plastic drifted on the gusts of wind. I moved along the front of the building and stopped at the corner.

In a side doorway of the next building a small mannequin arm lay a few feet from the entrance. It was the size of a child's, the fingers extended as if waving to a friend.

I stepped inside, pieces of the mannequins snapping under my feet with each step. The smell of discharged rounds still hung in the air. I passed through an empty room and then another. The walls were pockmarked with bullet holes. Empty shell casings littered the floor. There had been violence everywhere. But what part of it was real? There was no sign of blood anywhere.

I stepped into the front room and stopped. In the darkness out on the street I heard the sound of movement and I rushed over to the doorway. A solitary coyote trotting down the center of the road paused and looked back in my direction, then continued on down the street. I followed it past one building and then another, watching its every move for a sign of the presence of another predator waiting in a shadow.

The animal never looked to its right or left, just continued straight down the road as if following a prearranged plan. At the third building it turned to its left into an alley and I lost sight of it. I ran to the corner, took two steps into the alley and stopped.

The coyote was gone. The boy on his bicycle carrying his backpack was still in the center of the alley. I started to take a step, and then hesitated and stepped back, pressing myself against the building.

The painted lifeless eyes were looking directly at me. Something was different about the mannequin, or the bike or both. Was it the way the pack hung from the shoulders? Had the bike been moved or turned?

Half a dozen windows looked down on the alley where the boy and his bike sat. I stared into each of them, looking for movement or the faint electric tones of a cell phone being dialed. There was nothing there. I took a step into the alley toward the doorway on the other side, hesitated for any reaction, any sound, and then continued to the door.

As I approached the bike, a gust of wind swirled down the alley and the boy and the bicycle began to shake. I froze a few feet from his lifeless eyes. The front wheel pivoted back and forth on the pavement, its dry bearings squeaking with each turn, the handlebars quivering in the grip of the plastic hands. I heard the sound of Salem's voice in my head. *A flash of light.*

'No,' I whispered.

The breeze strengthened, rustling the cuffs of my pants. I took a shallow breath, and then the gust swirled past and the air stilled. The bike's wheel stopped moving and fell silent. The handlebars in the plastic hands settled. As I looked once more into the boy's face, I heard a cry come from the dark doorway on the other side of the alley.

I raised my weapon. The sound was high pitched, a child's maybe; there was another one, and then another. Lying on the floor just inside the doorway was the mannequin wearing combat fatigues. The sound was beyond it in the next room. A whimper came out of the darkness and then a sharp cry. Something was moving across the floor.

I knew these sounds – a child's cry, or a madman's. I ran across the first room to the door from where the sounds had come. The room fell silent and I raised the Glock into the darkness. The air was heavy with moisture like a freshly watered lawn, but it was the scent of death that hung in the room.

Their eyes slowly became visible – three sets, staring at me with a cold yellow light. The dull shape of something else was curled on the floor in front of the animals. It was in a fetal position, or something like one. I took a step closer; the coyotes' nails began to click against the concrete floor as they moved nervously back. I took another half step and stopped. The legs of the body had been stripped of their skin. The thin silvery tendons that wrapped the muscles appeared to glow next to the dark flesh. I couldn't tell what it had been, a small deer or maybe a calf. The taste of the air, rich with decay, began to turn my stomach.

I backed out of the room and then rushed over to the nearest exit, took a deep breath of fresh air. Behind the building was a small clearing in the desert. I stared in wonder at it for a moment and then pulled the hammer back on the pistol and gripped it with both hands.

'Irony,' I whispered.

A series of holes had been dug in the sandy soil, one after the other, every few yards. Some were little more than a few inches deep, others a foot or two. There was a manic quality to the digging, like the end of a child's scavenger hunt.

I walked out into the center of the clearing. Blowing sand was already beginning to fill the holes back up. In a matter of hours the desert would have erased all traces. On the far edge of the clearing lay a shovel. I walked over to it. Several dark specks of blood dotted the handle of the shovel.

A gust of wind carried another cry, but this was distinct from the coyotes' mad howls. This was human, and full of anguish. I ran back down the alley past the boy on the bicycle and stopped at the corner of the building. Another cry came from out on the street, only this time I could make out the words.

'Shoot me . . . shoot me.'

I froze. The voice belonged to Smith. He was moving. Each cry was drawing closer.

'Delillo,' he screamed.

I pressed myself back against the concrete. My hands holding the useless weapon began to shake.

'Delillo,' he yelled again.

I tried to take a breath, but could barely manage a sip of air. I looked out on to the street and the swirling dust and then stepped around the building into the open and raised the Glock. Smith was twenty yards away in the middle of the street. His face was bruised and bloodied. His hands were bound behind his back. A small backpack hung over his chest, the strap around his neck. A foot behind him stood Russell. He was a little taller than Smith, powerfully built. In his left hand he held a gun, in his other a cell phone.

'Shoot me,' pleaded Smith softly. 'Please . . . shoot me.'

I held my empty weapon on them and took a step forward.

'I want my money,' said Russell.

Smith shook his head, his wild eyes staring at me.

'Shoot me, do it!' he yelled.

'Let him go,' I said.

Russell shook his head. 'Where's my money?'

'I don't know.'

He raised the gun and cocked it, placing it against Smith's head.

'Then he dies.'

'Release him, I'll take you to it,' I yelled.

'Tell me now.'

'No,' I said.

Russell looked at me for a moment, the faint presence of a smile on his lips. He held up the cell phone and began to dial numbers.

'You bastard,' I said.

He nodded. 'Ever since birth. Now drop your weapon,' he ordered.

'Let him go, you can have it.'

'Don't,' yelled Smith.

'All right, you can have him. Walk to her,' said Russell.

Smith started to shake his head and Russell hit him on the side of the head with the gun.

'Walk,' he yelled.

Tears began to fall down Smith's face and he took the first step.

'Shoot me,' he pleaded. 'Don't let him do this to me.'

Russell dialed a fourth number on the cell, then a fifth.

'The money,' he said.

I started to lower the gun.

'No,' yelled Smith.

'Where is it?'

'Me for him,' I said.

Smith took another step, then another.

'Shoot me,' he screamed.

'The money,' yelled Russell.

'Don't,' Smith said.

I lowered the gun to my side.

'Drop it on the ground.'

'No,' screamed Smith.

'I'll tell you,' I said.

Russell dialed a sixth number.

'Let him go,' I yelled.

'Oh, God,' cried Smith.

'Let him go,' I repeated.

'Drop your weapon.'

I looked at Smith and let the Glock slip from my hand.

'Now let him walk away,' I said.

Smith began wildly shaking his head, trying to get the pack's strap off from around his neck.

'No,' said Russell.

His thumb slid across the keypad of the phone and stopped on the final number. I started to run toward Smith who began to scream, the pack bouncing off his chest as he tried to get it off.

'Smith—' I began to yell when the sound of a gunshot broke through the wind with a horrible dull thud followed by nearly instant silence.

Russell's body stiffened for a moment, his head obscured by a fine mist of crimson. The phone fell from his hand and then his body crumpled to the ground like a broken toy.

The silence lasted for another moment and then Smith fell to his knees and began to cry.

'Don't move,' I said to him.

There was nowhere I could run, or hide. I would be dead before I took a single step. A few seconds stretched to ten and then twenty. There was no second shot, only the wind. I glanced around, trying to determine where the shot had been fired, but I could see nothing in the darkness. I ran over to Smith and knelt down. He tried to pull away.

'No, no, no,' he began to shout.

I took his face in my hands.

'It's all right,' I said.

'Get it off, get it off,' he repeated again and again.

I lifted the pack off from around his neck and then tossed it toward one of the buildings where it landed without a sound. Smith leaned into me, his shoulders rising and falling with silent sobs.

'You're all right, it's over,' I said softly.

He looked up, his eyes finding mine.

'Is it?' he said.

'It will be.'

He shook his head. 'How will you know?'

I looked out into the darkness; a few stars were beginning to sparkle through. I imagined Crawford lying on the bottom of the ocean staring up, looking for the light.

'You'll know when you can't fall any further,' I said.

I reached round to his back and untied his hands, then got up, retrieved my weapon and walked over to where Russell lay face down in the dust. The shot had neatly entered the back of his head, taking out a large portion of his forehead as the round had exited. I reached down and picked up the cell phone, stared at the six numbers on the screen and then turned it off and threw it against the wall of the building where it shattered.

On a gust of wind I heard the faint drone of an engine and I ran to the top of the hill where I had first seen the town. There were no headlights anywhere in the darkness. The sound came and went with the gusts and then finally fell silent.

'Taylor,' I said.

But why only Russell, why had he let us walk away?

I looked out into the dark hills around the combat town. The sound of the engine seemed to have come from the road that led to the old water tank behind the hill. Taylor would be heading back to where it forked. It was quicker the way I had come. I could cut him off. I looked down the length of the town's street.

On one end lay Russell, on the other a pile of plastic body parts, slowly being consumed by flames. Smith was no longer where I had left him. I called his name as I ran back down the length of the town to the Volvo but there was no response. His SUV was still at the opening to the slit canyon. Whatever shelter he was seeking now, there seemed little I could do for him.

In the distance the sound of the engine came and went with the wind. I got back in the Volvo, spun it round and raced back through the canyon and past the warning signs. Where the two roads merged, I skidded to a stop and stepped out.

The sound of the other engine was gone. If Taylor

had come this way, I had missed him. To the south I could see the glow of the lights from Trona bleaching into the darkness. A rumble shook the ground, but it wasn't thunder, the storms had moved on. I looked back over the hills to the west where a series of faint flashes lit the darkness, followed a second or two later by the sound of more concussions.

China Lake. Bomb runs. War was being practiced.

thirty-eight

There was only one road back to Ridgecrest and the base. If I could intercept Taylor before he drove through the gates of China Lake and into its closely guarded secrets, it would have to be on this road.

The illusion that my form of justice still had a chance over Taylor's because it was connected even by the thinnest of threads to the law lasted until I reached the outskirts of Trona and stopped.

No other cars came down the road from Death Valley. Ten minutes passed, fifteen, then half an hour and on and on. With each tick of the clock, Taylor slipped further away, taking with him any chance of holding the truth of what had happened up to the light of day for all to see.

If I hadn't believed it before, I knew now that Salem had probably disappeared into the same void that had swallowed anyone who thought they had a chance of bringing something good out of the nightmare half a world away. In another couple of hours it would be dawn and just as the naval officer had said, it would all be over, and nothing could change that.

I was too tired to make the drive to LA so I drove into Trona and pulled off on to an empty side road lined with dead palm trees covered in white dust, and stopped to close my eyes.

What came with sleep was no more restful than any of the events that had overwhelmed the last handful of days. Drowning and falling, the click of the gun's hammer, drops of oil falling on the windshield like rain, Harrison's eyes, his touch, wet grass, the taste of salt and sand, my hand gripping the gun, an envelope, a secret, the faces of the dead. Salem's voice . . . *it's all true*.

I bolted awake at the sound of his words. The first light of the sun rising over the eastern horizon lit the empty sidewalks and dust-covered landscape around me. The ringing of a phone had woken me, not Salem's voice. I fumbled in my pockets, it was the phone Harrison had given me.

I hesitated before answering, not sure I wanted any part of wherever the words on the other end might take me. 'Just walk away,' I whispered, and then I answered it.

'Can you help me?'

It wasn't a question, but a plea. I recognized the voice.

'Lowery?' I said.

'Yes.'

'How did you get this number?'

382

'When you called me at the base.'

How long ago was that? A day – no, it was even less. Was that possible?

'Where are you?'

He hesitated. 'Can you?'

'I don't know,' I said. I wasn't sure I wanted to. What could come of it? 'How?' I asked.

'Get me out of Ridgecrest, they're watching the roads. You can get me out.'

'What makes you think I can do that?'

'You could get help.'

'You're a thief,' I said.

'Arrest me then.'

'Russell's dead. He's not after you any longer.'

Lowery was silent for moment. 'You're a cop, you have to.'

'What can you tell me about Salem?'

He paused. 'Nothing.'

'I can't help you,' I said.

'You can't just walk away, you've got to help me.'

'The money's been recovered, it's gone, they have it back,' I said. 'You haven't broken any law that I can arrest you for. You're the navy's problem, not mine.'

'Please.'

'What good will come of my helping you?' I said.

'It won't be over,' he said softly.

'It's already over.'

'No, it isn't.'

He was right, but I also knew that helping him wouldn't change that.

'What can you tell me that could do anyone any good?' I said.

'Everything.'

'I already know everything, and I can't do anything,' I said. 'Unless you can bring the dead back, or find Salem.'

'I can't do that.'

'No, you can't,' I said.

'I can tell the story.'

'To who?'

'Everyone. Get me to a reporter. Can you do that? I'll tell the whole story. A newspaper, TV.'

'You're a thief, why would anyone believe you?'

'Because you will be telling the same story.'

'Why should I do this?' I said.

'It's my only chance.'

'That's not good enough. You don't deserve saving.'

He fell silent.

'I'm sorry—' I started to say.

'It's your only chance,' he said.

I took a breath and imagined my fingers closing the phone. That would be the end of it.

'It's Salem's only chance,' Lowery said.

Drive away from this dying town; don't ever look back. This was the door out. Take it. I reached for the ignition and started to turn the key.

'Give me your number. When I reach a pay phone I'll call you back and you can tell me where you are.'

He hesitated. Then gave me the number.

'Hurry, Lieutenant.'

thirty-nine

The shift was changing at the potash plant as I drove out of Trona. Covered in the same pale white dust that blanketed the landscape, the workers walked to their cars, appearing like ghosts in the dawn light.

Lowery was hiding in a bar called the Blue Hanger. The same place Deputy Gilley had called the day he died. I didn't want to help Lowery, but here I was, driving through a dying town on the way to do just that. Why? It wasn't justice I was after any more, I wasn't even sure I believed in it any longer, or at least I didn't believe that if I had found Russell first, his end would have been any more just than what Taylor had had in store for him.

It would be nice to say this was for Salem, but I wasn't sure that was true. A man I hardly knew had stepped into my life and nothing was the same any longer, not the way I saw the world, not the way I saw myself.

It would be good to think I was doing it because the

only way to fight the grey men who were responsible for these nightmares was with truth, but they had long since co-opted that weapon and twisted it for their own devices, and what was worse, no one seemed to notice.

If I was helping Lowery for any reason, it was because I saw this as the only way to get back home, if not to the life I had had before I picked up the phone and heard the words, *I saw a boy on a bicycle vanish in a flash of light*.

I reached Ridgecrest and China Lake as the sun rose fully above the volcanic cones to the east of town. Traffic was beginning to move, most of it in the direction of the base. I found the Blue Hanger next to a strip mall on the eastern end of town. It was a square cinder-block building painted the bright blue of the desert sky with two blaze-orange windsocks flapping in the light breeze above the front entrance.

I stopped half a block away and studied every parked car on the street for anything that didn't fit the scene. There were no vehicles in the bar's parking lot. A doughnut shop and a Mexican restaurant appeared to be the only businesses in the mall with activity. An Hispanic man was carrying crates of vegetables from a white van into the restaurant. There were two cars at the doughnut shop. A man in his late sixties sat by the window of the shop holding a cup of coffee in both hands. A young woman with long jet-black hair sat at another booth staring at the empty seat on the other side of the table. If someone was waiting for Lowery, I didn't see it.

I drove around to the back of the bar. A trash truck was pulling away from a dumpster that sat a few yards from the rear entrance. I tried to get a look at the driver's face, but the sun reflected on the glass and his features were lost in the glare. I stopped the car and stepped out. There were no other buildings behind the bar, only the desert stretching toward the horizon.

I walked over to the door and started to reach for the handle to test it but stopped. A piece of trash hung from the lip of the dumpster, twisting in the breeze. I turned and watched the trash truck as it drove past the back of the strip mall without stopping.

A car alarm started wailing out beyond the front of the bar on the street. I walked over to the dumpster and lifted the lid. The stench of stale beer, food and liquor filled the air. The dumpster was still full.

I turned and ran toward the bar, pulling Smith's Beretta from my holster as I reached for the door. I flung it open and stepped inside, raising the gun.

A short hallway led to the darkened bar at the other end. The walls were painted the same bright blue as the outside of the building. Two doors on the left led to restrooms, a swinging door on the right led into the kitchen.

I pushed open the swinging door to the kitchen – it was empty. I stepped down the hall and pushed the restroom doors open with my foot, raising the gun into each – again empty.

At the end of the hallway I stopped. The bar stretched out into the darkness forty or more feet.

Rows of bottles behind the bar reflected the light bleeding in from the open door at the end of the hallway. A pool table occupied the center of the room. Booths lined the outside walls.

I took a step inside and caught the faint reflection of movement off the glass of the bottles.

'Lowery?' I said.

There was no response.

I started slowly walking across the room, watching for the slightest hint of movement on the bottles. The floor was covered with broken peanut shells that snapped with each step I took. A faint shadow moved across a bottle of vodka at the end of the bar. I raised the Beretta and stopped.

'Police, step out now,' I said. 'Your hands in the air.'

Nothing.

'Lowery,' I said.

A figure rose from behind the bar, a baseball bat clutched in his hands.

'Is that you, Lieutenant?'

'You can put the bat down,' I said.

Lowery set the bat on the bar and stepped round the end. His hair was a mess and he looked as if he had slept in one of the bottles of booze.

'Do you have any other weapons on you?' I asked.

'No.'

'Were you here all night?'

He nodded.

'Who knows about it?'

'Just the manager, he let me in after closing.'

'And no one saw you enter?'

He looked over toward the exit. 'Did you see something outside?'

'It was probably nothing,' I said.

His feet had trouble maintaining their place and he reached out a hand, steadying himself on the bar.

'You're drunk?' I said.

'Yes, ma'am, a little. Wouldn't you be?'

'Can you walk?'

He nodded, took a step, wavered for a moment and then steadied.

'I'm all right.'

'The picture of credibility,' I said.

'Truth is the truth,' he said.

'We'll see.'

I took his arm and walked him out the bar to the rear exit door. Nothing moved outside. My car was twenty feet away.

'You didn't bring back-up?' Lowery asked.

'There is no back-up,' I said.

He started shaking his head and chuckling. 'Maybe we should just paint a target on my chest and walk me past the main gate of China Lake.'

'Just do exactly what I tell you,' I said.

Lowery stopped laughing. I motioned toward the car.

'We're going to run, you're going to get in back and lie down.'

'I think I'm going to be sick,' he said. His eyes caught mine. 'I'm all right.'

'Run,' I said.

We sprinted the short distance to the car and I opened the back door. Lowery dove in and lay down on the seat as I rushed round and got behind the wheel.

'Miracles do happen,' he said.

I turned the ignition and shifted into gear. Lowery began to laugh.

'Goddamn, we made it.'

I stepped on the gas and started to move toward the far corner of the bar when a Humvee pulled out from around the corner and blocked the way. I slammed on the brakes and put the car in reverse as two more vehicles came from the other side of the bar to block that exit.

I spun the wheel and shifted back into drive, pointing the car at the open desert that stretched toward the horizon. Lowery started yelling.

'Go go go go.'

I stepped on the gas as the first Humvee swung to cut us off. I turned hard, just clipping the side of the Humvee as we slid past, heading into the open.

'Go, now, now,' yelled Lowery.

The Humvee touched our rear bumper and the car began to fishtail. I turned hard back the other way and started to straighten out. Lowery was yelling continuously. 'Now go now go.'

I accelerated, turning hard back toward the bar to avoid one of the other Humvees.

'You've got it,' Lowery yelled.

I swung around the third vehicle and pressed the pedal to the floor, heading toward the open desert again. The rear end fishtailed back and forth, the tires began to spin and then sank into the loose sand and we shuddered to a stop.

Half a dozen uniformed men were moving toward us. I started to reach for the door handle when I saw Lowery slip a pistol out from under his shirt.

'No,' I yelled.

I tried to grab his arm but he had already opened the door and was stepping out. I yanked the other door open and started out as the figures moving toward us began to shout instructions.

'On the ground now!'

Lowery began to raise the pistol.

'Lowery!' I yelled.

The men moving toward us stopped and in a blur of movement raised their weapons into firing positions.

'Goddamn it,' Lowery shouted.

'Drop the weapon,' they shouted.

'Goddamn you,' yelled Lowery as he turned toward the nearest figure and pointed the pistol.

I was running toward him.

'Drop the gun,' they shouted.

I slipped in the sand and nearly fell.

'Goddamn no,' yelled Lowery.

His arm holding the weapon stiffened and I jumped toward him. I caught his wrist holding the gun with my right hand and then wrapped my other arm around him as we fell to the ground in a heap. He struggled, trying to raise the gun back up, but I kept hold of his wrist and pressed it back into the sand.

'No, no, no,' he shouted.

'It's over,' I said.

His eyes found mine.

'Don't let me disappear,' he said.

In a second we were surrounded. The gun was pulled from Lowery's hand and then I was dragged off of him and my arms pulled behind my back.

'I'm a police officer!' I yelled to no effect.

'Don't let me disappear,' he shouted again as four men lifted him off the ground and started moving toward one of the vehicles.

'Lieutenant,' he shouted.

'I'm a police officer,' I started to say when the bag was slipped over my head.

'Tell it,' shouted Lowery. 'Tell it—' and then his voice abruptly fell silent. I tried to pull away from the hands holding me but it was no use.

'Lowery?' I yelled.

There wasn't a sound, and all I could see was the dull light of the sunrise filtering through the bag covering my head.

forty

Hands pressed me to the floor as we drove away. For a period we were on pavement and then the road surface became rough and I began to breathe dust.

How long we drove I was uncertain, though I could guess the direction or at least the destination. They were taking me into the desert, and there could be only one reason for that. They wouldn't even have to waste a bullet on me. Without water I would wander for a day or two and then I would begin to hallucinate.

My tracks, should anyone ever find them, would become erratic and possibly even turn back on themselves. If I was lucky I might find a tank or a hollow in a rock face where the rain from the previous night had left a handful or two of water. If I wasn't lucky I would find a crevice in a rock outcropping, curl up and wait to die. In another twelve hours I would begin to slip back and forth into unconsciousness. And by the end of that day, I would slip away completely, never opening my eyes again. My heart would struggle on for a time, but with each beat it would grow weaker until I died without so much as a whisper or a single thought.

I tried to picture the faces of the men who had taken me, but there had been too much movement, and I had been focused on Lowery instead of them. I tried talking to them like a cop about what they were doing, about the laws they were breaking, the penalties. Then I tried talking like a mother, and about memory, and regret and guilt. And then finally I fell into silence and just listened to the sound of the tires moving over the landscape.

When the vehicle stopped and the doors opened, my heart began to beat against my chest and my breathing began to race. This is how you die, I said silently to myself – for nothing. I could have stopped it. Go back to the beginning, all you had to do was put the phone down, hang up, that's all it would have taken, an act as small as that the difference between living and dying.

I was lifted off the floor of the vehicle and walked a dozen steps and stopped. The hands holding me by my arms released me and the men walked back to the vehicle.

'You have nothing to say,' I said.

The doors of the vehicle closed and then I heard it moving away.

I tried to speak, to yell, but instead I just listened to the sound of the Humvee's engine moving away into the distance until it vanished completely and I was left in silence.

I could feel the heat of the desert sun beginning to gather. A bead of perspiration or of fear slid down the side of my face. A faint breeze pressed the cloth of the hood against my face, bringing out a scent that lingered in the fabric. For an instant I believed it might be a drug and I tried to turn my head away from the cloth as I took a breath, but then I realized it wasn't that at all. It was oranges – as if the skin had just been peeled away from the fruit.

I took a deep breath of the scent, and for a moment there was the tree holding the fruit, and then my daughter picking the orange and holding it up for me to take a breath of it.

'I'm sorry about the bag,' said a voice, jarring me back to the moment.

I spun round to where I thought it had come from. I knew the voice, and I knew what would be coming next. I had been wrong about wandering the desert slowly dying. In Taylor's world, nothing was left to chance. I heard the click of a hammer being cocked. My legs began to tremble.

Run, the voice in my head said. I don't want to die like this, just another picture on Crawford's wall. *Run*. I took a step, stumbled and rolled, and then got back to my feet and began running. I was running toward the sun, I could feel its warmth on the bag's cloth. The ground was flat and my feet found each step without turning an ankle or slipping.

Faster, run, come on, come on.

I pulled at the restraints on my wrists, trying to free

them as I ran, and with each turn of the wrist a little tension was lost. *Faster, faster, don't run in a straight line.* I started to swerve to the left and right, trying to avoid the bullet coming from behind.

A wind was coming up. Air began to lift up the bottom of the bag over my chin. I turned my head to the left and a gust caught the bag and lifted it over my mouth. Breathing was easier now and with each breath I picked up the pace of my steps. The voice in my head began to shout. *Run, run, don't slow down, you can get tired.*

I started shaking my head back and forth and the bag began to crawl up my face. I could see glimpses of the ground under my feet. I pulled on the restraints and they cut into my wrists, but they gave a little more and then I pulled hard and they slipped off my hands and I reached up to pull the bag off my head.

'It was necessary to protect my men,' said Taylor.

I hadn't taken a single step, nothing more than a single heartbeat had passed. This is what you think of when you die by violence, I thought. Not people, or love, or right or wrong, you think of one more step, one more breath, one more second to cling to this world.

His hands touched my shoulders and then lifted the cloth off my head, and then with a slight pull my wrists were set free. I quickly spun round. Taylor stood several feet away. In his hands he was holding a knife. His hair had been cut short, and his beard shaved, but I recognized his eyes. They held the light as if saving it for another time. I tried to take a breath but I couldn't. My entire body began to tremble.

He lifted the knife and I began to lean away from the expected blow. And then with a flick of the wrist he folded it back up and slipped it in his pocket. I exhaled as if I had been punched in the stomach. Beyond him I saw my Volvo parked next to a Humvee.

We were standing in a small valley where tall minarets of rock and sand rose out of the landscape like long-ago buried mosques. Beyond them a dry lake bed as white as freshly fallen snow stretched for miles toward a distant set of hills. I took a deep breath, the trembling in my hands and legs beginning to settle.

'I don't understand,' I said.

He stared at me and I saw in his eyes a hardness I had witnessed in few other human beings.

'I'm a soldier not a murderer,' Taylor said.

We looked at each other for a moment.

'What's happened to Lowery?' I said.

'Shore Patrol has him, he'll be prosecuted according to military law.'

'Law?' I said. 'You murdered three people.'

He took a deep breath. 'Let it go, Lieutenant. Your rules aren't much good in a war. The guilty have been punished.'

'This isn't Baghdad,' I said.

He nodded. 'No, here a kid gets on a bicycle and always reaches the other end of the street.'

'There's a body lying back there, police are going to ask questions—'

'Are they?' he said.

I looked at him for a moment.

'It's gone already, isn't it?'

'I don't know. I was never there.'

Taylor reached into his jacket pocket and removed a plastic bag containing a pistol and a knife. He took a step and held it out to me.

'Russell's gun and knife, his prints are on them, the ballistics will match the round in Burns's head. The blade will correspond to the wounds in Henkel's neck.'

'And what about Deputy Gilley? There's nothing in this bag about him.'

'If there had been something to put in that bag, I would have.'

I stared at the bag for a moment. 'Just like that.'

'Who's to say otherwise?'

'I won't be a part of this.'

He tossed the bag on to the ground at my feet.

'Would you prefer Havoc's solution, blame it all on Salem?' he said.

'That's not the only choice.'

'No, but it's the best one.'

'And what about Salem?'

Taylor said nothing.

'He's dead, isn't he?'

Taylor nodded.

My heart sank. 'Where?'

He looked toward the dry lake bed. 'Out there somewhere. A hole in the sand.'

I looked out toward the white expanse. 'That's why you brought me here.'

'I thought you should know.'

We both fell into silence for a moment.

'Russell killed him,' I said.

Taylor looked at me and nodded. 'The war Salem was fighting wasn't winnable.'

'Why?'

'Because no one in power wanted him to win it.'

There it was, the final truth of it all. The moment Salem had stepped out into the light knowing what he knew, he didn't have a chance.

'It didn't have to happen this way,' I said.

'Of course it did,' said Taylor. 'All wars end just like this.'

A warm breeze picked up sand at our feet and sent it swirling off into the distance. Taylor watched it for a moment, then reached behind his back, removed a gun from his waist and held it out to me.

'Your weapon.'

I took it from him and checked the chamber. It was loaded. Taylor looked at it in my hand for a moment then turned away. He had killed three people and he had just handed a cop a loaded gun and looked away. Since the moment he had held me down in the sand and ripped my clothes, I had imagined this very moment, and he had just given it to me. Was this his way of slipping over the bow of the boat and ending his war? I looked at the back of his head and my hand tightened around the grip of the pistol.

Do it, said that voice in my head.

'If circumstances had been different that night, would I be dead?' I asked.

Taylor turned back to me, looked at the gun in my hand and took a slow, tired breath.

'Given the right circumstances, everyone dies.'

'Do you know what you did to me that night?'

He made eye contact with me and then looked away. 'When you're trained in Special Forces, regret isn't part of the course work. You learn that on your own. I know what I did that night, Lieutenant, and I also know that the wounds you learn to live with, and get to go home with, are preferable to the ones where you don't.'

'You know about going home, do you, Taylor?'

He shook his head. 'I haven't been home in a very long time.'

I looked at him for a moment.

'You saved mine and Smith's life,' I said.

Along with that hard light his eyes carried, there was something else, something he would never lose. A longing. For the past he had lost, or a future he knew he would never have. My hand relaxed around the gun.

'You knew my gun was empty back on that street.'

'Did I?' said Taylor.

I nodded. 'Yes.'

'What I know, Lieutenant, I'll take to my grave . . . all of it.'

He reached down and picked up the bag containing the gun and knife and held them out to me.

'You are a part of it,' he said.

I shook my head. 'No, I'm not.'

'Another cop will take it,' Taylor said. 'And then it will be over.'

'They may take it, but it won't be over. Lowery was right, someone will want this story,' I said. 'A newspaper, TV, someone will run it.'

'Are you sure?' he said.

'I'll make sure.'

'Nothing is for sure, Lieutenant.'

He looked at me for a moment.

'Who's going to stop me?' I asked. My hand tightened again around the Glock.

'Not me,' he said and turned toward his vehicle.

'Taylor.'

He stopped.

'What do I tell Salem's wife?'

'Tell her he died for the only thing worth dying for in war.'

'What would that be?'

'The truth.'

High overhead the contrails of an F-15 from China Lake began criss-crossing the bright blue sky.

'Does this place have a name?' I asked.

He nodded. 'Pinnacles. It's called the Pinnacles.'

I knew that name. The young girl I had met at the motel the first night in Trona had mentioned it. I looked out past the spires of rock toward the miles of empty desert and lake bed that concealed the grave of a policeman.

'Where the astronauts practiced walking on the moon,' I said.

Taylor looked past me into the distance for a moment.

'A giant leap for mankind,' I said.

His eyes found mine and for an instant the hardness they carried softened.

'Nothing ever lasts,' Taylor said, and then he turned and walked away.

forty-one

I walked the dry lake bed for hours after Taylor drove away. The rain that had fallen the previous night had washed away any tracks the crystalline soil might have held before the storms. If Salem's last steps had been imprinted in the white landscape, they were gone now.

In the days that followed, an official search took place, but no amount of manpower could reveal the secret concealed under the lake's surface. In time there will be another storm, and whether it comes in one year or ten or a hundred, the flood that will wash through this desert will reveal what it has hidden: the body of a young policeman preserved in the salt crystals of a dry lake, his features not looking a day older than the one on which he walked beyond the point of no return.

When the search had ended and everyone had left except Cathy Salem and me, we walked to the top of a rise that looked out on to the dry lake that stretched to the horizon. If what I had seen in her face that first day she visited my house was fear that her husband was lost, what I now saw reflected in her eyes as I told her what I knew was the finality of knowing, if not understanding.

'A bandage,' she whispered, looking out across the bleached white landscape. 'It's like a fresh bandage covering the wound where Jack lies.' She turned and looked at me. 'Tell me something good will come of this?'

I reached into my pocket, removed the photograph of her husband and a boy standing with a bicycle and handed it to her.

'The next boy never got on that bicycle,' I said.

'Can you promise me that?' she said.

I shook my head. 'Jack did.'

She stared at the photograph for a moment then out into the dry lake. 'Then he became the cop he always dreamed of being, didn't he?'

'Yes, I think he did.'

'If I could give you back these last few days,' she said.

I took her hand in mine. 'It's those days that give meaning to all the ones yet to come,' I said.

'Do you really believe that, Lieutenant?'

'I hadn't for a long time, your husband gave it back to me.'

'I don't think I'm quite ready to believe that,' Cathy said and then looked back out over the dry lake. 'Every year when we drove to Death Valley, Jack wanted to stop and look at this, but I never did, so we didn't.' She reached out and took my hand. 'Now I don't think I'll ever look away.'

Another cop did take the bag containing the gun and knife: Smith took it. In the end it was all he could do for Salem. He got him the funeral accorded to those who have given the last full measure in the line of duty. At the service I watched him hand Cathy Salem a folded flag, which she clutched to her heart along with a small photograph of her husband and a little boy who vanished in a flash of light.

The official story that a missing security contractor suspected in the theft of government funds had murdered a cop and three people ran in the days following my return from Trona. There was no mention of children being used as human weapons. No details of an operation with the name Havoc, or what had happened near a dying town named Trona. Within days, fiction had taken on the patina of truth.

I told my story to one paper after another until it finally ran in a small alternative press that few people read, but it was printed. Denials were immediately issued. Fingers began to be pointed. I met with a congressman who promised an investigation. A senator's aide said there would be hearings. I'm still waiting for their calls. For a few days the story was spread across the internet by conspiracy theorists where it was read and passed on by those crying wolf into cyberspace. Any chance of being taken seriously had vanished with the sound of typing keyboards. In the end, what I could prove was no match for the patina of truth; it was too painful.

I had been able to give Cathy Salem the knowledge of what had happened to her husband. But I couldn't give her justice. Taylor may have been right that the guilty had been punished, but no one had taken responsibility for what had happened. As Crawford had said, the worst thing in war for those who send other men to fight them is bad publicity.

Three months after that morning in the high desert the military reported the death of a soldier in a firefight in Anbar Province. There were no details of the action involved. Nothing more than his name and rank was released. Master Sergeant John Taylor. I would like to think he died for the one thing worth dying for in war, but in the end, that secret, along with all his others, he took to his grave just as he said he would.

The report said that he had left behind a wife and an eight-year-old son. What it didn't say about him and what I knew, and what the men who sent Taylor halfway around the world didn't care about, was that a part of him had been lost to them long before he took his final breath.

I drove slowly back to Los Angeles that day Taylor left me in the high desert on the road to Death Valley. At the top of the pass leading down into the basin I stopped and waited for the sun to set and for the marine layer to slip in from the coast and cover the city

406

in a blanket of fog. I didn't want the clarity of the desert's light any more.

As I reached the basin, everything I loved and hated about the city was just as I had left it a few days before. Traffic slowed to a crawl. The scent of exhaust and sweat and perfume, tortillas, smog, jasmine and the ocean, and then the sounds of nine million lives speaking a hundred different languages all became one, just trying to get through another day.

I drove to Santa Monica and parked outside Harrison's house. Through the windows I could see him moving about inside. I watched him cook dinner. I watched him eat. I watched the way his arm moved, the way his hand held a glass, the line of his neck as he read, the way his hair touched his forehead. I tried to place in memory every gesture, every move, as if they were gifts never to be forgotten.

An hour passed, then another and just before midnight the front door opened. Harrison stepped out and looked across the street to where I was sitting.

'It was all true,' I said softly into the darkness.

I reached down and slipped my gun out of the holster, removed the magazine and locked the weapon in the glove compartment. My war, for now, was over. As the clock moved on to a new day, I opened the door and took my first step back towards home.

acknowledgements

This work would not have been possible without the support of Elaine Koster, David Grossman and the wonderfully creative people at Headline Publishing, in particular my editor Vicki Mellor.

Now you can buy any of these other bestselling Headline books from your bookshop or *direct from the publisher*.